*To Tony J
with b
How*

Feathers Fur & Fins
A Trio of Unusual Animal Stories

Douglas Hill

Books for Free

You've rescued me from going to waste

healthyplanet.org
healthy_planet   healthyplanet

USA • Canada • UK • Ireland

© Copyright 2005 Douglas Hilt.
All rights reserved. No part of this publication may be reproduced, stored in a retrieval system, or transmitted, in any form or by any means, electronic, mechanical, photocopying, recording, or otherwise, without the written prior permission of the author.

Front Cover Photo Credits:
Cockatoo: Douglas Hilt
Coyote: Julie Davis
Dolphins: National Oceanic and Atmospheric Administration;
U.S. Department of Commerce.

This book is a work of fiction. Any resemblance(s) to any person living or dead is purely coincidental.
Note for Librarians: A cataloguing record for this book is available from Library and Archives Canada at www.collectionscanada.ca/amicus/index-e.html
ISBN 1-4120-5274-2

Printed in Victoria, BC, Canada. Printed on paper with minimum 30% recycled fibre. Trafford's print shop runs on "green energy" from solar, wind and other environmentally-friendly power sources.

TRAFFORD

Offices in Canada, USA, Ireland and UK
This book was published *on-demand* in cooperation with Trafford Publishing. On-demand publishing is a unique process and service of making a book available for retail sale to the public taking advantage of on-demand manufacturing and Internet marketing. On-demand publishing includes promotions, retail sales, manufacturing, order fulfilment, accounting and collecting royalties on behalf of the author.

Book sales for North America and international:
Trafford Publishing, 6E–2333 Government St.,
Victoria, BC v8t 4p4 CANADA
phone 250 383 6864 (toll-free 1 888 232 4444)
fax 250 383 6804; email to orders@trafford.com

Book sales in Europe:
Trafford Publishing (UK) Ltd., Enterprise House, Wistaston Road Business Centre, Wistaston Road, Crewe, Cheshire cw2 7rp UNITED KINGDOM
phone 01270 251 396 (local rate 0845 230 9601)
facsimile 01270 254 983; orders.uk@trafford.com

Order online at:
trafford.com/05-0169

10 9 8 7 6 5 4 3 2

For Marquita

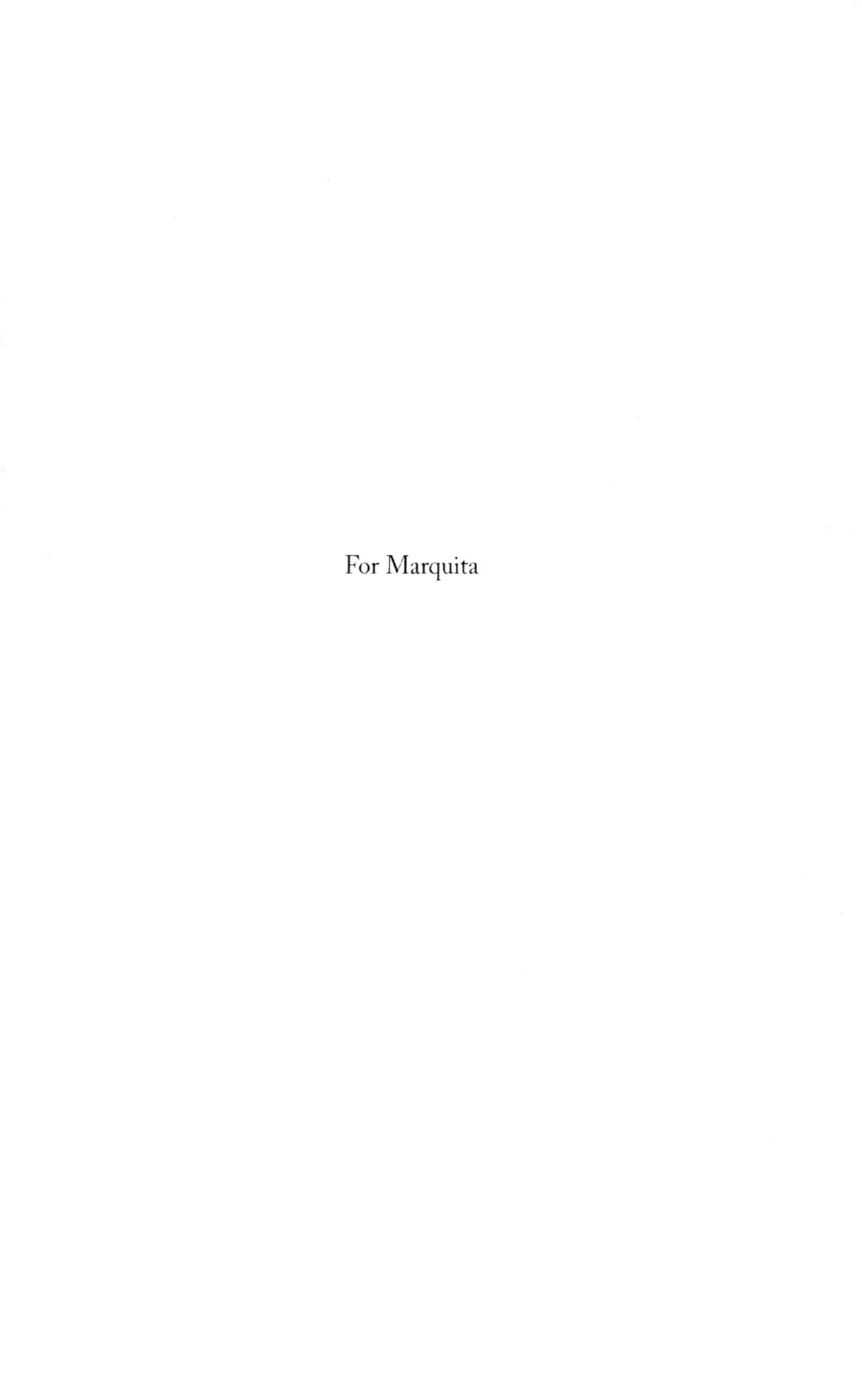

Acknowledgments:

Many thanks to the staff at Trafford Publishing for their unfailing courtesy and help. Special words of appreciation go to Scott Barrie and to Kathy Phillips for their professionalism and hard work. To my wife as always, my thanks and gratitude for everything.

For those readers who may wish to learn more about the background of *The Moluccan Manuscript* and its protagonist—the real Bikkia—may I draw their attention to Leigh Farris's *A Bird Shall Carry the Voice*, also published by Trafford.

The Ancients knew their world full well
And breathed the fullness of the land and sea;
Revered the songsters of the skies, and in tales did tell
How creatures oft had helped set mortals free.
These brothers, sisters that around us dwell
Were hymned by Aristotle, Plutarch and Pliny,
Loved by the gods and seers, who each foretell
A world of life and love, of universal harmony.
That Eden now is ended; we have lost the way
Of truth and trust; deep bitter strife,
Affronts to Nature mark our world today
Where exploitation of all forms is rife.
We need restore the ancient bonds, so may
The gods return and lead us to a gentler life!

Contents

Poem 7
The Moluccan Manuscript 11
    Translator's Foreword 13
Down to Earth 105
Beyond All Barriers 143

The Moluccan Manuscript

*Transcribed by
Dr. Hans-Jürgen Zuckmeyer
Translated from the German by
Douglas Hilt*

Translator's Foreword

Rarely has a single event divided the scientific world so bitterly. The publication of the manuscript in Germany last year—at the time hailed by many as the sensation of the century—gave rise to an acrimonious dispute among ornithologists that shows no signs of abating. No middle ground seems possible; either Dr. Hans-Jürgen Zuckmeyer is a genius to rank with Darwin and Wallace, or he must be reckoned the perpetrator of a crude hoax on his colleagues and the general public.

The basic question, as every reader knows by now, is simple enough: Did Dr. Zuckmeyer go beyond strict scientific observation of Bikkia, the cockatoo, by adding his own perceptions to what she had narrated to him in her own language? At no point did Zuckmeyer claim, as some of his critics allege, that the bird spoke English. Quite the contrary: the Moluccan, in fact, is a relatively poor imitator of human speech when compared, for example, with the mynah, and parrots such as the African Grey. For all that, her native tongue in which she related her story is far more complex and expressive than had hitherto been supposed. The bird's memory is truly amazing. No one can gainsay Dr. Zuckmeyer's unique achievement in bringing these irrefutable facts to light.

One wishes the matter could rest there. However, the untimely death of the distinguished ornithologist last October merely heightened the controversy. Had the world-famous author of the epochal twenty-one volume *Kleiner Beitrag zur Papuapapageisprach fähigkeitfrage* lived, he would no doubt have revised his handwritten notes. Understandably, given the trying conditions under which they were recorded in the equatorial rain forest, the notations are often hard to decipher. A man of single-minded determination, virtually a recluse, for years he immersed himself in the humid rain forest of the Moluccas, the fabled Spice Islands of another era, to study *Kakatoe moluccensis* and learn its language. His patience and dedication to his work were legendary in zoological circles. Even so, had Bikkia, or Beaka as she is more popularly known, not spent a considerable time in the United States before returning to her homeland it is doubtful whether even Zuckmeyer could have gained her confidence to such an astonishing degree.

Which brings us to the most controversial point of all: Did Bikkia, in fact, grasp the intricacies of the American idiom? The reader may well ask, how could a mere bird comprehend the language so quickly? A retentive memory, a quick mind, and lengthy exposure to human speech patterns seem to have been the determining factors. Some have maliciously suggested that Beaka had the unfair advantage of not being subjected to the American educational system. Be that as it may, she clearly is an extraordinary, intelligent creature as many older television viewers in this country can testify.

Where does all this leave Zuckmeyer? His rigorous methodology in the best German scientific tradition, his great personal integrity—even the most sceptical reader must allow the possibility that Zuckmeyer was the first to unlock the language of the Moluccan, a complex fusion of utterances involving pitch, inflection, and gesture. That Bikkia had experienced so many incredible adventures and had learned to understand, though not speak, everyday American English was, of course, a totally unexpected revelation.

A brief observation of my own, in my capacity as translator, is perhaps here in order. The reader will no doubt note the duality of Bikkia/Beaka as the manuscript progresses. Bikkia, the bird in the wild, reveals an innate lyricism that would indicate her close rapport with nature and the rhythm of the seasons. By way of contrast, the captive Beaka seems often to be a stranger to her true self as shown by her rather mordant outlook and her matter-of-fact manner of expression. Professor Zuckmeyer assured me that this was, indeed, the case, and that his notes stated no more than the truth.

The precise accuracy of Zuckmeyer's transcription will never be known. Clearly he helped with the syntax, but the main thrust of the manuscript is indisputably that of the avian protagonist, Bikkia/Beaka. As such, it is unique in the annals of literature. I have based my translation solely on Dr. Zuckmeyer's own notes, in contrast to the highly imaginative (and wildly inaccurate) versions which appeared last year in several popular magazines. Throughout I have endeavored to remain as faithful to the original as possible in the belief that the cockatoo should speak for herself. In this spirit the Moluccan Manuscript is presented to the American public for the first time in its entirety.

D. H.

The Moluccan Manuscript

I have but the vaguest idea how I came to America. You see, it all happened very suddenly. I had already been in Singapore several weeks. Of course, I only discovered the name of the city or where it was long afterwards. That morning in the store was like any other—dozens of us in all shapes and colors cooped up in stacked metal cages, the sultry air stale with the stench of rotting fruit, no hint of a welcome breeze. And the squabbling and screeching! Finally I had enough of it. I clambered down from my metal perch and clung to the front bars of the cage. A good deep breath, then I shrieked at the very top of my lungs. That did it. You could have heard a feather drop after that.

My next-cage companion was a striking lory, by chance also from the Moluccas. Our jailors had thrust us together, and we had become good friends. But Merbabu was not strong, I could tell that he was very sick. It saddened me greatly, for he was all that remained to me of my homeland. I happened to look down and there was Merbabu huddled in a corner. At once I knew he was dead.

Just then Tummy—from where I was stacked that was his most outstanding feature—threw open the door that led to the jangling street. The narrow entrance admitted faint amounts of light and air as well as the clamorous din of machines and voices. We knew that the first customers would soon enter. Tummy gave the sawdust-strewn floor an indifferent swish or two with a rag tied to the end of a stick. Ridiculous! After all, it was *our* floors that needed cleaning, not his. Every so often he would glance inside a cage to see what was going on. I'm sure he wasn't concentrating, for he walked right past my dead friend.

Years ago, back in the rain forest, Old Binaija, the oldest and wisest of cockatoos, had often warned us younger ones of the fate that awaited us if we were ever captured. He had seen a lot in his long life. Grim stories about bird markets in cities called Singapore, Hong Kong, and Ho Chi Minh City had filtered back to the jungle. Old Binaija had never seen these places, but he assured us that they existed. Dr. Z., I'm sure you've been to some of them, haven't you?

And now, here I was in one of those very places. My wire cell was just what Old Binaija had described, far too small for me to stand up straight. Like any other prisoner, all I could think of was escape. Heaven knows how many times I tried to bite through the metal bars, tried to break the lock on my cage. Why do I keep saying *my* cage? I hated that miserable contraption, though one gets used to anything eventually. Tummy and his young helper hardly ever opened the little gate. It was much simpler to toss the seed and scraps through the bars. After the freedom of the forest, captivity is almost too terrible to endure. I really believe that wild-caught birds die more of a broken heart than anything else.

I still have not introduced myself. Dr. Zuckmeyer, you know me well, of course, as do those who remember me from my television days. I can see I'm jumping ahead a bit, but please forgive me. It may sound strange, but it was only during my stay in America that I discovered that I was a Moluccan cockatoo, *Kakatoe moluccensis*, if I may show off the only two Latin words I'll ever know. They say I'm one of the larger tropical birds, about twenty inches long, even though I must admit a lot of it is tail feathers and noise. My plumage is mostly white, suffused with a pale rusty pink. Usually my crest is recumbent (you taught me that clever word, Dr. Z.) but when I'm excited I can't help raising it and displaying the reddish feathers underneath. This is why some people simply call me a Salmon-crested cockatoo. Two little drumsticks with scaly feet attached, a dark grey beak, ovoid eyes that seem jet black—that's about all there is to me. Oh, I nearly forgot: my name Bikkia is after the beautiful white flowers that grow in profusion along the rocky coast of my islands. But I must get back to my story now.

As I said, most of the time we were totally ignored. But you should have seen the attention showered on me if a customer showed any interest. *Then* they noticed me! And the sales pitch! "Beautiful talking bird—" I used to growl some gibberish that sounded a little like humans'— "Nearly tame, very docile—" Hmph! Just wait until I can get my beak into one of you! "Isn't that the cutest crest!" they'd say whenever I got so mad at the whole thing. I picked up Tummy's lingo in no time flat, at least the general drift of his nonsense. "Male bird, black eyes mean it's male." I screeched at him every time he said that but he never paid a bit of attention. He never mentioned my beak, of course. He steered well clear of it, I can tell you. What a jerk!

It must have been about mid-morning when the well-dressed man entered the store. I could see at once that he wasn't just the usual run-of-the-mill customer. This one was energetic, very self-assured. He gestured toward several of us with a knowing air. At first he hardly noticed me, he was so busy standing tiptoe and bending down to see who was in the less accessible cages. People aren't really interested in character, they're just looking for birds with flashy feathers.

Just then I remembered the counsel of Old Binaija: if caught by the humans, *do* something, don't just stand there like a stuffed owl, try to be different, *anything* to attract their attention. So I began to bow frantically up and down, at the same time flaring my crest. When competing with the gaudy lories and lorikeets one really has to try every trick in the book. I gave it all I had, up and down, up, down. Boy was I going to get out of there! Well, my impromptu show was enough to make the stranger pause briefly, murmur a couple of words to Tummy before moving on.

Only later did the meaning of all this dawn upon me. I'd been sold. Very shortly I regretted having drawn attention to myself. That evening Tummy and his assistant began to load all of us sold that day onto something I later discovered was called a panel truck. The two men quickly tired of carrying the cages one by one and started tossing them in. Then came my turn. Two hands descended on my cage, jerked it up, and presto! I was flying through the air—in a cage. I landed on top of some poor lories with a jolt that sent me crashing against the sharp edges of my tin seed can.

Blood oozed from a deep gash in my left wing. I was sure that I had broken it. The pain was intense, I screamed and screamed, but do you think anyone came? Once the last cage had been loaded, the tailgate was slammed shut and a tarpaulin securely tied. We found ourselves in total darkness. Suddenly there was a rumble underneath, the roar of a motor revving up. We lurched forward, bound for an unknown destination. Little did I know, but this was the first step on my way to a totally new country.

In my wretchedness I cast my mind back to happier times. My earliest memories are of a nest high up in the hollow of a majestic batai, with shafts of sunlight filtering through the occasional gap in the undulating green canopy. Below and all around lay the dense intertwining foliage of the rain forest. Curiously enough, the first sound I recall was not the voice of my mother but the incessant pounding of the monsoon rains that lashed the jungle with tropical fury. My brother Manhuru and I, snug in our shelter and protected by loving parents, felt perfectly safe from the storm raging outside.

I came from a happy home. The love bond between my father and mother was obvious. The only annoyance I felt was when Manhuru, so much bigger and stronger than his little sister, would push me aside and insist on being fed first when either of our parents returned to the nest with a morsel. But he didn't mean any ill, he was just that much bigger and hungrier. Even so, I always had enough to eat.

With each day I gained strength, and after a few weeks Manhuru and I could stand on the edge of the nest and flap our fledgling wings. The monsoon rains were now slackening into quicker bursts, followed by magnificent clearing skies. With each day I became more anxious to leave the hollow. Several weeks must have passed when one day Manhuru stood on the edge and jumped into space. I could hardly wait to follow.

My first attempts at flying were none too impressive, I'm afraid. Dr. Z., you'd have laughed to see me waggling my wings and going nowhere. One day I lost my footing and got really scared. Somehow I managed to flutter down to a lower bough. It wasn't far—really no more than a hop—but at least for a moment it gave me the sensation of flight. Manhuru of course made fun of me (*he* could already fly into the neighboring kanari nut tree) but my father was delighted. "Not to fly is not to be a bird," he kept saying. I soon overcame my fear, and the very next day flew up into the topmost branch of the batai.

Before long I could accompany my parents and scalawag brother down to the river and into the sago palms beyond. What a thrill it was! The surge of air between the feathers on the upstroke, the buoyant lift as the wings beat downward…

Dr. Z., bless you, but not even you can imagine what it is to fly. Complete freedom, nothing less.

The truck's brakes literally jolted me back to reality. Every single cage was tipped over, including mine. Blood once more began to ooze from the wing, again the searing pain. Outside it was pitch black. We were taken into a house through a side door and dumped in a room bathed in the wan light of a single bulb that dangled limply from the ceiling. The air was stale with an acrid smell, the languid blades of a small table fan spinning to no perceptible purpose. As soon as the last cage was stacked, the door was closed and a brighter light turned on.

The two Chinese (that's how I later heard them described) were furtive in everything they did. Obviously they were smugglers, but at that time I was totally ignorant and had no idea what was going on. The truth is I was terrified. One man would open a cage, thrust his heavily gloved hand inside, and extract a screaming bird. The second man cut out pieces of cardboard roughly the shape of the bird's wings and then clamped them on either side of the struggling creature. A piece of tape was run around the body, while a second strip secured the beak. A final plaintive whimper, and the trussed bird was set aside to make room for another.

I watched until it was my turn. I vowed that I would resist to the utmost despite my crippled wing. The cage door opened, and an outstretched palm descended on me. Instinctively I lunged at the fingers and bit into them with all my remaining strength. The Chinaman cursed volubly, my you should have heard him yell! It didn't help though, he still had his other hand free. The next thing I knew he was poking away at me with a stick through the bars. One thrust found my gaping wound, for the clotted blood was clearly visible against the powdery white of my wing. The pain was so intense that I must have fainted.

When I came to, I found myself bound and taped. It was darker than night in that container, not a breath of air. I thought I would suffocate. I couldn't move, but only felt the rhythmic drone of some machine and a vague sense of motion. I could never have imagined it, but I was flying, human fashion. I was on my way to America.

I remember the first time I saw humans. It was down by the seashore. I had never been there before, and I was fascinated by the deep blue expanse of the shimmering ocean lapping the sandy shore. Here the coastal palms and the screw pines grew in profusion. This part of the island was completely new to me. It was much more open and less protective than the luxuriant soaring growth of the interior, but my parents were anxious that Manhuru and I gain confidence.

As we flew over the cliffs of coralline limestone my mother warned us about the sea eagle whose territory we had dared challenge. Not a word about the creatures down below. Way down inside the forest I had seen the deer and wild pigs crash through the overgrown paths, and knew that they were not to be feared. As for the fur-coated cuscus, why that lazybones was usually fast asleep in a tree. The least threatening was the swift-footed cassowary—can you imagine being frightened of a bird that can't even *fly!*

Manhuru and I alighted on the frond of a coconut tree and watched our parents punch open the nuts, hard work, believe me. So far no sign of the sea eagle. Rather than reassure us, it should have placed us on our guard. Now seemingly from nowhere, two upright animals were standing on their hind legs below us, scrutinizing the upper branches. Looking down, I could clearly make out the dark frizzy fur on top of their heads, the flat noses and thick lips. Their muscular brown bodies were draped with material here and there—clothes, I later learned—and they seemed adept at grasping objects with their front paws.

These were the humans I had heard so much about. My parents and brother instinctively froze, but foolishly I descended to a lower branch to take a closer look at these strangers. They saw me at once, attracted by my sudden movement. With cool deliberation one of them pulled at a long string which made the curved sapling he held in his other hand bend even further. My parents screeched frantically "Bikkia! Bikkia!" and beat their wings to distract the man below. Out of sheer fright I launched myself into the air and gained height as quickly as my fledgling muscles would allow. Just then a sharp twig swished through the primaries—the long flight feathers—of my outspread right wing. I couldn't rest until I was back in the shelter of the batai. For a long time my heart beat bumpety-bump from terror.

Bumpety-bump, bumpety-bump. This was a different sensation, outside me. Thanks to you, Dr. Z., I now have a fair idea of what this monstrous flying machine really was. Swathed in my cardboard and tape cocoon, I could not move or see anything. A deafening roar, then a rapid deceleration, then rolling to a halt. In the stifling darkness the air pressure changed once more. A door must have swung open, letting in a welcome breeze. I was back by the sea! Home again! Yes, shake your head, dear Dr. Z. Poor fool that I was!

    A wait, three, four, perhaps five minutes (how I have learned to count time!). Then the suitcases (for that was my container) were removed from the monster's belly as if we were no more than lifeless cargo. To be fair, the men unloading the plane had no idea what the cases contained, the truth is by then many of the flock were indeed lifeless; none of us had eaten or drunk for hours. I've since heard that years ago black men and women came to America in much the same way.

    I would have given anything to open my wings and breathe fresh air. Outside, I heard the thumping of suitcases being stacked onto the waiting carts or cars or whatever. At long last it was my turn. First up, then down. The hideously screaming motors right next to us revved up one last time before subsiding and fading away. I know at least two of my friends died out of sheer fright. The smugglers accept such losses with a shrug of the shoulders, knowing that a few of us will somehow survive. When they say "he's a tough old bird," it's a real compliment.

Again the sound of a motor—a small one, mercifully—an abrupt jerk, and we were moving. The squeal of brakes or tires or something like that, a brief pause, followed by a ride along a bumpy incline. A sudden grab, a quick hoist, and the feeling of being deposited on a flat surface. Now I could hear human voices. Yet the tone and rhythm were quite unlike the sing-song cadence of Tummy and his customers. Just above me I heard something being inserted into the locks, a double click as they sprung open, and an awareness that the main part of the suitcase lay exposed. I vaguely felt a hand run through the articles in the section above me. I was dying to scream, "*Here* we are! Get us out!!" but my exhaustion and the tape around my beak prevented any sound from emerging.

Imagine, if you can, four of us stashed under a false bottom specially inserted by the gang in Singapore. It must have looked authentic, because after a few seconds the case was snapped shut, we were propped on our sides and hustled away. Soon we were in an earthbound vehicle, and after many stops and starts we came to what I later learned was called a freeway. Machines and endless pavement, a world without a soul. Freeway, ha! Free? What's free about it?

As the truck turned and then hurtled along what must have been a sideroad, my mind went back to a conversation I once had with Old Binaija. You never met him, did you? In his old age he could barely fly, his feathers had lost their sheen, and cataracts were forming over both eyes. Yet none had seen more of life than he. What saddened him most was the capture of birds. Even the destruction of the forest did not affect him as much as this. He had warned us how to recognize the traps: the inviting boughs coated with a viscous substance, luscious fruits and grains temptingly put out near the native villages, strange loops high in the trees to enmesh the unwary. We had been warned a thousand times, but scarcely a month passed without some tragic diminution in our number.

Old Binaija was resigned to this fact of life. In his great wisdom he had come to the following conclusion which he confided to me one day. "Bikkia, my dear, if you should ever be captured by the humans, there are two possibilities. You can remain wild and defiant, you can threaten, you can refuse to help in any way. But I must warn you. If you do this, man will clip your wings or even pinion them so that you will never fly again. You will be confined to a small cage from which there is no escape. The most you can hope for is to be placed in a zoo."

"A zoo?" I ventured in all innocence.

"A place where non-human animals are collected so that human ones can stare at them. Some zoos are quite good, in fact there are places where the people try their best to help the other animals. But many zoos are terrible." Old Binaija paused to note the effect of his words.

"You said there were two possibilities."

"So I did. In the zoos the humans study their captives. Well, Bikkia, you must study your captors, should that dread day ever come. Try to cooperate, see what makes them happy."

"How does that help?" I wondered.

Old Binaija pondered the question a moment or two before replying.

"Humans have a great need to be amused. Many of them live in dreary expanses made of something called concrete. It's sad, but they lost touch with nature long ago. So, instead of appreciating a bird in the wild, they prefer a tame bird that performs tricks. Take my advice, little Bikkia, if you should ever be captured—which the Great Power of the Skies forbid!—do as I tell you. Make yourself invaluable to man."

With all respect to Old Binaija's vast experience, inwardly I was seething. Remember, I was still very immature. I tried to contain my anger, but couldn't.

"I won't, I won't," I protested. "I'll never give in, never. No one can make me change. Besides, why should the Great Power of the Skies permit such a thing to happen?"

Old Binaija showed no sign of resentment. If anything, he became even more understanding.

"Bikkia, have you ever flown down to the native village? You haven't? Ask your father to take you there when the sun is high and the humans sleep off their midday meal. You must see for yourself."

I took my leave and related everything to my father. He quickly gave his assent. My brother had already seen the village and so felt even more superior towards me, a "mere" female. The next day, during the torrid heat of the early afternoon, my parents, Manhuru, and I flew southward, following the river but keeping close to the protective trees. Occasionally we glimpsed a bronze-skinned man paddling his prau, but I was far more thrilled by the sight of magnificently plumed birds such as I had rarely seen before. One flock filled the air with their shrill cries, while others darted into flower-entwined trees by the water's edge. Most breathtaking of all, forming their own multicolored flying carpets, were masses of butterflies that fluttered drowsily in the languid breeze.

Below us the swollen river described a long curve with only the crescent of a sandbar visible. It was again the season of the east monsoon when the current runs full spate. First one palm-thatched hut, then a whole settlement came into sight, some on stilts high above the swirling eddies but most huddled together in a clearing on shore. This was my first view of a village. Beyond the last row of huts lay open fields of varying shapes and colors. Father explained to me that this was where the natives raised their crops of rice, maize, and yams.

One field attracted me in particular. For there, right in the middle, eating his fill of grain to his heart's content, stood a cockatoo, one of our very own! Both Manhuru and I pleaded with our parents to be allowed to join our feasting comrade. To our intense dismay, Father refused with unusual vehemence. Dr. Z., can you imagine why?

"Was he a Judas-bird, a decoy?"

Precisely. That bird in the open field had been tamed by the natives and placed there to entice his own kind. What a mean trick! That's how so many of the flock had been shot at.

We flew on beyond the village, keeping to the river bank. I was surprised to see neat stacks of tree trunks lying about. Of course I'd seen plenty of fallen trees before—the termites here can eat their way through the mightiest of emergents—but never so many in one place. Father must have read my thoughts, for he quietly said, "Look further back, over to the right." Half the hillside had been stripped bare. Nothing was growing except tufts of coarse grass. Father later explained to us that the natives did it so as to plant crops. But now rivulets of muddy water were coursing down the exposed rock until they joined the main stream below, darkening the river to a murky earth brown. The forest, our home, was disappearing, and with it the thin topsoil which nourished life.

The village was very quiet. Apart from some idle wisps of smoke rising into the sultry air, nothing stirred. Father motioned me to follow him as he glided down, wings outstretched, to a cluster of plantain trees. Not a human in sight. We could make out the animal pens behind the huts. There, grunting contentedly in the shade, some pigs were lying on their side. Wandering in between, pecking at the ground, were five or six hens. I was puzzled. I couldn't understand why our fellow birds should wish to live with man. Why didn't they try to escape? You can see I still had a lot to learn.

At that moment a totally new sight caught my eye. Under the roof of a verandah hung a little piece of iron piping, and on it, with a chain around her foot, was a cockatoo, the same as myself! She kept trying to lift the chain and chew it. Then she would stop and look off into the distance. I could see how dejected she was, with no space to move or fly, no wood to chew, no freedom. Suddenly I was seized with an overwhelming anger, an urge to fly down and release my spiritual sister. My father, sensing my intention, leaned forward and sternly forbade me to move.

"It's no use," he said sadly. "Once a bird has been chained there is no escape."

"But there must be!" I insisted.

"Bikkia, you must never be caught. Those that are never return. Come, it is time to go before the humans awaken."

As we flew back to the batai, for the first time I was filled with a premonition of disaster. Innocence alone was no defense. It would require more, much more.

My reverie was rudely interrupted as the vehicle jarred to a halt. Doors were opened, voices raised. Once again I felt myself being carried, then dumped. The locks sprung open, the contents above me were tossed out, the false bottom removed. One by one we were unwrapped by a man and a woman. The room was ill lit, but you can imagine that even that meager light blinded us. The words meant nothing to me at the time, but I could tell that the two humans were angry. Not much of a market for dead birds, I guess.

The man stared straight at me. I was terrified. I tried to wriggle free, but my strength was sapped. With one hand he grabbed me behind my neck, with the other my feet, and thrust me into a waiting cage which the woman held open. Then the metal gate clanged shut. At least there was a tray with the seeds of the sunflower—not that it grows in *my* rain forest! Also a piece of withered apple—just as strange to me—and a filthy basin with stale water. I ate and drank so ravenously (that has nothing to do with a raven, does it, Dr. Z.?) that I felt sick for the next couple of days. But at least my wing was on the mend.

As I looked around the dingy room I saw that there were about six other cages of various shapes and sizes. A fidgety toucan was cooped up in a bell-shaped structure so narrow that he could barely move his head without his long curved beak rattling the bars. He reminded me of the hornbills on our island, but as for the blue and yellow macaw, well, I'd never seen the likes of him before. He wasn't caged, but chained to a short perch, which is just as bad if you ask me. Both Pepe and Juanito were from South America, wherever that is. Evidently they went through a lot worse than I did, something having to do with car hoods and hubcaps...

The other birds in the room were all smaller. One tiny cage held a couple of vivid red and blue lories such as I had seen that sultry afternoon down by the river. And now fate, in the shape of man, had brought us together thousands of miles away.

Talking about the shape of man brings me to my latest captor. Unlike Tummy, his limbs were long and lanky, just like bamboo shoots. The most I saw of his face was some greyish hair and sallow skin. And those teeth! You should have seen them. He kept popping them in and out of his mouth, in and out the whole time. Amazing! Sometimes he would eat in front of us. We stopped nibbling seeds or whatever we were doing just to watch his teeth go up and down, but somehow he kept them in place. I'm just glad my beak's so well attached. Anyway, after feeding himself, Toothy gave us one last inspection and turned the light out.

We so-called parrots aren't the quietest types, I'm afraid. Once Toothy had left, all hell broke loose. I'm not bragging or anything, but I can easily hold my own when it comes to lung power. That first evening, though, I was too beat to contribute to the evening concert. Within a minute or two I was sound asleep.

The next morning they showed up again, Toothy and his mate. They made a perfect pair, really they did. Those two would have made a fine display in a nice tall cage—no, I take that back, I wouldn't wish that on anyone. Well, hardly anyone. This couple was something else, though. The moment one opened the door to the street, the other shut it pronto. They kept the shades pulled down all the time, but I knew when it was broad daylight because of the chink of light under the door. Years later I heard someone call this a "fly-by-night outfit." That's a good one! The only flying done in that dump day or night was by the dozens of flies and mosquitoes that buzzed around our cages. Toothy and wife took off once in a while, but not in the bird sense. My little joke, Dr. Z.

Occasionally a visitor would drop in to have a look at us. They always had a furtive look about them for some reason or other. I remember one day a man gestured to me and asked Toothy, "Black market bird?" I still can't figure it out, I, among the whitest of creatures, being called black, as if I were a Palm cockatoo! I thought maybe he was just referring to what some ignoramus once termed my "beady" black eyes. Beady, my foot! I'd sure like to give *him* a black eye!

One day—it must have been late morning—the door opened, and in came two youngish fellows followed by Toothy. An overhead light snapped on, presumably to show us off to our best advantage. I remembered Old Binaija's advice, so immediately I put on my full show, you know, the crest-raising bit, bobbing up and down like crazy, twisting my head and neck in a rapid figure eight. Let me show you, Dr. Z. See, just like this. And this! Whew, that's tiring—I'm no longer a spring chicken now. Anyway, these two seemed faintly amused, but I could see that they were more interested in my flashier companions.

I can still picture the four of them sitting on the lumpy sofa and chair, haggling away for all they were worth. Pretty soon they got up and went over to have a look at Juanito, the macaw. Juanito started growling horribly. This, together with a wicked lunge or two, hardly made for a favorable impression. He just wasn't going to have anything to do with humans, period. All of a sudden he let out an almighty squawk, raised his tail, and—well, I needn't tell you the rest. No sale that day.

The two fellows didn't waste much time on the smaller birds. The parakeets were too plentiful, and even on the rarer lories there wasn't that much of a markup since the demand was apparently less. For some reason they never considered Pepe—all that beak, I suppose. Or maybe it's because toucans don't "talk" so well, a point in their favor, I'd say.

So it was back to me. I must say I made every effort to attract their attention—more crest-raising and the rest of that nonsense, even a wolf whistle I'd picked up from an African Grey old Toothy kept in the bathroom, of all places. I know, because sometimes he'd leave me in there too. More haggling. I recall certain words they kept repeating—"twelve hundred," "tame as they come", "fabulous pet." Don't laugh, that's *me* they were talking about!

Old Toothy was as anxious to clinch the deal as I was to get the hell—I mean heck—out. All of a sudden I had an inspiration. Grabbing the upper bars with my beak, I pulled myself up and turned a complete somersault before landing on the horrid iron perch again. That clinched it. I was quite proud of myself. As for Toothy, he was positively gleeful. You could see he'd made a small fortune out of me.

The four of them kept saying "*he*" this, "*he*" that. For some reason that dumb Toothy thought I was male. Come to think of it, so do most humans the first time they see me. Why is that, I wonder? Some even have the nerve to call me "*it*," as if I were some table or chair. At any rate, those two bargain-hunters must have made a good buy because they laughed and joked as they carried me out in my portable prison and shoved me into the back of a station wagon. Across the street I caught sight of a tall tree shaped like the palms growing along our island shores. Instinctively I thought of my brother Manhuru.

As you can imagine, there was a fair amount of sibling rivalry between Manhuru and myself. He was older by all of two days, but quite a bit stronger and bigger. I suppose we Moluccans look very intimidating with our aquiline beaks and curved talons—they're not really talons, they're just curved toenails. My parents never did another creature any harm that I know of, except rid the world of a few destructive bugs, perhaps. Manhuru, for all his boasting, was content to live and let live.

Unlike the eagles—now, they've got *real* talons!—unlike those and other predators, we're largely vegetarians and never attack another bird. Well, let's say, not unless it's an intruder. We much prefer to munch on the nuts and fruits of our forest. Some may think we're wasteful—atrocious table manners, fussy people would say—but, after all, what we drop to the forest floor helps nature reseed herself. You'll laugh, Dr. Z., but when I first saw American kids tossing cans and bottles out of car windows I assumed they were reseeding them. Huh! Have I smartened up since then.

Life in the rain forest took on a familiar pattern. Weeks turned to months, and gradually the monsoon abated, allowing a tranquil beauty to descend over the islands. By now I was used to the earth tremors which shook even the loftiest boughs. I could fly as high as any in the flock, so high that even the praus on the river receded to small specks far down below. Each day we soared between islands on the warm air currents. Sometimes we flew many miles in search of tasty durian. To feel the cool air of the evening as we beat our way homeward was sheer joy.

I knew it couldn't last. I had heard too many stories from others in the flock. Some told of loud explosions that blasted birds out of the sky. Others still bore the jagged marks where pellets had grazed their flesh or lodged in hollow bones. Sadder still, some of those died agonizingly slow deaths when gangrene had festered the wounds.

That wasn't all. I also knew of some who ate of the bananas, mangoes, mangosteens, papayas and other such temptingly laid out fruit near the humans' habitations. They had bitten into the luscious pulp, only to die shortly of a violent seizure. Old Binaija said that the birds had been poisoned, and warned us to stay away from the crops and gardens near the villages.

Late one afternoon Manhuru and I flew to the salt lick, the one near the grey-trunked mangrove trees. It was nearing twilight, and the other forest inhabitants were making their way to the same sandy spot. You've often said that everyone needs minerals, Dr. Z. And that's where we got ours. Even the spotted civet cat and the stealthy python came there. Those creatures scare me silly! Before alighting, Manhuru and I made sure that no such animal lurked near. We edged closer to the mangrove roots. A wary hornbill perched on a nearby pandanus was savoring his meal. We no longer hesitated, and joined the others to take our fill.

There must have been at least two dozen of us at the salt lick that evening. You've no idea how satisfying it was. We must have let our guard down, for suddenly, without any warning the air was filled with a sharp cracking sound and whoosh! a mist-like curtain rose all around. At that moment several humans emerged from their hiding places. I froze on the spot, not daring to move. I could see others struggling to free themselves from the fine mesh of the net. They didn't even call out very much, they were too busy trying to get loose. But it was no good. Even now I can't forget that scene. Those still free desperately clawed at the netting. It was a race against time. The harder they tried, the more hopelessly entangled they became.

There was no sign of Manhuru in the confusion. By the merest chance, I was protected by the gnarled roots of a mangrove, though I too was under the net. I crouched low, taking advantage of the cover, such as it was. And then—I still can't believe it to this day—one of the men just for a second raised the edge of the net to reach for a quivering lorikeet. I saw my chance, and with the strength born of sheer fright I launched myself through the narrow space upwards to freedom. Not until I reached the batai did I halt my frantic flight.

My parents knew immediately that a great tragedy had befallen us. We do not weep outwardly, but our sorrow is no less for all that. Manhuru never returned. He has been lost to us ever since that terrible day.

If I thought that I would no longer be confined to a cell, I was sadly mistaken. The two young men, Gus and Robin (yes, all two hundred pounds of him) took me to the place they ran, an outfit called the Purrfect Pet. Some name, isn't it? My cage (or rather Toothy's old one, I'd been sold as a package deal) was placed on a stand by the main counter. Right next to me was a pair of Blue-Headed Parrots in a wrought iron cylinder with fancy curlicues sticking out in all directions. On the floor were other containers with furry animals I didn't recognize. Later I found out they were rabbits and hamsters, also for sale. Near the back of the store were rows of lit-up water tanks with colorful darting fish. If I really craned my neck I could see a pen that enclosed some placid-looking tortoises. The rest of the shop was cluttered up with an assortment of packages, novelties, and plain old junk—you name it. At least on sunny days some rays streamed in through the front window, and with customers looking us over something was always happening.

My latest captors were—well, different. Gus and Robin looked about the same age with masses of hair growing this way and that. I quickly found an easy way to separate the two. Gus emitted smoke all the time, a bit like an angry volcano on our island, while Robin, besides being the bigger of the two, just couldn't keep his jaws still for one moment. At first I was afraid that he'd swallowed a frog, but thank goodness it was only some kind of rubber he was chewing.

As the latest arrival I was immediately the center of attention. Gus couldn't wait to show me off to everyone. He had all the facts at his fingertips—*his* facts, that is. One day a fussy little lady came into the store looking for a "feathered friend." The first thing she did was thrust her face close up to the cage. From where I stood, I thought *she* was the one behind bars, honest I did. As I watched her darting eyes, her beak-like nose, I couldn't help thinking, the only thing missing is the feathers.

Next she started asking Gus the same old questions, you know, how old I was, where did I come from, was I tame, girl or boy, that sort of thing. I'll say this for Gus, he was never at a loss for an answer. In quick order I discovered I was supposedly from Malaysia, not a day over two years old, tame as a kitten—I *hate* cats—and obviously male because of my black eyes. It was only when the lady asked if I had any "official papers" that Gus nearly choked on his cigarette. Robin quickly came to his rescue with some nimble double talk that was way beyond me at that time.

Luckily for them, the bird-lady had turned her full attention to me and didn't notice their embarrassment. "Pretty bird, there's a pretty bird," she cooed, at the same time stretching her bony fingers through the bars to touch my crest. I started to snap at those inviting digitals, but thought better of it. Old Binaija had warned us you don't get goodies thrown in your cell that way. So I dutifully raised my crest and let her touch a feather or two. Finally Gus saw that she wasn't going to buy me or anyone else and deftly steered her out of the store.

Except for the need to make a fast buck the two boys rarely agreed on anything. For the same reason they had trouble finding me a name. So help me, for a time Gus wanted to call me Napoleon, said I had the regal bearing of an emperor. (Looking back now, I think Josephine would have been far more appropriate). Anyway, Gus kept repeating, "Nappy, there's a good boy," and idiotic things like "Nappy like a peanut," an offense against history, grammar, and intelligence alike. To show my annoyance, I raised the small feathers on either side of my beak as disapprovingly as I could. It took some time, but eventually Gus got the message.

"Let's try a new name," Robin suggested.

"Such as?"

"Well, something special. Hey, how about Flame? You know, the crest."

My reaction must have been exceptionally violent—I think I hissed and puffed out all of my feathers for fully half a minute—because Flame was given a quick burial.

"There's always that big beak of his," Robin noted defensively. "Wait, I've got it—Beaka!"

I could hardly contain my pleasure. If Beaka wasn't exactly Bikkia, it was close enough. Anything better than that horrid Nappy! I thanked the boys the only way I could by hanging on to the bars, displaying the famous crest and squeaking with delight, all at the same time. Gus and Robin were thrilled. Let's face it, in this racket a happy bird is a profitable one.

Even so, no one bought me that first month. Not for any lack of admirers, let me assure you, but simply because my owners (there I go using that word!) wouldn't come down in price. The fact is, they were in this strictly for the money. Just to show you, Dr. Z., they split up a pair of Blue-Headed parrots to make a quick sale. They weren't intentionally cruel, I never saw either one strike an animal, they just didn't stop to think, which at times is just as bad. They really kidded themselves that they were animal lovers and were doing us a good turn. Can you beat that?

I soon got used to the routine. In between screeching when the other birds struck up, I would sometimes sing a little aria of my own invention. Gus soon realized that I wasn't all that fierce. One evening, just after he had locked up the store, he had an inspiration. Why not let me out of the cage on the end of a broomstick? With some reluctance, Robin agreed. So, for the first time since captivity, I emerged from my cell.

The temptation to fly off the handle—or rather broomstick—was very strong. My wings had not been clipped. But with every door and window covered, what use were they? Where could I fly? I therefore decided to cooperate fully and even cocked my head coyly to one side. The boys were delighted at this proof of my docility. As a reward, I was allowed to walk along the counter top. You don't know what a relief it was to splay my feet after so many weeks' close confinement on a single stick. I wasn't yet free of the cage—Gus popped me back in for the night—but I was planning ahead.

I'm sure the idea of finding me a mate was motivated by greed as much as anything else. Those two had a vision of an unending production line of high-priced young birds for sale with me siring the lot, if you please. Even with their dubious connections, getting hold of another Moluccan wasn't easy. Finally Robin heard about one in a private home and rushed off to make a deal.

A couple of hours later he was back with the scruffiest thing you ever saw, the feathers picked over, the breast plucked bare, not only that, but unmistakably female! There we stood, side by side on the same iron rod, wondering what on earth those two had in mind. But even if Gus and Robin had brought a handsome male, it wouldn't have worked out. Long before, I had bound myself to Hantu Raya, and nothing would ever induce me to break that tie.

All life in the rain forest must replenish itself or perish. In due time the monsoon from the west was over, the winds from the east returned, and so the cycles continued, the seasons and the years. I was now fully grown, healthy, and ready to assume my role.

The choice of a partner is no casual matter for us, for we remain faithful to the same partner for life. Oh, I remember many a swain who would flash his wings and try to win me over with a vigorous courtship, bowing and displaying his fiery crest. I remained hesitant and coy, unwilling to give myself to the first strutting male who presented himself, nor to the second or third for that matter. I suppose that I was more than a trifle flirtatious. Sometimes I led my rival suitors a pretty dance, just to see them threaten and chase one another. Nothing came of these quarrels, and once they saw what my little game was, they looked for happier hunting elsewhere.

It began like any other day in the monsoon season. The azure morning skies gradually gave way to low banks of menacing leaden clouds, the assured harbinger of a torrential thunderstorm. In a matter of minutes Mount Hella completely disappeared from view. Daylight surrendered to darkness, illuminated only by the searing flash of lightning, closely followed by the antiphonal rumble of thunder. The first heavy drops fell, accelerating until the very heavens seemed bent on disgorging their plenitude.

To my surprise and secret delight, I saw that I was not alone. Next to me stood a magnificent young male, virile and self-assured. His gestures, his every movement betokened a greatness of spirit. His name was Hantu Raya, which means, appropriately, Great Spirit of the Jungle. Even as the storm reached its tropical fury I knew that I had found my companion for life. In the midst of the downpour we nuzzled our curved grey beaks and pressed close together.

The next two days we spent in search of a suitable nest. Hantu knew that he must not trespass on the territory of the older cockatoos who had already established their homes. But he also knew that he must be courageous and assert himself. At last, high up in the crown of a meranti, we found a depression which we could enlarge. We were impressed by its safety, for we had heard of native boys climbing the lower trees to steal hatchlings from the nest. And so we prepared the hollow by whittling away the rotted wood. I reduced the chips to finer and finer pieces and then flicked them away to make a comfortable place to settle in. Hantu brought back food and other material from his forays, and at the end of a week we had our first home.

Now was the time we had waited for so anxiously. One afternoon Hantu Raya bowed and lowered his handsome crown before me, all the while singing a song of rapture. Aroused by some age-old instinct, we were united. We do these things our own way. This is what humans do not understand. So often they place any two of us in a cage and expect a miracle. They themselves would be outraged if ordered to marry a total stranger, no matter how old, dissimilar, or incompatible. Why should they expect us to be any different?

─◆─

Esmeralda and I soon became close friends. She had grown up in captivity, she told me. Anyway, she had only the dimmest recollection of the rain forest and so just assumed that she was quite a young chick when she came to America. As to her age, she reckoned that she must be on the far side of fifty, though with all the homes and zoos she had seen—poor dear, she sometimes had trouble keeping the two apart—there was no telling how old she really was. Her language was hardly becoming an elderly lady, but that I ascribed to her long exposure to ill-bred owners. I was amazed at how much she knew. She'd been around a lot, of course, and had kept her eyes open. If she had one regret, it was that she had catered far too much to the whims of humans instead of thinking of herself. I asked her what she meant.

"Well, take those kids, for example. All I ever did was knock myself out to amuse them. Didn't do me a damn bit of good."

"What kids?" I inquired in all innocence.

"Mostly spoiled ones. Just when you think they love you along they come and tug at a feather or get their gooey fingers all over you. Don't ever expect them to give you a bath or a shower. You might as well face it, you're just another object lying around the house. That was my big mistake."

"I don't get you."

"Trouble is, Bikkia, over the years I never changed. Oh, I was cute all right, but always the same old Esmeralda. I'm a bit lazy, I have to admit, that's why I never learned any tricks that made me really special. Not like those birds in the shows and on TV."

My ignorance was all too apparent. Patiently Esmeralda explained what television was and how cockatoos and other non-humans had been trained to perform all sorts of tricks that sent people into convulsive laughter. Esmeralda was really concerned about my future and took me under her wing, so to speak.

"What your Old Binaija told you is absolutely true. But that's only half of it. Bikkia, I'm now going to let you in on a secret that will make all the difference. Now listen. The humans also have their language so they can communicate."

To be candid, Dr. Z., this was nothing new to me. Right from the start I was aware that some sounds always produced the same reaction. Take Gus and Robin, for instance, I learned their names merely by listening to them call one another. Other words, such as cage, seed, bird, were obvious from the beginning. Frankly, I was at a loss to see what good this could do.

"Language is everything," Esmeralda explained. "With it humans exchange ideas, make plans, decide what happens to us. Anyone who understands what they're up to has a tremendous advantage. You see, they consider themselves so damn superior that it would never occur to them for one moment that any of us could get the hang of their lingo. We have a heck of a time getting out idiot phrases like "Polly want a cracker" not because we're dumb, but simply because we weren't intended to express ourselves that way. At least we can understand their language, even if we can't speak it."

"But Esmeralda, how come you didn't learn more of it then?" I asked. Really, I didn't mean it the way it sounds, I was just anxious to find out everything I could. Anyway, Esmeralda didn't take it amiss, bless her heart.

"I wish I had," she replied sadly. "It would have made a lot of difference. I'd have known right away what they were up to."

"How's that?"

"I kept getting sold and sent to different places all the time. You see, the kids grow up and go elsewhere, then the older folks find it a bother cleaning up after you, not that they ever did it that often. And then the humans keep having rows and splitting up. Do you know I was once part of a divorce settlement?"

"Are you sure that you weren't the cause with all your screaming?" I asked maliciously.

"I'll ignore that," Esmeralda said, puffing out what was left of her body feathers in mock anger. "No, I became more and more fed up with myself. It took me a long time to realize that nobody really gave a hoot what happened to me. That's when I started picking my feathers, just to have something to do. You should have heard my owners yell at me. One I remember shouting, 'Pretty soon that overpriced chicken won't be worth fifteen cents!' Not much of a compliment, was it?"

"Not exactly. So that's how you landed up here?"

"More or less. Boy, did my last owner get mad at me. He read somewhere that the best investment was exotic birds—*us!* I'd only just started nibbling here and there when he bought me. I know what was going through his crummy mind. I'm sure he'd landed me fairly cheap as I had one or two bare spots. The guy was hoping to break me of my bad habit and then sell me at a fat profit. Mercenary little bastard."

"You must have broken his heart," I ventured.

"Damn right I did. Couldn't stand him—I was lucky if he cleaned my tray once a week, not a scrap of wood to chew on in that useless black iron cage of his. I was determined to get even, so I really started working on my feathers. Honest, I thought the man was going to go stark crazy seeing his investment go down the drain. Once, the jerk threw the table lamp at me but forgot to pull out the cord."

"I wish I could have seen that!"

"Made him madder than hell when it smashed against the floor. His girl friend tried to hold him back when he came charging to beat the crap out of me with a kitchen chair. Best part was when he tripped over the lamp cord and fell flat on his fanny. You should have seen him! That's about the only time I've been glad to be stuck in a cage. With my screeching and their yelling the neighbors were soon banging at the door to find out what the hell was going on.

That's when the guy decided to get rid of me. A couple of days later Robin came to collect me, and here I am."

I was glad to have Esmeralda as a companion. She was a good old gal and taught me a lot. Some of her joints were arthritic, and she had trouble climbing up to her perch from the floor of the cage, but she rarely complained. As I said, most of the time she had been around humans. She had never been a bird in the real sense. All her life she had been neither flesh nor fowl, to borrow a phrase.

And now something was beginning to stir within me. I immediately recognized the signs, for in the wild it had happened many times. I was forming an egg which, if my past experience counted for anything, I would expel in two or three days. Only this one would be different. Separated from Hantu Raya, this forlorn effort bore no hope of fruition.

―――❖―――

Even the rain forest knows a barren season between the vitalizing monsoons. For weeks the equatorial sun beat down relentlessly, shriveling up all in its path, drying out the very sap from the upper branches. How glad we were for the umbrella of foliage above us to filter out the cruel rays!

One day we were in for a great surprise. The dark monsoon cloud appeared in due course, but instead of bringing rain, it was rising up from the earth! I climbed quickly to an upper branch. To my consternation I saw a dense pall of smoke billowing above the treetops.

Immediately I knew what it was. Old Binaija and Father, too, had told us how the humans would clear away the jungle undergrowth by setting fires so that the cattle could take over. Sometimes the people grew careless or the wind shifted unexpectedly. Before they knew it, the trees would be aflame. And now the fire and smoke were advancing directly towards us! There was no escape for many of the land creatures. In desperation they ran hither and thither until overcome by the acrid smoke. At least we could fly away—if we had enough warning.

At first there was no more than a light rustle from the south, then a stiffening breeze. The wind was veering round, forcing the fire back on itself. Down below we could see men, women, even children hacking at the underbrush, trying to contain the blaze. The sparks and ashen vapors were no longer gaining. We were safe, but hundreds—no, thousands—of creatures had perished. Early the next morning a mute expanse of charred stumps was all that remained.

As so often in nature, destruction was followed by an act of creation. The rains came, and now I was about to initiate the birth of my first chick. It was painful, for my vent had never been called upon to stretch so wide. I couldn't suppress a cry at the moment of expelling the egg. The sight of the white oval shell full of life at the bottom of the nest immediately made me forget the pain.

All the while Hantu Raya stood guard, ready to defend us with his life if need be. An egg is most vulnerable, both from the depredations of native boys who climb trees to raid the nest and also, I hate to admit, from animals like the tree shrew. Fortunately, the hollow we had chosen was so high that we felt safely out of reach. As I nestled that warm ovoid part of me beneath my breast I was awestruck by the miracle of life that was about to unfold.

Hantu Raya was the perfect father-to-be. He foraged wide for both of us, and when I needed to exercise my wings and slake my thirst, he assumed my duties. Three days later there was a second egg, somewhat smaller than the first, but just as precious to us, for we knew that was to be our daughter. Out of the ashes of the forest fire, life was about to be renewed.

※

Gus and Robin weren't exactly the most sensitive of people. Even so, they could see I was below par and anxious to crouch down in a corner of the cage. The dopes were still convinced I was male, and could only conclude that I was desperately ill. To save a few bucks on a vet they consulted a book on parrots by some self-styled expert. Heaven knows what chapter they looked up, for all I got was some rubbery white bread barely fit for human consumption, let alone an expectant cockatoo. Once they fed me hot dogs—now *there's* a horrid name—and some greasy French fries as a special treat. Even the dumbest cuscus in the rain forest eats better than that. If only they'd thought of giving me fruits and nuts, and some grit on the side to help me replenish my minerals lost in making the eggshell.

Thanks to all that junk food, I wasn't feeling at all well. One night with Esmeralda in attendance I laid my egg on the floor of the cage, not with much enthusiasm, I must say. It wasn't easy for me, and I was glad when it was all over.

When Gus and Robin came in next morning, I was turning it around just for something to do. Dr. Z., you should have seen their faces! They stared at me as if I were the goose that laid the golden egg.

"Who put an egg in their cage?" Gus wanted to know.

"Esmeralda?" Robin ventured.

"Then how come Beaka's hugging it like that?"

"Maybe Esmeralda's a boy too."

At this I just stared at them in disgust.

"But one of them's gotta be a girl, stupid."

"O.K. If Esmeralda's the father, then that makes Beaka the mother. Hey, she's *female!*"

After that, the boys lavished every possible attention on me, nothing was too much. Gus even went to the trash pile and found a cardboard box for me. Out of maternal instinct I tended the egg; after all, though fatherless, it was still part of me. Those guys really thought they were going to strike it rich.

I soon tired of the whole nonsense, and before long spent more time up on the perch with Esmeralda than in the box. Robin tried to coax me down with pieces of peanut, but you don't fool me that way. It took this pair a couple of weeks to realize that I'd laid an egg in every sense. They hated to admit defeat, but eventually one of them took it away. I'm sure to this day they haven't figured out what went wrong.

I'll say this for those two—they never ran out of ideas. I was now going to be given a chance to redeem myself. Their new project was to make me something of a linguist (Robin kept saying languist—how's that for modern education, Dr. Z.?). Esmeralda had kept uncharacteristically quiet during the egg fiasco, but this new attempt to boost my monetary value was too much.

"It won't help you one bit," she warned me. "Any bird can rattle off a few stupid words like 'Happy New Year', 'What's your name?', that sort of crap. I once heard a mynah recite half the Declaration of Independence, fat lot of independence it got him, never once got out of his cage. Repeating words is a waste of time. You have to find out what humans are actually *planning*."

Esmeralda's advice made a lot of sense. Now I really began to pay heed to human sounds and speech rhythms. It's surprising how much vocabulary repeats itself. For some, a couple of hundred words and a few grunts is all they need. Some kids get by on next to nothing. That's why Robin thought he had to spend hours and hours trying to get me to repeat the same old stuff. He didn't realize I was way ahead of him.

Now, thanks to Esmeralda, once more I had a purpose in life. I really worked my tail off, pardon the expression. Quite a bit was beyond me at first—I *do* wish some humans would enunciate more clearly—but soon I could follow the gist of most conversations. One day a funny thing happened. A customer came in and started talking to Gus, but I couldn't understand a single word he said. This had never happened before. Then I saw that Gus was just as puzzled, and Robin wasn't much help, either. The man started waving his arms, and then they started waving theirs. Finally Gus turned his back on the customer and said, "Why the hell can't everyone speak English?" I guess that included me, too.

By now my two owners were getting absolutely fed up with me. First no chick, and now no more than a croaky "My name is Bikkia," which I insisted on pronouncing my way just to annoy them. They thought I was useless and told me so to my face.

"Dodo bird," Gus said more than once, "can't talk, won't reproduce."

Robin nodded. "The old buzzard's just as useless. I just hope we can find someone clueless enough to buy the pair of them." Buzzard, indeed! At that point Esmeralda started screeching as loud as she could.

"You can't teach an old bird new tricks," Gus opined. Is that so? I'll show him!

Something happened one night that brought matters to a head. Every evening at five those two would lock up the store, check that all the cages were escape-proof, pull down the blinds, and then leave by the back door that led to the alleyway. Sometimes things got pretty noisy, especially when Esmeralda started complaining about the lack of fruits and greens. "Carrots without the tops on, never heard of such a thing," she screeched full blast. "Haven't seen a coconut once in this crummy joint. I'm telling you, it's a goddam disgrace." Esmeralda had been rather spoiled by some of her previous owners, as you might have guessed.

It must have been around midnight when I first heard it. All the others had finally shut up and were fast asleep. As usual, I had my beak resting on my right shoulder—I never know why, but it always amuses people to see the way I sleep. Well, as least I don't snore. I thought I heard something stirring in the back of the shop. I opened my right eye, but couldn't see anything, so I dozed off again.

The next thing I knew all heck had broken loose. Two beams of light were stabbing the darkness, and a man—he looked like one I had seen hanging around outside the store earlier in the day—was rushing from cage to cage, glancing at the contents of each. By now everyone in the place—bird, dog, cat, hamster, rabbit, you name it—everybody was yelling and screaming. Even the fish and tortoises joined in as best they could. On top of it all, a bell somewhere was clanging furiously. What a racket! The rain forest can be clamorous, but nothing like this. A cage with two conures was already on the floor, ready to be taken away. Just then I saw this kidnapper coming straight at me. Esmeralda and I were about to be stolen!

Locked in as we were, all we could do was shriek and peck at the gloved fingers that held the cage. Before we knew it, two more thieves were there to dump us and the conures in the back of a van. Just at that moment there was a blaring whine and a flashing light at the end of the alley. "The cops!" one of the men shouted, "let's go!" "Not with this hot stuff," another said and promptly threw the cages out of the van. With a sickening thud we hit the pavement. I landed right on top of poor Esmeralda which probably saved me from more serious injury. I wish it had been the other way round. Esmeralda never fully recovered from the shock. We found out later she had broken a wing and that something had jabbed her left eye. She was an older bird, and so couldn't bounce back like us younger ones.

Am I going too fast for you, Dr. Z.? I'll try to slow down, but I get so worked up when I think about it. I'm sure the crooks got away, because the police were back almost immediately. They carried us back into the store, turned off the alarm, and made some calls. Gus and Robin showed up about twenty minutes later. They were hopping mad that they'd been woken up in the middle of the night. I found out later that they wished we *had* been stolen so that they could have picked up a nice insurance check. Anyway, the police asked them a few questions, jotted down some notes, and that was the last we saw of them.

Our keepers sat down to take stock of the situation. Both were thoroughly fed up with the bird business, that much was obvious. They soon started arguing, each blaming the other.

"You're the bright one who got us into this," Gus snapped as he lit up another cigarette. "And now you want to bug out. Typical."

"Quit your gritching, man. Listen, I've been thinking we ought to have a clearance sale, put lots of catchy ads in the local rag, get rid of the whole damn lot. No more of this messy cages stuff."

"Right on, man! Grab me that pencil. Hey, how's this: 'Fabulous deal on Moluccan breeding pair, going cheep.' Cheep, cheap, get it?"

Robin sounded dubious. "How about 'Rainy Day Special. 50% off on old merchandise. Moluccan pair under $3000. Who can turn down this poultry figure?' See, poultry, paltry? Not bad, eh?"

Us? Old merchandise? The nerve of those guys! Just imagine, us on sale, just like dishwashers, used cars, cat food, second-hand lawnmowers. Our lives counted for nothing.

─❖─

Now I mustn't give the impression that by contrast life on our little island is idyllic. You know better, of course, Dr. Z. The Great Power of the Skies bequeaths life on all living things, but just as readily allows it to be snuffed out.

Under my breast the two eggs felt warm and snug. They had lain there a full lunar cycle when I felt a slight rocking motion, then a definite throb concentrated in one area. The first to emerge was our son, pecking his way through the shell, only to crawl around helplessly in his blind state. I licked his bare little body to reassure him that all was well. Hantu Raya looked on, awed by the wonder that had just taken place. Two days later, a little female joined her hatchling brother.

Both chicks were born healthy and peeped all the time for nourishment. In a few days' time their eyes opened. We never questioned our duty to protect them, and never left them alone for a single moment. There were always nest-raiders on the prowl, from native boys to tree shrews.

We named our son Putih, for he would one day resemble his father down to the last white feather. His little sister already delighted in clicking her tiny tongue, so naturally we called her Meka.

Within a few weeks the first pin feathers thrust their way through the tender skin. Before long our two fledglings were making hesitant attempts to open their young wings.

On the jungle paths far below us we could often discern groups of humans. Many were hunters and trappers, but the nest was so high, so protected from view by the leafy canopy beneath, that we felt completely safe. No villager would risk his footing to climb such a lofty giant. And supposing he were so foolhardy, then there was the full fury of Hantu Raya to contend with!

There was much we did not know. Only later did we learn that the humans took careful note to which tree an adult bird kept returning. They knew exactly where the nests were located, no matter how high off the ground.

It began as a faint rumbling, somewhere down at the base of the tree. At first we paid no attention. We were used to earthquakes, and so dismissed it as yet another of the hundreds of tremors that shake our island each year. Yet this one was different. This sensation had a rhythmic pulse, back and forth, in and out, a steady beat. Slowly, to our horror, we realized that our tree was swaying not from the earth shaking or from the wind…

Suddenly the trunk gave a sickening lurch, followed by a succession of cracking sounds as the wood snapped beneath us. Hantu and I dug in our claws and tried desperately to hang on to the nest and our loved ones. It was all in vain. Within seconds the mighty batai, so proud and erect, was tearing and crashing in its death agony through boughs and other growth that but briefly impeded its downward descent. At the last instant Hantu and I took flight as what had been our home hurtled to the ground.

We never saw Putih and Meka again. With cruel deliberation the natives had struck down this greatest of giants. And why? Just to snatch our youngsters away from us. The trunk remained there, soon a rotting hulk stretched lifeless on the ground to remind us of our loss. To this day, we have no idea whether our young ones are still alive, and if so, where they may be.

Now it was the prospect of losing Esmeralda that worried me. She'd been patched up by a vet but she still looked in bad shape. I was itching to get out of the Purrfect Pet, but the thought of leaving her behind made me very sad. I could see that she was suffering a great deal and did not have much longer to live. That's why I quit performing my somersaults in front of perspective buyers, I knew it shook the cage and made her feel even worse. Unable to show off my big trick, I was reduced to raising my crest and preening demurely. Everyone was intrigued, but not to the tune of what Gus and Robin were asking.

They may not have been the world's most convincing salesmen, but they never gave up. What rubbish those two put out! "Birds of a feather should be sold together" was the least of it. I heard Gus explain to one young couple what a fabulous investment a matched pair was—Esmeralda and me, who else? But what saddened me most was his readiness to separate us if that's what it needed to clinch a deal. What if we really had been a pair? Supposing instead of poor Esmeralda it had been Hantu Raya?

But enough of that. Nothing worked. I was getting desperate. Can you imagine, condemned to the same dismal four walls a whole lifetime? I'd rather have died. Just when I was feeling most dejected, something happened. It must have been near closing time when I noticed this little girl peering up at me through the bars. I have only the vaguest idea how old humans are—I know you have the same problem with us—but what I did notice was her dark brown hair neatly parted in the middle with barettes on either side, and the way she watched everything I did. Every time she stretched out her hand trustingly towards me, I leaned forward and gave each of her little fingers a playful nibble. She wasn't at all afraid.

I was so wrapped up with her that I failed to notice that she had been joined by her parents. Big as they were, you'd think I couldn't miss them. You know, seen from a cage all humans seem enormous, it's not at all like in the rain forest where they were mere specks far below us. What's more, at the beginning they all look pretty much the same. I suppose what really counts is how they treat us, whether they're kind or cruel, that sort of thing.

Well, I could tell immediately that the mother was dead scared of Esmeralda and me. She kept telling the little girl to keep her hands away from the cage, and made darn sure she herself didn't come anywhere near biting range. The girl pleaded with her parents to buy us, but her mama wasn't having any of it. I even heard her say that we'd just be a lot of trouble to look after. The nerve of that woman!

By now, Gus and Robin, smelling a sale, joined in. As it was me they were all discussing, I saw no reason why I shouldn't put in a squawk or two. "Take me with you," I tried to say, but it must have come out an incoherent jabber, because the father thought it a huge joke and tried to imitate me. I was so embarrassed that I hid my head under my wing and sidled up to Esmeralda. The numskull husband found this hilarious and began to laugh in such a stupid way that I was sorely tempted to mimic him. The urge was tremendous, but luckily I thought better of it. How's that for self-control, Dr. Z.?

Just then I had a happy inspiration. Esmeralda, poor thing, was leaning against the side of the cage, so I practically had the whole perch to myself. What I did was place my beak on the crossbar and run along it, not the usual sideways shuffle, but with one foot in front of the other. Here, let me show you on this branch. See? At the same time I wagged my tail furiously, like this. As soon as I reached one end, I turned round and charged off in the other direction, squeaking like a rusty wheel. Not that I could go more than a foot or two each way. Esmeralda, good old trouper that she was, also got into the act and hung upside down from the perch—actually, I think she was just trying to get out of my way. Come hell or high water, we were getting out of that crummy pet shop. Purrfect Pet! Perfect rot!

No thanks to Gus and Robin, we had sold ourselves. When he finally quit laughing his head off, the father reached into his inside pocket, tore off a slip of paper from a pad and scribbled something on it before handing it over to Gus. It all happened so quickly, there was no time for the usual haggling. The boys were beside themselves, the girl was thrilled, the father fatuously self-satisfied, and the mother as distrustful as ever. Our opinion was not solicited.

Esmeralda, of course, had seen this happen dozens of times before. For me it was completely new. With the stroke of a pen the pair of us had become the property of the Wingford-Simons family. Now we had hopes, prospects, in other words, a future. Odd, but at that moment I glanced down and saw my deformed left foot. Immediately my thoughts swarmed back to the past.

＊

In the rain forest all creatures acknowledge one supreme law: whatever the odds, the species must renew itself. Personal tragedy must be set aside, the work of securing the next generation begun anew. Putih and Meka were gone from us, never to return. Our duty was abundantly clear.

And so Hantu Raya and I set ourselves to the laborious task of building a new home. It was no longer a simple matter. We were determined to retreat as far from human habitation as possible, only to discover that rows and rows of alien dwellings had encroached upon the forest. Down where the river spilled into the sea were machines that gouged out the sand and disgorged it onto other machines that hauled it away. We saw houses on the beach where none had been before, not the raised native huts of bamboo and matting with roofs of sago fronds, but ugly boxes roofed with shiny metallic material. Nor had we seen the long wide paths along which the humans drove their noisy smoke-belching monsters. One thing was clear. We could never return to that part of the island.

So we decided to scout the northernmost reaches of our island. Few of the flock knew the area well, and Old Binaija made no secret that he disapproved of our leaving the others. By nature we are gregarious, but Hantu had become convinced there no longer was safety in our dwindling numbers. In the last few seasons the flock had suffered great losses. So many had fallen victim to farmers and trappers that our very survival was at stake. Hantu was determined that this time our young ones would reach adulthood.

We flew north, over the furrowed volcanic hills that form the spine of the island, past the familiar cleft cone of Mount Hella, and off in the direction of the marshlands. For us the area was less than ideal. We were unsure of so much. Would we live in harmony with the red and green parrots, the great hornbills, the fruit pigeons, with the long-tailed kingfisher and the moundmaker birds? Hopefully the very isolation would more than offset any disadvantage.

Such were our thoughts as we winged high over the serried treetops. Except for a passing flock of crimson lories, we had the skies all to ourselves. Just over the horizon we could make out a solitary bird hovering in flight, wings outstretched. Our long-distance vision is excellent, of course, so I was not mistaken in what I saw. This strange creature was suspended in space without any apparent motion. As we drew closer, I became all the more puzzled. A sea eagle, perhaps, soaring on a thermal? Then to my alarm I saw that it was flying directly toward us and rapidly closing the gap. How could a bird possibly fly so fast and straight without flapping its wings?

Then we heard the most unearthly sound—not like the piercing cries of our noisy race, but the whining reverberation of some aerial robot. Instinctively, Hantu placed himself between me and the intruder. We could now see it in sharp detail. From its beak a disk was whirring around at tremendous speed, and mounted on its neck was a little glass house. Inside was the face of a human! Our enemy had captured some huge creature and forced it to carry him into space! Man could fly just like one of us, only much faster. Hantu and I were badly shaken. Without saying a word we banked and hurried back to the flock.

To our surprise, Old Binaija evinced no reaction. "Of course those are not fellow animals," he stated matter-of-factly, "those are machines made by humans. They are called airplanes. They are driven by propellers which can cut up birds. Some larger planes even have engines which suck in birds."

I was so naïve that I asked Old Binaija if the birds ever came back out alive.

"No, my dear. Never. Now you know why I did not want you to go to the northern part of the island."

We were glad to return to familiar surroundings. The sight of dozens of our own, the sound of beating wings, even the raucous chatter—to which I confess we contributed mightily—it was all very reassuring after our harrowing experience. We even found a suitable spot for a new nest in the fork of a lofty batai like the one I remembered from my earliest days. If only they would leave us in peace…

Even as I say this, I must admit to a certain inconsistency. It's man, after all, who has planted the fields of grain which we find so irresistible. I wish they wouldn't place such great temptation our way. Mmm, the luscious maize, the reddish panicles of rice— I just *love* the rice you cook, Dr. Z. I suppose we're also at fault because we've learned to eat food that once was foreign to us. No, we're not perfect!

Well, to continue. It was late afternoon, I remember. Hantu and I, along with several others of the flock, had crossed the river and were headed for the wide open fields that lay beyond the edge of the forest. We skirted around the fields, for at times men with guns guarded the ripening crops. As luck would have it, no one was in sight except for an old peasant woman sitting on a raised stand in the middle of the field. She was holding the ends of some strings which she tugged at every so often, causing rows of bells and rattles to dance in the air and tinkle and clatter. The lady was a familiar figure, so we weren't afraid. Even so, two sentinels of our group kept watch as we alighted in the field of maize to eat our fill. No humans came. The risk was well worth it.

Soon we had filled our crops—odd, isn't it, that word? We filled our crops with crops! After all that good food we needed to rest before returning home. The others flew on beyond the edge of the fields, but Hantu and I were only too happy to alight at a grove of coconut palms which obligingly grew nearby. As we descended, we spied an inviting stem of just the right width, perfectly suited to our grasp. What rapture it is to stand beside one's partner and feel the cooling breeze waft in from the ocean!

But somehow the branch just didn't *feel* right. For that matter it even looked different. Hantu Raya tried to come closer to me. To his consternation he found that his feet were firmly attached to the branch. As he became more and more agitated his feathers took on a flushed appearance. I wanted to help him, only to find that I, too, was glued to the spot. Both of us were hopelessly mired in an adhesive sap which had somehow formed on the stem. Flight was impossible. We beat our wings furiously, but it was no use.

It was Hantu Raya who first realized what had happened. He remembered having heard about humans coating a bough with a viscous substance so that the birds' feet would stick to it. The idea was that the entrapped animal—humans aren't too fussy what they catch—would finally exhaust itself in a vain effort to escape. Hantu told me to calm down and garner my precious energy. No one in sight, thank goodness. Now was the time to concentrate.

Over and over again we tried to launch ourselves free. It was a terrible struggle—my strength was simply not enough. Each time I tried to lift off, I sank back exhausted. Even Hantu with his powerful wings and leg muscles made painfully scant progress. But I was thrilled when, with a truly heroic effort, he lunged forward, stretched his neck to the full and grasped a higher stalk with the hook of his beak. Slowly, toe by toe, he heaved himself loose, gave one last tug, and took to the air. He would have done anything to help me, but all he could do was flap around helplessly and shout encouragement.

I was certain I was done for. Already I pictured the gloating native boys who would pry me loose and thrust me into a sack. The same fear must have passed through Hantu's mind. He kept exhorting me again and again to summon my remaining strength and make one last attempt to free myself. Out in the distance I saw Mount Hella rising majestically above the old lava streams, in my mind I could hear the familiar sounds of the rain forest. The effort I made was as much mental as physical. With one last intense resolve I followed Hantu Raya's example. I lunged for the same stalk that had offered him freedom, grasped a tendril with my beak, and pulled with all my ebbing strength.

The pain was excruciating. I felt a front claw being wrenched from my foot, a searing rent. Then slowly, oh so slowly, my feet came loose. I was free! We circled the grove wishing to alight somewhere again, we were so breathless, but we didn't dare and so made straight for home. Only then was I able to survey my injury. Blood was still spurting from the wound, another front toe was twisted grotesquely—probably broken—and a stabbing pain made even the slightest movement agony.

And yet my feelings were overwhelmingly of love and gratitude. I was thankful to be back, back where everything had meaning. I had life, the freedom to fly, and Hantu Raya. We had been bound together still more closely. Like the infinite ocean, the future lay all before us.

⤞✦⤝

Dear Dr. Zuckmeyer, these sad events are but memories now. As you can imagine, my departure from the Purrfect Pet gave me plenty to think about. Poor Esmeralda! She was suffering a great deal, though to see her you'd never know it, that's how brave she was. The Wingford-Simons had no idea she was so sick. But then they had little idea how to take care of anything, as I soon discovered.

Our move to Beverly Hills made no real difference. At first we were placed on a table in what was called the family room. The floor was cluttered with games and gadgets in various states of disrepair. On the shelves were tangles of electronic equipment—computers, all sorts of cameras, projectors, you name it—with wires running in every direction. Esmeralda and I were just two more knicknacks to join the others.

A few days after our arrival we acquired a new cage. Mrs. W-S was especially proud of the contraption, another of those useless black wrought-iron cylinders with scrolls and curlicues in the very places that made climbing practically impossible. No visitor to the house was allowed to escape without first admiring it and its contents. It might have been fine for a couple of cage-born canaries, but for two cockatoos? No way! I wouldn't even wish Mrs. W-S to be stuck in a broom closet for years on end, not that she'd fit in, anyway.

Mrs. W-S liked to throw her weight around. I must say she had plenty of it. Her husband—Claud, more often "you big creep"—worked at a place called a film studio. He was what humans call henpecked. I hate that word! I've never seen a hen treat her mate the way Melissa—Mrs. W-S—went after her husband. Everyone was scared of her. And she in turn was scared of us. Yes, really! Scared of a couple of caged birds!

By way of contrast their little girl, Cathy, gleefully opened our cage whenever she got the chance. Then she would take the pair of us out on the shaft of one of her father's golf clubs. That was a sure sign that both parents were away. The first time Cathy held us I was so excited I would have flown straight into the glass of the sliding door to the outside but for a sharp nip from Esmeralda. That darling bird saved me from breaking my neck.

But what an enticement the back garden offered! How I longed to climb up one of those fruit trees, I mean just to look around and give my wings a good workout. But then the temptation to fly away in search of Hantu Raya would have been too great. That and looking after Esmeralda was all I thought about.

Except when Billy was around. Sheer survival was all that counted when he came near. He must have been two or three years older than Cathy. Maybe it was his age that accounts for some of the things he said and did. Esmeralda told me she'd seen plenty worse in her time and not to worry. Then there was Alicia, the pretty black-haired lady who had the job of feeding us and cleaning up. She used to speak to us in a language that didn't help my English very much, though I loved the musical sounds of her voice.

Cha-Cha, a wooly mutt of a dog, and Miaow, the Siamese cat, had the run of the house. They could go outside whenever they wanted to. No cages for them! They really weren't that smart at all. Cha-Cha was a real nuisance, planting her dirty paws on everyone who entered the house. As for Miaow—now there's a silly name, don't you think?—all he could do was sleep *in*side and kill birds *out*side. That's about the only wild instinct he had left in him, that over-pampered predatory pet.

My favorite, of course, was Cathy. Every evening before dinner she used to practice the piano. The tunes were simple, and soon I found myself improvising little melodies of my own to accompany her. Cathy loved my compositions, but Billy would ruin everything by rattling the cage and telling me to shut up. He kept calling me and Esmeralda a couple of "bird brains" and "stool pigeons", and making cutting remarks such as "the only good parrots are stuffed ones." I suppose he was only repeating what he'd heard grown-ups say.

Billy liked to pose as an authority on wildlife, especially when he had an audience. About once a month this instant ornithologist would flip through the pages of a magazine with colored pictures of birds. "They like living in cages," he assured his friends. "All they do in the wild is sit around and preen all day anyway." I hopped up and down furiously whenever I heard that nonsense. All the kids had a good laugh—except me. How could I explain to that brat that feather cleaning and combing were vital for us to keep in flight condition? Especially as he never seemed to wash or comb his hair. That wasn't all. Any bugs crawling around the house he immediately blamed on Esmeralda and me. How do you like that!

That wasn't the end of Billy's expertise. "Parrots don't really like to fly," he pontificated to anyone who cared to listen. That's a bit like saying that humans don't like to walk or run. "Don't listen to him," Cathy whispered in my ear. "I know better." I nodded my head in assent, and Esmeralda chimed in with an appreciative bar or two. Finally, when Billy left the room, Cathy let us climb out on top of the cage. Esmeralda and I had the greatest time up there beating our wings, you should have seen the cloud of white dust from our feathers. Well, nobody ever gave us a shower, so what else could they expect?

Sorry, I'm getting all worked up again. You see, except for those few special moments it was so monotonous, day after day, week and after week, month after month, always the same. Well, sure, we like to depend on getting our food at the same time of day and have some kind of routine. But who likes to depend on boredom? True enough, Cathy used to fuss over us and tickle us under the wings for a few seconds before running off somewhere else. Sometimes Esmeralda and I had a little tiff and started pecking one another, we were so frustrated. Now and then the whole family took off for several days leaving us entirely on our own except for a minute or two each morning, just long enough for Alicia to dump some seeds in, say something like, "Adiós, mis pajaritos," and before you knew it she was gone, too.

You won't believe me, Dr. Z., but I owe a lot to television for keeping me sane during those nerve-deadening months. In one corner of the room stood a color TV that blabbed all day from morning till late at night. Claud called it the boobtube, maybe that's why he was always camped in front of it when he was home. I never could figure out why the humans on the screen kept hitting and shooting one another, but I guess they had a good reason.

Well, as I said, TV helped me a lot. Especially with my English. That's how I kept my mind busy all day, trying to figure out what they were saying. I liked the commercials because they kept repeating the same words over and over again. They're really aimed at folks with low intelligence, so-called bird-brains, if you please. I never figured out why people need to have the same dumb message repeated over and over. Anyhow, that way I could test myself to see how much I was learning. Now I know all about things like hemorrhoids, constipation, diarrhea, flatulence and halitosis. I'm just sorry that humans seem to have so much trouble at both ends.

I have to confess to something wicked I did. In the evening the youngsters were supposed to do something called homework. I don't wish to boast, but in all honesty I was learning faster than both of them put together. Instead of studying, Billy used to play the same grating CD hour after hour, a top of the charts album called "Hey, Babe, We're Gonna Screw The Whole Night Through" played by a group called the Loose Screws. Gosh, it got on my nerves! Any bird in the forest sings a thousand times more melodiously. Cathy used to play charming pieces on the piano by a man called Mozart, but all Billy could say was "Man, he's as dead as they come." Well, so strictly speaking is Old Binaija, though no spirit lives more today than his.

I see I'm wandering again, as usual. One day Cathy put Esmeralda and me on top of the cage and then left the room when the phone rang. I happened to look down and there, lying on the floor, was that hideous record. I simply couldn't resist hopping down and biting a big hunk out of it. You should have heard the language Billy used when he found out. I learned a lot of new words that day.

One evening on the news there was something about a major earthquake in central Indonesia with thousands feared dead and homeless. I craned forward to listen, but just then the announcer said that first there was this important message from Kittikat, the meaty meal cats like best. I never got to hear about the earthquake as a tremendous row had broken out among the family as to where Indonesia was located. Billy had it confused with India, Cathy thought it had something to do with Indiana, while Mrs. W-S swore she couldn't care less where it was, as long as it wasn't Southern California. Claud merely swore, which made Cathy shout at the others to stop shouting. For all I knew, my island home might have been destroyed. Only with the rundown of the basketball scores was peace restored.

Much as I liked Cathy, neither she nor the others had any idea how to look after Esmeralda and me. The worst thing was the food, nothing but seeds, seeds, seeds, morning, noon and night, with the occasional bit of apple tossed in. Every so often they would go to the opposite extreme. After fancy dinners Alicia fed us pieces of greasy steak and rich gooey leftovers. We could cheerfully have done without that frilly fat, but since it was there we both gave it an indifferent peck or two. One evening Mrs. W-S sailed in with a bevy of friends. Keeping her usual safe distance, she proclaimed to one and all that "a hell of a lot of people in China don't get fed as well as those birds." Come to that, the birds in China don't do too well, either.

I dreaded it most when Billy came back with white paper cartons full of pieces of cooked birds. I refused to have anything to do with feasting on one of my own kind. Once he poked a piece through the bars, and I moved as far away from it as I could, Esmeralda too. That's when Billy said, "Chicken is for the birds." Humans have a lot of expressions like that. For instance, they often talk about "killing two birds with one stone." Then there's the one about "a bird in the hand is worth two in the bush." That's their opinion, not mine.

By now Esmeralda was in really bad shape. For hours on end she would crouch listlessly on the floor of her cage. The sparkle had gone from her eyes, and often she wouldn't touch her dry seeds. If only someone had thought of giving her a mineral block and a vitamin supplement! Now it was too late for that. She had a strong will to live and could have lived a lot longer, but the inadequate foods and lack of exercise over the years had taken their toll.

The end came quite suddenly. It was in the middle of winter. In the corner of the living room a fir tree was loaded with baubles and winking lights, with all sorts of gaily wrapped packages underneath. Claud called it Christmastime, which seems to be some sort of commercial carnival to celebrate the winter solstice. Anyway, quite a few relatives and friends joined the family for dinner and drinks. As they filed back into the living room after the meal some of them looked none too steady on their feet.

Soon people gathered round our cage guffawing and imitating us in their boozy way. Billy thought that Esmeralda and I should also contribute something to the life of the party. So I did a few half-hearted hops and bowings, but poor Esmeralda just huddled in a corner on the cage floor. Then it happened. Someone I'd never seen before said, "The old bird needs livening up." The jerk then began to pour something from a flask into our water bowl. All except Cathy thought it a huge joke.

I knew something dreadful was about to happen. I think Esmeralda sensed it as well, but she was too ill and too tired to care any more. For some reason, she felt thirsty. I screeched at her and tried to get her away, but she just wouldn't listen to me. Dutifully, she drank from the bowl, to hoots of laughter from the bystanders. From my perch I saw her straighten up, stagger round for a moment or two, and then collapse in a heap on the cage floor. I was saddened beyond measure.

The next few minutes were pandemonium. Claud was phoning frantically amid Cha-Cha's incessant barking. Everyone blamed someone else. For once in his life Billy looked chagrined, while Cathy tearfully stroked Esmeralda's crest. I knew that it was already too late. Through the window I watched Mrs. W-S back the car out of the garage. They wrapped Esmeralda's inert body in a towel and placed it on the back seat. I never saw her again. Strange, isn't it, but in her last minutes on earth Esmeralda received more care from the family than in all her life there put together.

Later I pieced together what happened that night. Mrs. W-S bewailed the fact that the vet had to be paid extra for going down to the animal clinic after business hours. From what I gather he was more used to high-priced cats and society poodles than to tropical birds. Claud later maintained that the vet had made the wrong diagnosis and was responsible for Esmeralda's death. That's nonsense, of course. She really died of ignorance, cruelty, and crass insensitivity.

In their own peculiar way the family tried to make it up to her. They ordered a special satin-lined coffin made for Esmeralda, and Alicia took the kids to her funeral at the Precious Pet animal cemetery. For two thousand bucks they got something called piped organ music and a headstone with a gilt-lettered inscription thrown in. I wouldn't swear to it, Dr. Z., but I believe Esmeralda died a good Episcopalian at no extra charge.

Humans have strange attitudes about death, don't you think? I mean, they keep talking about heaven, but they don't seem too anxious to get there. I've never really thought about the afterlife, but I feel sure that the Great Power of the Skies has a plan for all of us.

In the rain forest we see death everywhere. It's a fact we cannot change. I just mention this so you won't think me indifferent to Esmeralda's death. I missed her terribly, yet I fully accepted what had happened.

Likewise no amount of entreaty could restore Putih and Meka to us. Hantu Raya and I knew what we had to do. So we set aside our grief and determinedly prepared for new life. This time there was only one egg. From it emerged our son Liamatei, as helpless and blind as Putih and Meka had been at birth. We had seen it happen before, but we were as awestruck with wonder as if it had been the first time.

Liamatei grew up strong of wing and as radiant as the morning sun for which he was named. The three of us flew the length and breadth of the island together so that he would learn how to fend for himself. We also passed on to him our knowledge and experience, hoping that he would be spared the terrible things we had endured.

One day close to the river bank we caught sight of something out of the ordinary. Some half dozen men had erected two tents in a clearing they had made. These people were quite different from the local natives. Most surprising was the large number of boxes lying around. Hantu was all for turning back, but you know me, I've got to stick my beak into anything unusual. A couple of wing flaps, and I was up in a tree right on the edge of the forest.

Almost immediately I had my first look at one of the men. I'd never seen one like him before—tall, light complexioned above all that fur on his face, khaki clothes, and with heavy boots on his feet. Who were they? Where had they come from? And what were they doing there? Suddenly I saw two long tubes on a camp table. Guns! I should have known, of course. What a fool I was not to listen to Hantu! There I was, exposed on an open bough, no more than a few feet from those awful weapons, and nowhere to hide. Just then one of the men spotted me, for he grabbed the nearest gun, pointed it straight at me, and then—

"And then—click!"

"You know, then! Dr. Z., you've spoiled my whole story."

By now you've all guessed what it was. Yes, the man was going to shoot me all right, but not with a gun. The tube was a telescopic lens attached to a camera. Since then I've faced dozens of cameras, but this was my first time. Dr. Z., I'm glad you explained that these were scientists, like yourself, trying to help us. It's sad, isn't it, that we can't tell our friends from our enemies among humans. You know, even some of your fellow scientists just come here to capture us. Supposedly it's to study us and to make sure that our group survives, but wouldn't it be better to leave us alone and get people to quit destroying the forest? Then Liamatei and all the others could grow up the way the Great Power of the Skies intended. That's not asking too much now, is it?

⇝⋄⇜

I really missed Esmeralda. Now I had no one to turn to. Cathy was very sweet and meant well enough, but she had little idea of what I needed. I was her pet, and that was that. None of the family understood that an adult wild bird can never be fully domesticated. Claud kept saying that I would live to be at least a hundred and that he was going to leave me to his kids (that Billy, ugh!) in his will. Then Mrs W-S would tell everyone how I just loved being around people, that's why I was as happy as a lark. Now I don't mind the old gal being all mixed up, but why confuse me with a totally different bird? That's a bit like comparing her with a sumo wrestler which anyway is much closer.

Esmeralda's death had no lasting effect on that adolescent squirt of a Billy. I dreaded it most when both parents were away. That invariably was the sign for Billy's pals to drop by. They loved teasing me and saying insulting things like, "Hey, Squeakbeak," and "Jabberjabberjab." One brat said that I must really be dumb to have been caught. He knew he was much smarter than me because I was stuck in a cage and he wasn't. Now I ask you, what's Beverly Hills if not a gilded cage?

The boys loved teaching me naughty phrases that made them double up with laughter. One day those kids really worked on me. For once I couldn't care less what anything meant—after all, we're just supposed to parrot words. I rattled them off as best I could, anything to get Billy and his buddies off my back. Dr. Z., you'd be shocked at some of the words I learned. Anyway, I must have done well, because they soon got tired of it and roared off on their motorbikes.

Only slightly more bearable were the society matrons who flocked to the house every other Tuesday afternoon. If I've got it right, they were there to discuss great literary landmarks, whatever those are. I bet you've never seen a phonier collection in your life. Even I could spot those mink eyelashes and polyester wigs that changed every time. I can tell you, nobody's going to get me to change *my* crest feathers. Now comes the best part: I only had to cock my head for all of them, fur coats, fancy plumes and all, to protest what ardent animal lovers they were. Pardon the expression, but the whole pack was nothing but a pain in the cloaca.

One afternoon I really had more than enough. The ladies were off in the living room discussing the merit of two literary landmarks, one entitled "How to Manage Your Own Nervous Breakdown" and the other something like "Confessions of a Heavyweight Housewife." It couldn't have been that interesting, because one of the women wandered in with a drink in her hand and thrust her painted features right up against the bars of my cage. "Beaka dahling," she gushed woozily, "just look at you, naked as a jaybird." Somehow I managed to keep my big beak shut. I knew my chance would come soon with all those words I'd learned from Billy's pals.

The discussion group moved to the kitchen where Mrs. W-S was proudly showing her friends some new gadget Claud had bought her. Opinions were invited.

"It's our contribution to ecology," Mrs. W-S trilled encouragingly. Now was the time to try out my new vocabulary.

"Load of crap," I retorted from the family room.

At first there was stunned silence, then: "Uh, well, uh—Claud thought we could produce a little less garbage—"

"Load of crap, load of crap, load of crap." I really gave it to them.

"Uh—well, I—really, uh, no, it's even better than a trash compactor, you see, it—"

I tried another one from my new repertoire. "Get screwed," I chirped cheerfully at the top of my voice.

By now it was all too clear who the villain was. The ladies were standing in a semicircle in front of my cage, rather amused, I must say. Not so the hostess. She came storming out of the kitchen. I've never seen Mrs. W-S so mad, not even the time Claud backed her Cadillac into the fish pond.

"Beaka, you're a wicked, wicked bird! I've never heard such vulgar language in all my life!" she screeched. Evidently she'd never listened to Billy.

I decided to try my last phrase. Well, I'd better not repeat it here. It must have been really bad, though. So help me, I've never seen such a reaction. Mrs. W-S's mouth flew open wide as a hornbill's, but before I could admire her bridgework she had commanded Alicia to help her grab hold of the wrought ironwork and drag me into a guest bedroom at the back of the house. There she threw a white cover over the cage, and ordered me never never ever—what grammar!—to utter a word again and stomped out of the room. Really, such a big fuss over a mere trifle.

Mrs. W-S soon realized who had taught me those awful words. For once she cracked down on Billy and forbade him to ride his motorbike for a whole week. Being the bully he is, he decided to take it out on me. When no one was looking he sneaked into the back bedroom. Suddenly he threw back the sheet, opened the cage, and began to hit me all over with a folded newspaper.

Luckily, my head movements are very rapid, also I can make my neck stretch a long way. Billy didn't know this, and stuck his hand further into the cage to take a better whack at me. That's all I needed. I lunged forward and took two or three really good bites at his fingers. I'm telling you, Billy's yelping would have roused the sleepiest of cuscuses back in the rain forest. His mama rushed in to see what all the noise was about. That crybaby quit his hollering just long enough to say he'd come to pet me but that I'd turned vicious. You'll never believe this, Dr. Z., but she swallowed every word.

I could already see myself back in the pet shop. Only Cathy's entreaties saved me. She was a good kid. She knew that I hadn't really changed. But that didn't get me out of solitary in that back room. I had no idea how long I would be stuck in there, but the days were already becoming weeks.

Cathy's brief visits were the only break in the loneliness. When the others were out of the house she would visit me for a few minutes. How I loved it when she scratched gently under my wings and ran her fingers sweetly through my crest feathers. Best of all, she let me scamper about the room and beat my wings. Then she gave me a hug before putting me back in the cage and replacing the bedsheet. With that, darkness descended once more, and I was left wondering what was to become of me.

Nobody wants a bird that bites, least of all one that uses foul language—sorry, Dr. Z., just another of my awful puns. I was fairly sure that sooner or later I would be sold again. Esmeralda and I had found out long ago that we're listed in the newspaper ads along with used cars and second-hand junk. We're something special—weekend specials, that is.

I'm used to sad farewells. Hantu Raya and I knew that one day Liamatei would leave us forever. He had grown up to be as strong as any in the flock, and now he flew more and more on his own. We had taught him all we knew, how to forage and protect himself, also to be wary of the ever-present dangers. One day he did not return to us. I was saddened, but also proud in a way. We had given to life, and we were confident that Liamatei in turn would raise young ones on his own. Occasionally we saw him skimming the treetops or traveling with the flock, but we knew he was gone from us, just as we had once left our parents.

It was soon afterwards that Old Binaija died. He simply had completed his sojourn on earth. One morning we found him motionless in the crook of his favorite branch. There was no funeral, and none of that nonsense to which Esmeralda was subjected. Nature had followed her ancient course, allowing flesh and bone to return to earth and air. His spirit, I am convinced, is with us still to lend us courage and hope.

※

My disgrace was complete. I was never allowed back into the living room. Except for Cathy's occasional visits, I was all but forgotten. I was thoroughly miserable with that bedsheet draped over the cage, with nothing to do or see day or night. The only consolation was that Billy kept his distance from me. At least I had taught that rascal a good lesson which is more than any of his teachers ever managed to do.

Quite unexpectedly my luck changed. Claud never came into the room, so I was all the more surprised when he stopped by with another man to have a look at me. Claud had a habit of showing off his latest gadgets, so maybe that was it. Whatever the reason, it was a relief to have that bedsheet-blinder pulled off, I can tell you. From their conversation I gathered that Claud's friend was a television producer. Suddenly I remembered that bumptious cat in the commercials and saw my chance. Boy, did I act up! You should have seen me hang upside down, twist my head in every direction, waggle my wings like crazy. I didn't miss a single trick. This was my big moment, and I made the most of it.

I could see that I'd made a favorable impression. The man looked huge to me, very red in the face. I was fascinated to watch his bushy mustache move up and down with every word he spoke, just like a furry flying squirrel breathing in and out.

"That's a clever bird you've got there, Claud. Maybe we can do something with him," he said. At least I'd progressed from an *it* to a *him*. Anyway, I wasn't interested in starting an avian women's lib, just liberation, plain and simple. So why argue the point as long as Brush-face got me out of there? I decided to toss in a few more bows for good measure as well as the old beak-along-the-perch routine. As a grand finale I threw my head back, fluttered my wings, and belted out my catchiest tunes. That clinched it.

Once more I had changed hands. Cathy was completely brokenhearted when she heard the news. To be honest, she was the only one I would miss. All in all, I was glad to bid farewell to the Wingford-Simons ménage, or menagerie, I should say.

So I was about to embark on a new career. Brush-face's real name was Joel, and his job was to come up with bright ideas for TV. The first thing he did was to hand me over to a younger fellow called Butch. He was in charge of a lot of animals, including a pair of loquacious macaws and various parrots the likes of which I'd never seen before. He put me in with a Sulphur-crested cockatoo named Matilda, I guess because we looked vaguely similar. Despite her strong Australian accent, we got along famously.

She told me that Butch was there to teach us tricks. So *this* was what Old Binaija had heard about. "Make yourself invaluable to man," he'd often counseled us. From the word go I was determined to outshine my fellow cagelings. I don't mean to sound superior, but Matilda and the others were a little on the slow side and had to be shown everything dozens of times. Not me. This is where understanding human talk really paid off. Butch was amazed that he only had to name an object and off I'd run to fetch it. Needless to say, all the tricks were things people do, like raising and saluting the flag, that sort of thing. Often I added a little improvement of my own. For instance, in one routine I stood at attention with my wing across my breast to take the Pledge of Allegiance. They really went for that.

At first Butch had me riding a bird-sized bicycle on a tightrope and running around on miniature roller skates just like the rest. He understood how to train animals, that's why he got so much out of us. I've heard of trainers who get hopping mad the moment you do something wrong. That also gets results, not always the ones intended, though. Kindness and patience work a whole lot better.

That was Butch's way. He soon realized that I was capable of much more. He even let me improvise. One day he gave me an empty beer bottle and a newspaper, just to see what I'd do with them. That was the chance I'd been waiting for. I remembered one evening Claud put a bottle to his mouth over and over again and couldn't walk straight afterwards. So I went one better and lay on my back with a bottle between my feet while pretending to take a few nips. Then I got up and staggered around, just the way Claud did before Mrs. W-S collared him. To round off my act I perused the newspaper, turning over the pages with my beak and taking a peck at the photos of people I didn't like. Butch loved every minute of it and rushed off to find Joel. I obliged with a repeat performance, ad-libbing as I went along. I've never seen two men laugh so much in all my life.

The next day I was given a so-called screen test. Butch had crammed his coat pockets full of odds and ends—a handkerchief, a billfold, a pair of glasses, and so on—and pretended to work at his desk. At a signal from Joel I crept up on him and started emptying his pockets one by one. Each time Butch looked down to see what was going on I would dash to the other side. Finally he got down on his hands and knees, searching, which gave me a chance to climb up onto his shoulder and scream "Whee-Wheeoo!" right in his ear.

They must have liked it, because they even let me have a look at myself when they ran the film. To be honest, Dr. Z., I was very sad to see what had become of me. All I saw was Beaka, the caricature of a bird. Of Bikkia, the mate of Hantu Raya, there was no sign.

The humans, of course, had no idea what I was thinking, or for that matter, that I was thinking at all. Besides, they had enough problems of their own. They were all worried about a sit-com called "Daddy's Darlings" that was a real dud. It was Joel's inspiration to work me into the series to give it a lift. For some reason the plot, about this nitwit of a father who can't manage his three kids, was supposed to be hilarious. In the rain forest it would be a tragedy, over here it's a big joke.

Butch taught me some special tricks for the show, such as playing dead, putting coins in a piggy bank, retrieving his car keys, that sort of thing. Every week my job was to rescue the nincompoop father from his own offspring just in the nick of time. Thank goodness the howls of canned laughter drowned out most of the inane conversation. Everyone thought me terrific, but I can tell you I was really ashamed for having come down to this.

In a matter of days they rewrote the scripts to make me the lead character. The father, played by a rough type called Hank Hubbins, was furious at being upstaged by a bird. Now there's gratitude for you! But for me, the clod would have gotten the ax. My part was easy. I just aped (is that the right word, Dr. Z?) the humans as I saw them. Within four weeks we were the top TV show in the nation.

You'll never believe what happened next. First I was given a canvas chair with "Beaka" printed on the back, then my own dressing room. Personally, I would much rather have had a fresh-cut eucalyptus perch. That wasn't half of it, though. I was amazed to see a sketch of myself on T-shirts that everyone was wearing. Butch told me that the letters underneath read BEAKA FOR PRESIDENT. Now that's going a little too far—I mean, I wasn't even born in America. Talking about letters, Butch got me to hold a pen in my right hand-foot and scrawl a big B whenever someone shoved a piece of paper in front of me. It all made me very sad, especially when I stopped to remember the past and all that I had lost.

Now there was no holding Joel back. It was his bright idea for Hank and me to do the commercials for "Daddy's Darlings." Most of them plugged some soggy pet food that I personally wouldn't touch with a ten-foot banana stalk. The filmed commercials turned out to be a great disappointment, too stagey, not enough snap. Joel suggested that one Saturday morning we go "live" on a kiddies' program to introduce Corn-u-Copia, a new artificially flavored natural cereal just out on the market. The idea was to be spontaneous, you know, nothing phony.

So they started the cameras rolling with me and some youngster having breakfast together while Hank supplied the corn, I mean the background blurb. While the kid was shoveling the stuff into his face I was supposed to be hopping round the table in sheer ecstasy at the thought of what Corn-u-Copia did to growing bodies. Trouble was, the brat was more interested in me than in his cereal. Every time I got close enough he'd reach out and grab my tail feathers. I'm usually very patient, you know that, Dr. Z., but there are limits. The last time he did it I tried to struggle free, but in the excitement I inadvertently upped the guano content in the cereal bowl at the very moment Hank was extolling the vital nutrients that went into Corn-u-Copia.

There was a tremendous row afterwards. I was confined to my cage for three weeks and put back on dry seeds and water, which at least was a whole lot better than being put on Corn-u-Copia. Butch was ordered to make sure that I was properly housebroken. Joel got the worst punishment though. The last I heard he was having to dress up as a cockroach in a commercial for "Bug-Off, the roach-ridder for happy homes."

⊱✧⊰

My disgrace gave me plenty of time in which to think things over. Naturally my thoughts always returned to Hantu Raya. Where was he now? Realistically, I had no hope of ever seeing him again, but a stubborn streak within me insisted that one day we might be reunited. I had been tempted to escape many times. My wings had not been clipped (it wouldn't have looked good on TV) and Butch often took me out of the cage during training sessions. These were always held indoors, but I prayed for a lucky day when we might get to go outside.

My only hope was that Hantu had been brought to the same part of the world. I tried to see things from the humans' point of view. Despite my regrettable lapse, I knew that I was valuable to them. Ever since Esmeralda's death, I had hoped another Moluccan might join me. What if they decided to find me a male partner? Mightn't he—well, just possibly—be Hantu Raya? I can see you're smiling, Dr. Z., but I assure you that faint hope was all that kept me going. As for fame, it meant absolutely nothing to me. You see, it was all on human terms. I was admired as a freak, something for them to laugh at, an extension of their own world.

I missed Hantu so much. In the rain forest he was my companion and provider. Our joys were simple. We would perch on a bough and preen one another's crown and just enjoy belonging together. No human, however well-meaning, can take his place. Cathy and Butch had both been kind, and I quite liked them. But they couldn't understand me fully any more than I could understand them. People see us, but only the dispirited outer shell. Our true selves remain in the skies and in the forest. That's the simple truth.

I knew that one day I must find a way to return to my island home and be reunited with my own kind. Only then would I be a bird again.

＊＊＊

If anything, my escapade on TV had made me more famous than ever. There was talk of a full-length movie and of inducting me into the Animal Hall of Fame. I really didn't mind the Beaka Fan-Club meetings so much or even the supermarket openings, what I couldn't stand was having to perform my tricks on inane TV talk shows. I even had my own agent, lawyer, psychiatrist, and feather-groomer, Dr. Z!

"Not to mention providing meal-tickets for the whole crew, Bikkia."

Huh! Didn't get *me* a ticket back home. No way. Well, soon the time for the annual Petsy awards rolled round. These are given to the non-humans that perform best in movies and on TV. There's something called categories so that there'll be plenty of prizes and the evening can be stretched out. For some reason I wasn't entered for doing the best commercial, but other than that I was the favorite to win just about everything else. Butch taught me some new tricks, as the studio boss reckoned the cameras would concentrate mostly on me. That didn't bother me half as much as the news that Hank Hubbins was going to do the introductions. The clown once had the nerve to say to me, "Cockatoos—cockapoos—same difference. Featherbrained, the whole bunch." Which shows how much *he* cared about wild animals.

The evening really was a bloody bore. I've never seen so many people slobbering over one another, you know, kissing, hugging, dahling-this, dahling-that, phony as hell. The movie stars are the worst, they'll kiss anything that moves, just to get on camera. I remember one blonde that looked as if she had a couple of coconuts stuffed into her chest, she kissed both Hank and a chimp. Maybe she had trouble telling them apart.

Finally it was time for the show to begin. At first I couldn't figure out what Hubbins was up to. Here he came waddling up to the microphone bent forwards with both feet turned in like this, see, one hand on top of his head and the other wagging back and forth on his fat fanny like a tail. One of his famous imitations, I guessed. Anyway, the studio audience laughed themselves silly. Then it dawned on me—that was supposed to be *me!* That creep! I wanted to take a peck out of him then and there, but Butch held me back.

"Hi, all you wonderful people," Hank drooled, "it's Petsy time again." By now he was surrounded by an assortment including a tap-dancing dog, a toothless lion, a sway-backed horse, an infuriatingly smug tomcat, a bewildered doe, a clawless cougar on a leash, a mischievous monkey, and an owl who wisely kept her thoughts to herself. As for me, I was stuck on a stand with a predacious raven, while on a nearby perch an eagle and a hawk eyed me with ill-concealed relish.

A bit more of this foolishness, then it was time for the awards. I was extremely nervous. I just wanted to get the hell out of there. Not the dahlings, though. They opened envelopes, dished out awards, all the time laughing at Hank's feeble jokes. Some of the things the other candidates did were really clever, but it made me sad to see them have to put on such an act.

My turn was coming soon. The moment Hank pasted on his smile to announce the best performer on TV I knew I'd be going into action. You should have seen that boob try to look surprised when he read off my name. Butch gave me a cue to get off the perch and clamber down the stand, then walk across the stage and climb up a rope he was holding. "Ladies and Gentlemen, Beaka the Salmon-crested cockatoo will now perform the Indian rope trick!" Hank announced in that unctuous voice of his. My only thought right then was to bite him in the ankle and get it over with. Somehow I controlled myself. I climbed up, raised my crest, and accepted the award. You see what a good bird I am.

I wish it had stopped there. Out of the corner of my eye I could see Hank hugging and kissing everyone within reach. I don't know what got into him, but the dope came over and tried to give me a buss on the beak too. That did it. As he bent down I grabbed for his hair. It lifted right off like a patch of peat moss, revealing a crown bald as a cassowary's egg! He was madder than Mrs. W-S the day she dragged me into the back bedroom. I took off fast, I'm telling you. I'd just gotten airborne when I suddenly got real nervous, nature called, and I just had to—. How was I to know that gleaming pate was just below me? Oo, the language!

Down on the stage it was pandemonium. Hank had backed into a donkey, which started a chain reaction. A goat was butting a bear who was taking round-house swipes at a horse who in turn kicked the cougar. The tomcat and the dancing dog were going at one another tooth and tail, the raccoon bit anything at ground level, the monkey jumped on top of everyone, while the raven flapped his wings and cawed full blast. In the middle of it Hank charged around threatening to sue everyone, including me. The crowd just loved it. Everyone agreed that Hank Hubbins deserved a special Petsy award for his performance.

It wasn't quite so funny afterwards. This time my disgrace was total. I was declared untrainable and my contract torn up. "Daddy's Darlings" was cancelled, and Butch demoted to breaking in donkeys for the kiddies' carnival ride. I was really fed up with the whole circus. In sheer frustration I started picking my feathers out here and there. Very soon I had a motheaten look which did little to enhance my monetary value. One day I saw myself in the mirror, all pecked over, not a feather in place. All I can say is, served them right, even if it was at my expense.

After a couple of weeks the studio decided to offer me for sale as a wild specimen. That was the greatest compliment they ever paid me. At long last I had been credited with being myself again. No longer was I Beaka, the pathetic parody of myself, but once more Bikkia, the bird from the Moluccas.

⨯⋄⨯

To tell the truth, I was glad to be back in a cage full time, away from the lights and cameras. You know, Dr. Z., it's an uncanny feeling not being yourself, I mean a sort of hybrid that's neither one thing nor the other. I'm glad Hantu never saw me in that state.

Our last months in the forest were the happiest. We had a sense of accomplishment, and our son Liamatei was there to ensure the continuity of our little group. The Great Power of the Skies willing, Hantu Raya and I would produce further offspring. In that way, should anything befall us, we would have done all we could.

Following our narrow escape from the sticky coco palm, Hantu and I scrutinized every branch before alighting. When we flew with the flock to the fields of grain, we all took turns as sentinels to watch for the approach of humans. As for the native villages, we avoided them altogether. If we saw a man carrying something long and narrow which he could raise to his shoulder, we stayed well out of range. We even varied the trees in which we landed in case the islanders were watching us.

One sultry late afternoon we decided to fly down to the ocean with some others of the flock. It was a part we often visited and, so far as we knew, was inaccessible to the villagers on account of the dense forest and coastal escarpment. Even so, we took our usual precautions before descending. The bough under our feet felt secure, a welcome resting place. Below the cliffs we could survey the breakers lapping the white sands, on the horizon we discerned the low profile of the next island. Some distance away the dark silhouette of a coral reef protruded through pale green lagoon waters. And behind us rose the familiar curtain of the rain forest, our sanctuary.

To watch a large bird in a cage one might conclude, as Billy did, that even in our native environment we're content to remain rooted for hours to the same spot. But as you know, Dr. Z., we only do that when we've just had a lot of activity, or need to recondition our feathers. So Hantu and I, after we had finally finished preening, decided to climb into the upper branches. Somehow it was unexpectedly difficult. We kept getting our toes caught in the tendrils. This was all the more surprising as they had never caused us any trouble before.

The more we tried to free ourselves, the more ensnared we became. It was a terrifying sensation. This was no ordinary tree! To our horror we noticed that interspersed between the leaves was a maze of fine loops. We had never seen this sort of growth before. At once we realized that this was yet another trap! We feared that no amount of courage would be enough this time. Soon we were hopelessly entangled. As dusk settled, our cries for help merely evoked a derisive echo from the inland hills. With night and our ebbing hopes came the bitter awareness that we were prisoners.

The natives came for us shortly after dawn. There were three of them, each with a large sack and a sharp knife. Hantu and I had struggled all night, but by now we were too exhausted to resist very much. We screamed and scratched, but those practised hands encased in thick gloves quickly grasped us behind the neck.

A deft slash with the knife to cut the loops, a cord around our feet, and before we knew it we were trussed as securely as any turkey at Thanksgiving.

My last glimpse of Hantu Raya nearly broke my heart. That magnificent spirit remained defiant to the end. Our eyes met one last time, and then darkness descended as we were thrust into separate sacks. Then and there I vowed that I would never rest until Hantu and I were free again—together!

※ ❖ ※

I have never forgotten that vow, not even at the moment of my deepest disgrace. It won't surprise you that the TV and radio commentators had a field day at my expense. One newspaper headline blared: BAD BIRD ENDS UP IN DOGHOUSE. Now what's that supposed to mean? It was the studio's fault for exploiting me so shamefully, but of course they didn't see it that way.

Someone had the bright idea that if I couldn't be trained, then maybe my offspring could. So they packed me off to a bird farm near Bilbordia, just outside Los Angeles. I've never seen so many different birds crammed into such a small area. There must have been hundreds from all over the world—macaws, parrots, parakeets, conures, lories and lorikeets, cockatiels, parrotlets—as well as half a dozen kind of cockatoos. As you can imagine, I eagerly looked round for Hantu Raya. I only saw a few birds as I entered, for the sides of the pens were covered with sheet metal panels to prevent any contacts except for breeding. I kept calling out his name, but there was no answering cry.

Despite the partitions, I got the hang of the place in just a few days. Tierra Exotica was run by a middle-aged couple, Les and Doris Biswell. My new overseers placed me all on my own in a pen some twenty feet long, the most generous space to date. At one end of my enclosure, suspended about six feet up, was a box with a small circular opening, no doubt for nesting. By now I was regarded as female—I should darn well think so, after all this time—so in all probability my future companion would be my mate-presumptive. Mate-presumptuous, more like it, if he wasn't Hantu Raya.

On both sides I had very noisy neighbors. To my left was a pair of rasping macaws, while on the other side was a couple of vociferous Hawk-Headed Parrots who informed me they came from an immense rain forest through which flowed a river so wide that only the strongest of birds could fly across. Once I had settled down all of us became the best of friends.

They were all amazed at my story. Yet in a way, what they had to tell me was just as extraordinary. You see, up till then I had naïvely assumed that only birds from my part of the world and Pepe and Juanito's homeland were smuggled in. Now I learned that thousands and thousands of exotic creatures—and not just birds—were captured elsewhere on a scale that staggered the imagination. I heard how people stupified some of their captives with tequila in corn mash so that they wouldn't protest when sneaked across the border. That's terribly cruel. Why should people want to do that, Dr. Z?

"Because of their market value, Bikkia. But of course they don't realize your true value, otherwise they wouldn't do it."

That's sweet of you. Well, I wish someone would tell them. But back to the Biswells. All I knew was that they were searching high and low to find me a mate. Using the underground communication system—taps of the beak on the sheet metal—I asked the other jailbirds if they had seen Hantu Raya. Of course none of them had. The same way I heard about some Sulphur-cresteds who had used small stones to tunnel their way to freedom right under the chain link of the compound. The Biswells quickly found out and cemented the wire in all round. Pity, because I'd been toying with a similar escape plan myself.

My spell in solitary soon ended. One evening the Biswells entered my pen carrying a small travel cage. My excitement was immediately dashed when I saw that the lively inmate was not Hantu Raya. Les and Doris could hardly wait to let this Moluccan

Casanova loose on me. They opened his cage, and within a couple of wingbeats he was right next to me, practically on top of me. That's all I needed. I spun round and gave him a swipe he'll never forget. I've never seen anyone look so crestfallen.

Wouldn't you know, a couple of days later he tried his luck again. This time Casanova snuck up on me when I was munching my sunflower seeds. Luckily I spotted him out of the corner of my eye—we have fantastic peripheral vision—just as he was advancing towards me. Did I ever give it to him! I chased him from one end of the cage to the other, feathers flying, up and down, from corner to corner. I got in some pretty fierce pecks as I did so. Talk about ruffled feathers! It took a few weeks before the Biswells sadly concluded that the great romance had fallen flat. Doris came to remove the deflated suitor, and that was the last I saw of him.

I'm not as proud of myself as I probably sound. After all, Casanova was just as miserable all alone in a cage as I had been. He was a fellow unfortunate who had been snatched away from the rain forest and had gone through a lot, too. But I couldn't help it if the past refused to be forgotten. The rainy season came and went, then the long dry summer, and so back again to the hot autumn winds from the desert. I knew that if I didn't do something decisive I would eventually be traded off and sent somewhere.

Not that there was any lack of human visitors—in fact, quite the contrary. I often heard people say, "So *that's* the bird that got kicked off TV!" or a hesitant "Well, she *looks* harmless enough now," followed by "You can never be too careful with wild animals," a sentiment with which I entirely agree. I used to hop down to the perch at the far end to have a good look at my gallery of spectators. It's funny the way they'd peer at me—I'd never seen so many humans behind bars before. One good thing about all those comments I overheard, they enabled me to keep up my English. In the end that's what saved my life.

Early one morning some men dressed exactly alike in long white coats marched into the compound. I knew immediately they were no ordinary visitors. They all behaved very officiously, carrying clipboards with lots of paper attached. Les and Doris tagged along after them, looking quite worried. As luck would have it, the entire group stopped in front of my cage. Immediately I scurried across and hung onto the wire to hear what they were saying.

"You've got to be kidding. Surely you can't mean the whole lot?" Doris protested.

"I'm afraid so," the leader replied matter-of-factly. "Government regulations."

"But they're perfectly healthy! Look, Beaka here's beautiful, she couldn't be healthier. You mean you're going to do it to her, too?"

I was puzzled, even a little frightened. Do what? To me? Why? How? I pressed my ear as close to the wire as possible.

The leader remained totally unmoved. Not a flicker of feeling in his eyes. "We're just following orders from above. There has to be a final solution to this thing. And the only way is to depopulate every bird in the place. Otherwise this Newcastle disease could get out of hand and threaten the whole chicken industry."

"Depopulate!" Doris exclaimed. "Do you mean *kill*? But our birds don't have any disease!"

"Sorry, ma'am. But they might get it."

"Let's wait and see, can't we?" Doris pleaded. "And anyway, what about ducks and pigeons and migratory birds? Not to mention all the mice and rats in those chicken factories! They can all carry the same disease, can't they? Our birds aren't even sick!"

Good, good, keep it up! I tried desperately to say.

"I don't know what you're so worried about, Mrs. Biswell. You'll receive a check for whatever your stock is worth. That's what we have to do now, appraise each one." The official turned and looked me straight in the eye. "Not a bad looking Moluccan, name's Beaka, you say? Not the same Beaka that messed up that TV show?"

"She's here for breeding, like the rest of them."

"No great loss," he said, ignoring Doris' comment. From his inside pocket he drew a little book, flipped a few pages, and ran a practised finger across several columns of figures. "Mm-hm, a bit ragged around the edges, but otherwise not too bad. We'll see what we can do. Let's go on up to the house and come to a final figure. We can start depopulating first thing in the morning."

"Gassing them! In the morning?!"

"Depopulating, *please*. Let's watch our language, now."

The group moved away and headed up the path between the aviaries. I could see that Les was now thinking more about the check than about us. The men were already proceeding from cage to cage, jotting down notes. Notes? Often the birds in all innocence greeted their murderers of the morrow with full-throated song. None suspected that their voices would soon be stilled forever.

It took some time for the full impact to sink in. I knew what populating was—but *de*populating? As for gas, well, I had always thought that was what people put into their cars. But I was absolutely certain that the officials planned something really terrible. My first duty was to warn the other birds. I began with my neighbors. They all thought I was crazy—humans wouldn't hurt, much less kill, creatures that were so profitable to them, it just didn't make sense. I couldn't convince any of them.

Believe me, I did a lot of thinking that night. I'd often heard people say disparaging things about us, bird-brained, chicken-livered, that sort of thing. Well, now I was going to show those smart guys a thing or two. I'm sure none of them thought me capable of planning my escape in advance.

When the task force came the next morning I was ready for them. Speed and surprise were vital. I waited for my cue. The moment I saw the figures in jackboots and white coveralls turn the corner, I hunched over with my eyes half-closed and wing over my head as if I were ill, see, like this, Dr. Z. I'm a good actress—I didn't win a Petsy for nothing. There were two of them, one apparently the chief, grasping a pole with a net attached, the other holding a large plastic bag wide open. They were coming for me first! As they approached I crouched down even further and closed my left eye completely. My heart was pounding, but thank heaven they couldn't see or hear it. In fact they seemed relieved—sick birds don't cause as much trouble.

They were so sure of themselves, they didn't even bother to fasten the gate behind them. This was it! The instant the first man reached out to net me, I pushed against the perch with all my might and shot past the raised pole, right between the two outstretched hands of his startled helper, right out of the cage! Up, up, over the cellblock, the path below, through the trees, away to the open sky. *I was free!* For the first time in years I felt the air rush by with each downward thrust, each exhilarating upstroke. Never mind the tired, overlabored muscles—I knew then that I would never again allow myself to be captured… *never!*

Captivity! It is more than mere deprivation of freedom, it is the ultimate outrage—no trial, no reason given, no consent. I shall never forget that early morning when the natives seized Hantu Raya and me. Totally uncaring, they had separated us immediately. Inside the sack all was darkness, even as the sun rose over the ocean to proclaim another day. From the labored breathing and rhythmic jolting I knew that I had been slung over a man's shoulders. The sounds told me we were descending the rough trail that led down to the shore. At first I could hear Hantu Raya's imploring cries, and in turn did my best to respond. But eventually a total numbness overcame me, brought on in part by the deep shame I felt at having been caught.

It was about mid-morning when we arrived at the kampong. A hubbub of voices rose on all sides as the villagers pressed round us. A thrust from an unseen hand, a blinding shaft of sunlight, the clang of a metal gate, and I found myself locked inside a small cage of the type I had once seen at a distance when I first saw the village with my parents.

I looked around for any sign of Hantu Raya. There was none. Later I discovered why we had been separated. The daughter of the village chieftain wanted a white bird to call her own, and as I was the smaller of the pair and so presumably more amenable, I was chosen as Uta's playmate.

Her father's house was the most important in the village. Like all the other huts, the wooden framework was filled in with the leaf stems of the sago palm, but as a mark of distinction the floor was raised higher than all the others above the bare black earth. My cage was placed outside on the long verandah. From that vantage point my eyes followed everything that passed along the muddy path. The first day or two I was confident that I would soon be set free again. I truly believed that the natives would release both Hantu and myself the moment they realized what they had done. How naïve I was!

One morning I saw a shriveled old woman carrying a hen by its feet. From its limp neck I could tell that the bird had just been killed. I was still in a state of shock when the woman sat down on a chair right next to my cage and began to pluck the hen feather by feather. Every so often she would press the lifeless body against the bars and taunt me with a toothless grin as if to say, "It's your turn next!" I recalled horrible stories we had heard of birds being cooked and eaten by the natives. So they were true then!

I became very depressed, not caring if I lived or died. Uta, the young girl who so much wanted a bird of her own, did her best to cheer me up. Once she took me to a room inside the house which was separated from the rest by hanging mats. Then she carefully removed the spindles that held one side of my cage closed. At first I was too startled to move, but Uta encouraged me by holding a piece of ripe mango. I was very scared and suspected a trap. Uta coaxed me out eventually, and soon I was stumbling around on the floor, even climbing up the rattan chairs. Already I felt much happier.

The urge to fly was compelling. I tried a short flap across the room. This proved my undoing. You see, in a closed area one loses all sense of distance. Everything seems so big, but really there is so little space. The take-off was easy, but I misjudged my landing and ended up on top of some utensils on a table.

The clatter brought Uta's father and the old woman hurrying into the house from the back garden. They were both angry with Uta. Her father gave a curt order, the woman went out and returned with a length of bamboo. Inch by inch they backed me into a corner. I'll never forget those leathery hands descending on me. I screamed, tried to bite into them again and again, but it was no use. The woman had her hand behind my neck, while the man was hacking away at my flight feathers with a sharp instrument. I was terrified. I was positive I would never fly again. Maybe my feathers would never grow back.

My misadventure produced one minor consolation. No longer able to fly, I was allowed to pace up and down the log that served as a verandah rail. If only they hadn't attached that irksome chain to my right foot! I'm right-handed, sorry, I mean right-footed, and every time I wanted to hold a morsel that chain made it so heavy. But at least I was now out of the cage for the greater part of the day. I'll let you in on a little secret. When no one was looking, I'd take a peck or two from the back of a wooden upright to keep my mandibles in proper shape. Nobody found out, or if they did, they probably blamed the termites. Soon I became a great favorite with the villagers. It was then that I first honed some of the attention-getting tricks that were to prove so useful later on.

It all ended quite suddenly. For some time I had noticed that there was less food to go around. The villagers were desperately poor and always had to sell something to outsiders just to eke out a bare living. It was about then that the short-nosed stranger came and looked me over. He flashed his teeth a lot, to inspire confidence I suppose, but I could tell that his eyes felt something different from his mouth. From the moment I saw him I sensed that my troubles had only just begun.

Later I discovered that the Chinaman was a bird dealer from an enormous market place called Singapore. All I knew then was that I was being taken from familiar surroundings. When the man picked up the cage into which I had again been thrust, Uta betrayed little outward emotion, but I could see that she was fighting to hold back the tears. As I was carried aboard the rickety river steamer I caught a last glimpse of her waving goodbye to me before turning back to the village. She looked sad, as if a part of her were leaving with me. Could it be that she felt the way I did when Putih and Meka were so cruelly snatched away?

On the boat I was placed atop a much larger cage that housed at a rough guess some two dozen chattering lories. Further back stood a crate stuffed with bright green lorikeets. The steam whistle's piercing hoot terrified us all. As we chugged into midstream the unfeeling pulse of the engine drowned out a cacophony of captive outcries.

With each bend the river widened, and the waterborne traffic steadily increased. Often our helmsman took evasive action to steer wide of the less maneuverable praus. The evening sun had already begun its sudden tropical descent when we headed for shore. Upon landing, the cages were stacked on the quayside, one on top of the other, with me ruling the roost, so to speak.

I had never seen so many people before. Some were pushing two-wheeled carts piled high with produce, others were carrying poles slung across shoulders bent under the heavy loads suspended from either side, still others were pedaling trishaws and driving all sorts of machines, the whole intermingling in a constant clamor that bewildered the senses.

We did not remain on the quayside long. With the onset of darkness, we were placed on the flat bed of what I know now to be a truck. You can't imagine how frightening this all was at first. Then came an even more fearful experience. I knew it was night, yet the humans changed it to day with bright beams of light! A still bigger surprise followed. Suddenly I found myself being whisked through the air by a giant arm that pivoted and then just as quickly lowered me into some black chasm. A slight bump, unseen hands grasping the cages and then setting us down. Where was I? Where? Where?

Only with the light of day did it become clear. All around me I heard the hiss and clang of powerful pistons going in and out and of wheels turning. From the undulating motion I felt that this was no longer the river but the open sea. I sensed—I knew—that we were heading away from the island that had always been my home. Farewell Mount Hella and my beloved batai! As I clung to the bars of my cell in the cavernous depths of the sea monster I despaired of ever seeing the rain forest or Hantu Raya again.

※

And now just the reverse was happening. I had, as they say, flown the coop. Whether Les and Doris would ever be reimbursed by the Department of Depopulation was the least of my concerns. For the first hour I dashed from tree to tree, caught my breath, and flew on, anything to put distance between myself and those men with their plastic bags. Thank goodness my primaries had grown back long ago! I had kept up my flying exercises faithfully. Even so, I was in no condition for such an undertaking.

I had little idea of where I was headed, even less what the strange sights were that I gazed upon for the first time. Toward mid-day I alighted on a high wooden wall with huge colored letters and pictures on both sides. Further ahead, I saw a whole series strung along the roadside—men puffing smoke rings, giant bottles, near naked women lying in the sun, cars floating in the sky, and other amazing sights. I had never learned to read, so for the life of me couldn't imagine what the messages said. They must have been very important, though, for the humans to use up so much valuable material. Personally, I still prefer to see the hills and trees and sky, but that's just my ignorance showing.

The houses went on forever. All I saw were roofs and gardens and pools and streets and cars and boards repeated a hundred hundred times. And then there were row after row of peculiar bare trees, boles straight as could be with crossbars and wires in place of boughs and leaves. The air was acrid and hung heavy with a yellowish pall. Of the rain forest there was no sign. It was now late afternoon and I was hungry and tired. Other than a few buds and the sap from some young twigs, I had nothing to eat or drink that first day.

I had to stop frequently for rest at one strange place after another. Once I tried to take a breather in a palm tree that reminded me of my homeland. Immediately flocks of sparrows and starlings squawking to high heaven banded together to prevent my intrusion. I felt most conspicuous on the wires next to the mockingbirds and doves, so exhausted as I was, I flew on.

Twilight had set in when I found the flowering eucalyptus. Its location was not ideal, for nearby a boisterous group of gaudily attired partygoers was cooking something at the edge of a bluish pool of water. All that noise and nonsense! Thank goodness, they were far too busy to glance up. As for me, I was terrified to move even a feather. Even when they finally went indoors I kept myself hidden in the upper branches.

Only with the first morning light did I venture down. Not a soul was stirring. On the ground were some crumbs and other leftovers which I gobbled down ravenously. Ugh! What junk these humans eat! Isn't there *anything* from nature? The water from the pool tasted just as bad—nothing like rainwater, even worse than the sludge Tummy used to leave in our cages. Well, I quenched my thirst as best as I could, then returned to my lofty refuge to survey my surroundings.

The man-city stretched in every direction as far as the eye could see. Was it possible that this strange land had no forests or rivers? There was only one way to discover if the concrete ribbons had any end. Higher and higher I flew, heedless of fatigue and danger, reveling every moment of my newfound freedom. And there, no more than a purple fringe above the yellowish haze, I could discern hills that rose to mountains beyond. I needed no further beckoning. High above the squat buildings I directed my anxious flight to the open spaces denied me for so long.

The gaps between the houses grew larger, then the first fields appeared. For the first time I felt confident I would survive. Food, mostly scattered seeds and grasses, became plentiful. My endurance rapidly increased. Occasionally I came upon a field of maize or savored from a tree laden with ripening fruit, such as I had last done in my homeland long ago. Even the sight of a hawk circling hungrily in the sky did not disturb me. From the islands I knew they much preferred meeker prey which could not strike back. Best of all, there were few signs of human presence.

At times I was absurdly optimistic, expecting at any moment to see Hantu winging towards me. That was really silly of me. If he had been brought to this country, he would almost certainly still be a prisoner. Much as I hated the idea, the only real hope of finding him was to stay close to human habitation. But where? He could easily be penned up in a home like the Wingford-Simons' or languishing on a pet shop stand. And then there was no reason why he should not be in some other part of this vast terrain. The more I thought of it, the more hopeless it all seemed. There was only one possibility I refused to consider: that Hantu Raya was dead.

So I decided to look for some place like Tierra Exotica where there might be hundreds of birds. All that second day and the next I scoured the countryside, but in vain. Late on the third evening I spied something that gave me hope. In an open field stood a long tin-roofed barn from which issued a sustained cackling and chattering such as I had never heard before. I could already make out hundreds and hundreds of white forms packed closely together. Surely these could not all be cockatoos! I see you're having a little laugh at my expense, Dr. Z.

In the failing light the rows of wire pens and feeding troughs took on an eerie aspect. One look at the inflated size of the birds and I could tell that they were never allowed to exercise, but were being fattened up for the humans. From my stay at the Wingford-Simons I knew they would be killed for their rubbery flesh. I cried out for them to escape, but it was no use. With a feeling of utter helplessness I ascended into the evening sky to find a resting place for the night.

In the following weeks my search for Hantu took me over meadow and forest, over mountain ranges and ravines, across deserts and scrubland. By the first light of morning or at dusk I would venture into human communities for any sign of him. The result was always the same. Once in a while I heard the strident call of captive macaws and similar relatives, but never that of my own kind.

And now the season was already changing, no longer the friendly warmth of late summer, but the first chilly rains of autumn. With the fruit trees bare and the fields all harvested, I was faced with a struggle just to exist. Still I was determined never to give up my quest.

I set out early one raw fall morning upon my daily search. From afar I caught sight of a strange spectacle. On the outskirts of a small town an immense construction looking for all the world like a dozen billowing lateen sails sewn together had been erected. Oh, you've guessed already, Dr. Z! Yes, it was the big top of a circus. On all sides were parked garishly painted vans and other vehicles. There were no people about, so I decided to investigate.

Now came the big surprise. On one of the trailers stood a pair of sturdy cages. Cages! No one was awake, so I glided silently toward them. Yet even as I drew near, I saw how foolish I had been. Inside the nearest was a pair of bengal tigers, animals I recognized from a TV program I used to watch. Another cage contained a large furry creature that was as far removed from a bird as one could possibly imagine.

I was about to give up when a slight movement caught my attention. A door opening, a curtain being parted—it could have been anything. I watched from the safety of a huge oak tree, not knowing whether to stay or be on my way again. And then I heard the sound, the thrilling sound of a great bird's call to herald another day. There was no mistaking those magnificent quavers! There, confined in a miniscule cage chained to a trailer, was Hantu Raya! With one flurry of my wings I was next to him. At first he gave a cry of alarm, then one of unbelieving joy. I clung to the wire as we tried to touch one another after such a long separation.

Just then I heard the creaking sound of footsteps on the trailer floor and the outside door swing open. Luckily I had the good sense to fly up to the roof and hide behind a metal pipe. Below on the steps, an orange wig with a fleshy woman underneath turned around slowly and went inside again. By now several people were astir. I had no choice but to remain where I was.

Shortly people began to busy themselves on the grounds. Several of the horses were being exercised, at the same time other animals were led into the big tent. For the tigers a special cage-tunnel was assembled by the circus hands. Finally it was Hantu's turn. I don't know how they did it as they first took him inside the trailer. When he came out, a muscular man with pictures all over his arms was holding him on a long stick. *Hantu, fly off, fly off!* I wanted to shout. Why didn't he? My heart sank, for I felt sure that his wings must have been clipped. Just then I noticed that Muscles was dangling coils of a long cord attached to Hantu's right foot. Good! That meant there was a chance he could still fly. I placed all my hopes on that fact.

A few minutes later Hantu reemerged from the big tent. A minute or so in the trailer, then back in the tiny cage. I could see that the heavy steel mesh and padlock were far too strong even for our combined efforts. Hantu looked up to me imploringly. But we had to bide our time, there was nothing else to do. As the day wore on I became famished, yet I didn't dare move. If only Muscles would take Hantu out of the cage just once more!

Toward sunset the fairground was all abustle. A crowd had gathered in front of the trailer next to mine. To the thumping blare of a calliope a barker was haranguing the bystanders. "Ladies and Gentlemen, you are about to witness the greatest circus show on earth. See Zoltan defy the man-eating tigers—" Ridiculous! They were about as dangerous as old Toothy with his dentures out. "—followed by the Raquel sisters on the high wire with no, I repeat, no safety net." So what? I don't use one either. "And specially for the kiddies there's Snowy, the magnificent flying Salmon-crested cockatoo, just like on TV…"

So that was it! Hantu Raya, at the end of a long cord, forced to fly round and round in endless circles for the amusement of the circusgoers. No doubt the performance would end with a sharp tug as the jess was pulled in.

There was no time to lose. Everything depended on whether Muscles followed the same routine as that morning. When night at last fell, I remained absolutely still at my post. Nearly everyone was inside the large tent. From my hiding place I could see Hantu cooped in his cell. The wait seemed interminable. Perhaps I had misjudged everything.

Finally Muscles, this time with a cape thrown over his shoulders, came to take Hantu inside the trailer and attach the cord. Another eternity. Then came the crucial moment as the trailer door swung open. I waited until Muscles stepped outside. It was now or never. In an instant I swooped down and plunged my mandibles first into one painted forearm, then the other. Muscles cursed and tried to wave me off, but he wouldn't let go until I had bitten deeply into his right hand. Without wasting a second I gathered up the cord in my feet and beak, and urged Hantu to take flight. He needed no further bidding. Together we rose from the ground, at last, at long last, both free!

On we soared into the night until we reached a forest of live oaks. Our flinty beaks acting in unison made short shrift of the cord. Only when we saw it slip to earth did we feel truly free. What perfect bliss to nuzzle up against one another after so many years apart! And so much to relate without knowing where to begin! Hantu listened with amazement to my adventures. He had nothing comparable to recount, only a deadening succession of unfeeling keepers who could not, or would not, understand that he was a wild spirit. If anything, the traveling circus had marked an upswing in his life. At least there he had a chance to fly, even if at the end of a jess. Now, all that belonged to the past. What of the future?

Our happiness was tinged with the sad realization that we were so far from home. How we missed the majestic batai, the fruiting durians and palms, the familiar plants and creatures that together made up our island refuge! Was it even possible to reach the tropics? In which direction should we fly? Always more questions. As the cold grey rainclouds swept the hillsides our dreams seemed so distant as to be out of reach.

Hantu Raya became suddenly animated. "Bikkia, there *is* one who can help us," he said. "I heard from a captive hornbill about a venerable cockatoo as wise as Old Binaija. He sits all day on an open perch in a zoo set amid a beautiful park. He is named King Tut because he holds court to all who enter. He will know."

I remained dubious. "How can we find him?" I asked.

Hantu refused to become discouraged. "We must travel south to where the ocean makes a wide bay. There we will find King Tut."

Our plan entailed great risk, for it meant flying where the humans were most densely settled. We were loath to return to the man-city, but there was no other way. Fortunately, Hantu had kept his wing muscles strong, and somehow he knew where to find nourishment. I was overjoyed to see that the years of captivity had not deprived him of his resourcefulness. After no more than two or three days his flight was as sure and strong as it had been in the rain forest.

By and by we reached the coast and headed south. Each dawn the sun climbed higher over the inland hills to disperse the seaboard fog and warm the chill air. By noon we had already crisscrossed many miles in our search for the big bay. Sometimes the coastline would describe a gentle curve, then for brief stretches the cliffs ascended to imposing heights. Small estuaries abounded, but nowhere was there a sign of the deep inlet we sought. You have no idea how disappointed we were. Maybe it didn't even exist.

One day we thought we had found it. A shallow channel meandering inland from the shore widened into a lagoon landward of the main highway. Other than the steady traffic and a stand of billboards there was no sign of habitation, certainly not of enclosures housing thousands of fellow animals. Hantu reckoned the gardens with their presiding King Tut might be found on the far side of a high promontory that jutted out into the expanse of water. But with each wingbeat it became clearer that no zoo was here. Dejectedly, we wheeled round to return to the coast.

Just then, seemingly from nowhere, the air resounded to the crack of whining pellets. In our anxiety we had let caution slip. Down in the scrubland below, advancing into the open, were two young boys, guns brazenly in hand. They had already reloaded and were taking careful aim at us in our confused flight. At the sound of the double report we instinctively pulled in our wings. Perhaps this is what saved us, for the slugs missed their intended mark. We were badly shaken and didn't stop to rest until we were well clear of our would-be assassins.

On and on we flew, ever southwards in search of the bay. All around us scudded banks of rainclouds that teasingly cast their dark shadow on sea and land, only to withhold their moisture from the parched fields below. Finally they relented and released their life-giving showers as we rested in a eucalyptus grove. For Hantu and me this was a rare delectable moment to spread out our wings as the rain subsided and feel the fine drops trickle down our feathers. For an hour or two we fondly imagined that we were back home.

An iridescent sun brought an end to such reveries. The storm had blown itself out, not a cloud was visible for miles around. The rain had cleansed the air so thoroughly that even the most distant object was brilliantly clear. And then we saw it! At first no more than a silver sliver on the horizon, but with each downthrust it loomed larger. We had found the bay! It was an incredible sight, with sails and ships of every kind and size flecking the glistening waters. To the south an imposing bridge arched gracefully over the harbor. Beyond a doubt this was our goal. Our next task was to locate the zoo and the venerable greeter with the regal name.

But where to look in such a large city? Again the never-ending masses of buildings, streets, traffic. There must be another place, an oasis of trees and plants, maybe a small lake or two, a green island set apart from the engulfing waves of houses.

This city was unlike any other we had viewed on our travels. Here the gigantic machines swept out of the sky and descended into the very midst of the highest buildings. Late one morning we found ourselves right in the path of one of these monsters, just like that day long ago on our island. But this one was many times larger. Out of sheer fright we fled from its screaming approach, heedless of where our headlong rush took us.

We were all the more amazed to find that we had landed in a grove of lavender-flowered jacaranda trees with tropical bushes and palms on every side. More incredibly still, at the end of a flamingo-filled lagoon, perched on his very own branch, stood the unmistakable august figure of King Tut! Paying no attention to the other inhabitants or the crowd of people, we hurried over to join our noble ancestor.

I could see that King Tut was very old indeed. Only when he failed to recognize two of his fellow Moluccans did I notice that cataracts had formed over both his eyes. He seemed more frightened by the presence of strangers sharing his perch than by the onlookers behind the railing.

It was only when Hantu explained who we were that King Tut warmed to us. In his rusty native accents he told us that he had been taken from the rain forest more than sixty years ago. He was, so he assured us, the oldest resident of this zoo in a city called San Diego, and he had been honored with the title of Official Greeter. As to the original King Tut, he had no idea of who that was—certainly no Moluccan.

King Tut generously offered us his royal counsel. "I am far too old to join you," he declared. "Besides, this has been my home for too long. My keepers have been kind to me, and have looked after me for many seasons. I know I will soon die. No, don't cry, Bikkia, we must all face the truth. You are both young and strong. You must return to your island home."

"But how?" I pleaded. "We're so far away. We can't just fly across the ocean."

"That's true enough, my dear. But there is a way. What man has done he can also undo. You must fly down to the harbor and seek out the largest of the ships. When it prepares to leave, you must find a home on board."

"But the humans!" Hantu protested.

"Some are cruel, I have to admit, but most wish to be kind. Remember, from where I stand thousands of men, women, and children pass by every day. I cannot see them, but none has ever harmed me. Go now, do as I say, and my prayers be with you, my children."

"Dr. Z., I was so sad when you told me that King Tut had died shortly after our visit. You called him a *rara avis*, which in some clever language means a very special bird. Well, Dr. Z., you're a *rara prof*, if I may say so."

"Bikkia, now you're embarrassing me. But I'm anxious to hear the rest of your story."

Very well then. Sorrowfully, we took our leave both of King Tut and his pleasant surroundings. Buoyed by his words, we winged our way to the harbor. So many ships lay at anchor, we had no way of telling which might be the right one. Now that we had to make a choice, our task seemed more difficult than ever.

Just then the decision was made for us. At the harbor entrance, steaming resolutely toward the open sea, was the most splendid vessel you can imagine. In a flash we made up our minds and gave chase. You should have seen how startled the resident seagulls were—not to mention the more dignified cormorants and pelicans—at the sight of two exotic strangers hurtling through the air at breakneck speed!

In a matter of minutes we had closed the gap with the ship and were holding tightly on to a railing high up in the superstructure. On the deck below, a group of sailors was gazing up at us, puzzled no doubt by our unfamiliar contour. As for Hantu and myself, we were too keyed up and far too scared to descend from our eyrie. One favorable sign: at least the sailors gestured with their hands and held nothing more menacing than mops and squeegees.

For several hours we sailed on, clinging to our perch. By now we had left the land far astern, and the ship was gently heaving in the ocean swell. At dusk the first shipboard lights came on. To ward off the chill, Hantu and I snuggled up close, but still the biting night wind penetrated through to the skin. Had we come this far merely to die of cold and hunger?

No, dear Dr. Z., I would not care to relive that first night. We were lucky enough to find a warm niche close to the funnel, but that did little to assuage the pangs of hunger and thirst. So much water around us, yet not a drop to slake our parched gullets! Even so, we would not have traded our freedom for the most magnificent cage in the world.

With the first light of dawn a small knot of sailors had gathered to see if we were still there. One, wearing an apron and a tall white hat, tossed something on to the deck. Bread! At the same time the men withdrew a few steps. Our famished crops gave us no choice. We fluttered down to a lower railing, ready to dash up to the masthead at the first sign of danger. Keeping a wary eye on the crew, we slowly edged along the railing toward the bread crumbs. We could hold back no longer. Abandoning our vigilance, we gobbled up every piece in sight.

The men were delighted. One of them pushed a small basin of water toward us. How good it tasted! To our surprise they made no attempt to approach us. By now a sizable crowd had assembled. They were obviously at a loss to explain our presence. One described us as Mexican seagulls, another was positive we were snowy owls. Can you beat that, Dr. Z? A third sailor darkly assured his shipmates that we were albatrosses which invariably portended bad luck for all mariners. He was deservedly ridiculed by the others. No one knew who or what we were, but it was clear they had taken a liking to us.

Already a more southerly sun suffused its warmth. And thanks to the crew, food and housing were no longer a problem. One of them had been thoughtful enough to fashion a wooden perch from an old broomstick which was given the place of honor on the captain's bridge, no less. From the captain on down, everyone seemed determined that we were to travel first class. With each hour we became less apprehensive. Soon we accepted the crew performing their chores in much the same way we viewed the hardy gulls that followed in the ship's wake.

By the third day I had completely overcome my fear of the seamen. Hantu was far more distrustful, and kept urging me not to approach them too closely. I tried to tell him that from what I had overheard of the sailors' conversation they had no wish to harm us, in fact quite the contrary. He still didn't believe me, though now he no longer flew off each time one of the crewmen sauntered by.

Late one sultry afternoon we sighted land. We couldn't contain our excitement at the thought that this might be our island. I nudged closer to where a group of sailors were leaning over the rail. One pointed to the horizon, and I was sure that I caught the word Moluccas. We were home! I rushed off to tell Hantu.

Leaving our sailor friends shipboard, we scaled the air currents to catch a better glimpse of the smudge in the distance. And there, off to the right, was the faint outline of a mountain! Mount Hella, it must be! In our imagination we already saw the towering emergents thrusting their crowns above the forest, the graceful palms bowing their heads to the ocean. Yet as we approached, it became all too clear that the headland was not our familiar Hella. Our disappointment was all the more intense when we caught sight of the wall of white buildings that lined the shoreline and the steady stream of traffic along the coast road. We were still far from home.

We returned to the ship, by now our familiar surroundings. Of course we'd been foolishly optimistic. The ship was now sailing towards another isle in the island chain. A few hours later, as the sun set we anchored in a beautifully sheltered harbor in a busy city. The sailors kept repeating the names Honolulu and Hawai'i, and one burly officer who seemed to be at home there once said something about Moloka'i to his companions. So *that* was our Moluccas!

"What is it, Dr. Z? Something the matter?"

"Not at all, Bikkia. Quite the opposite. You just mentioned the island of Moloka'i. That's where Father Damien did his wonderful work among the leper colony. These people were outcasts who suffered a great deal, and Father Damien devoted his whole life to helping them. That's why they've made him a saint."

"A saint?"

"Someone who through personal example and sacrifice teaches humans how we should act. There aren't many of them."

"You're one of them, Dr. Z. You're a real saint!"

"Bless you Bikkia. But you don't quite understand…"

"Yes I do. You've also spent your whole life helping others. Dr. Z., you really are for the birds. Really."

Dr. Z. smiled in a way that I had never seen before.

"Bikkia, that is the most wonderful thing that has ever been said to me. I will treasure it for ever. But you've got to finish your story now."

You're right. Well, as you can imagine, Hantu and I were getting desperate. We had no idea how far away we were from home. Should we stay on this unfamiliar isle or strike off on our own? The longer the ship remained at anchor, the more we began to lose heart. Perhaps we should try to find another ship leaving harbor. But what if the new sailors were unfriendly, even hostile?

One morning we noticed unusual activity on board. A tender had drawn up alongside, all manner of supplies were being transferred from the smaller craft to our own. As we peered down from the rigging, the bustle at first meant little to us. About midday the cook came on deck to toss a few tidbits our way. "Well, my two old salts," he called out lustily, "are you sailing with us or not? Tonight it's anchors aweigh and off again." *Where? Where?* I screamed, quite forgetting that I couldn't enunciate the word. In any case the cook would never have understood. At times humans use very little imagination.

There was a magnificent sunset when the ship sailed out of harbor, the striated clouds suffused with the same hints of vermilion that permeate ourselves. Gradually the shore lights receded and were snuffed out one by one. Once more we were on our own, surrounded by an endless watery expanse. The air became heavier with the onset of tropical rain storms. No longer did the sailors move with their earlier alacrity.

Every evening Hantu Raya and I would stretch our wings as we tracked the ship's furrow in the twilight breeze. Usually the railing was lined with half the crew. From their cheerful faces and waving I could tell they derived true pleasure from watching our uninhibited flight. They called us "our lucky mascots," which made me especially happy.

A week later we found ourselves sailing through an archipelago to the accompaniment of the monsoon rains. Each time Hantu and I sighted an island we would lift away in fervent expectation, only to return disappointed. There were so many coral strands and volcanic peaks that we hardly knew which way to direct our flight.

As the days slipped by, so did our optimism. Sometimes we thought we had recognized a feature—a headland, a familiar contour—only to see our hopes dashed again. The crew seemed to sense our bewilderment, and were not even sure whether to be happy or sad upon our return to the ship.

We had just about given up all hope when we saw it. Like a beckoning mirage, the ascending shape rose out of the ocean early one morning. This time there was no mistaking it: the cleft cone of our beloved Mount Hella rising above the island, the beaches we had known from our earliest days, the mangrove cluster by the tidal pool, the stately durian trees, the majestic batais, merbaus, merantis, and there the clove trees protecting the nutmeg trees beneath. No place on earth could possibly compare with this.

It was time to bid a sad farewell to our seafaring friends who had cared for us so well. To show our thanks, we circled the ship three times and dipped our wings. I'm sure the sailors knew what was in our hearts, for we could see them waving up to us. As we left the ship for the last time we sang a song of delirious joy. With each downstroke our island came closer.

And there, high above the canopy of the rain forest, winging its way oceanwards, was a cloud of birds—our own!—coming out to welcome us. We were home, home at last.

Down To Earth

When good men die, their spirits go to a good place; when bad men die, their spirits go back into coyotes.

Old Indian saying.

Down To Earth

Already it had been one of the worst winters in living memory. The first snow had carpeted the open range as early as mid-October, and ever since, the wind-blown drifts had piled up relentlessly. Small wonder that the sheep were in such pitiable condition. In past years a mild thaw around Christmas had enabled the flock to batten briefly on the exposed clumps of grass. But not this winter. The provender was running dangerously low. The drought of the previous summer had lasted for months, reducing the land to a dry-brown desert. And now this.

To old sheep ranchers like Bill Bakewell and the few others who hung on tenaciously in this inhospitable high plateau country there was a biblical element to life: either feast or famine, with little in between.

Bill had plenty of other worries. As if the weather were not enough, several pairs of ravenous coyotes had now made their ominous appearance. Usually the marauders were content to molest the weaker animals, the old and infirm, sheep that in any case had scant hope of surviving the harsh winter. Up till this year Bill had managed to keep the upper hand. The trap lines had taught the coyotes to stay a safe distance from the main body of the flock. For the unwary predator who ventured too close, Bill was ready with his hunting rifle. One way or another he had always held the critters in check. Until a month ago, that is.

It was in late January that Bill first sighted the wily newcomer. As bad luck would have it, that was one of the rare occasions when the rancher found himself out of reach of a gun. That very morning Jeanie had remarked how much it needed cleaning, and conscientious farmer's wife that she was, had immediately set about the task herself. If only Bill had had his .22 with him in the truck, he could have rid himself of the varmint then and there. The coyote couldn't have been more than two hundred feet away. There, in broad daylight, hunkered down in the snow on the far side of the swale, the animal stared straight at him through those cold yellow eye slits of his. Why didn't he turn tail and run? Strange, Bill mused, it was almost as if the coyote sensed he was in no danger. A cunning devil, for sure.

Bill had recognized the marauder at once, the type of coyote a veteran rancher feared most of all: a strong mature male, some twelve or so years old, wary of men and their traps, with an intelligence honed by the constant struggle for survival. As his adversary guardedly rose to his feet, Bill could make out his earthy coloration, the tawny yellowish coat with irregular flecks of white under the neck and belly, the lower legs trimmed in black, something diabolical about the creature he couldn't quite identify. Lucifer, he deserves the name of Lucifer, the rancher decided. That same moment the coyote, alerted by some slight movement, pointed his ears, turned tail, and trotted off to safer ground.

Lucifer had first attracted attention to himself soon after the New Year by brazenly killing a ewe at least twice his own weight. Then barely a week later the killer had severely mauled and finished off Jack, a ram penned close to the farmhouse, something hitherto unheard of. After that scarcely more than two days went by without some further depredation. Although new to the vicinity, the trespasser had quickly proved himself the most cunning of creatures, possessed of an amazing ability to outwit his human foe. Bill had tried everything, all the old proven devices, but nothing had worked.

Once, in fact, he had squinted straight at Lucifer as he sought to hold him in the crosshairs of his telescopic sight. But darned if the cur didn't keep moving just enough to prevent a steady aim, besides staying a smidgen out of range. Then another time Bill was sure he had him caught in a leghold trap—no other thief would have dared come that close to the chicken run—but incredibly the coyote had kicked just enough snow and dirt onto the pan to spring the jaws shut. All that remained of his nocturnal visit was a dead hen and some telltale hairs as if to mock the thwarted farmer.

It was this latest incident that prompted him to seek the advice of Harry Lind, a widower who ran the neighboring ranch some two miles to the east. Bill hated to admit to a fellow sheepman that he couldn't outfox a coyote, but then Lucifer wasn't what you might call your common critter. As Bill drove over the snow-encrusted country road he couldn't help but feel that there was something uncanny, even supernatural about it all. But then as he turned off toward the low buildings of Harry's spread, his basic common sense took hold again. Once he was rid of that sneaky varmint the whole affair would soon be forgotten.

Harry was standing at the front door to welcome him. Both men were hardy oldtimers, their faces creased by a lifetime's exposure to the elements. Like so many of the sheepfarmers thereabouts, they seemed to have been carved out of their very surroundings.

"Come on in," Harry said, waving his friend into the clapboard house. "How's it going, Bill? Hope ol' Jack's still earning his keep," he added with a knowing wink.

Instead of a responsive laugh, Bill could barely muster a groan. With more than a trace of embarrassment in his voice he related the incident about his prize ram getting killed.

"Never seen anything like it," he confessed. "I always knew coyotes were smart, but this one takes the prize. You know that fence I put up last fall back of the chicken run? Well, this devil snuck right underneath it and grabbed two of my best hens. Didn't even eat 'em, oh no—just killed 'em for the heck of it. So me and the boys dug real deep the whole way round and put in sheet metal under the wire. Took us a whole day. You'd think that ought to do it, wouldn't you?"

Harry poured out two stiff bourbon-on-the rocks and sat down.

"You'd think so. Here's to you, Bill."

"Thanks, I needed that. Well, three days later this same coyote—I know damn well it was the same one—out he comes in the middle of the night and you know what he does? Sonofabitch climbs on to the roof of the shed, he sneaks around the side of the house, right past my bedroom, smack across the backyard and into the chicken run. No chickens for him this time, oh no, not good enough for his fancy tastes, so the s.o.b. goes and helps himself to my best goose."

Harry had never seen his neighbor look more pained and tried his best to sound reassuring. "The geese must have raised the roof?" he ventured, none too convincingly.

"That's the funny thing. I didn't hear a sound, nothing. It's spooky, I'm telling you."

Harry thought for a moment and narrowed his eyes. "You sure it wasn't one of them wetbacks you got working for you?"

"Hell, no, Harry, couldn't be. They've been with me for years." Bill took a generous sip of bourbon to fortify himself. "Besides, why should they do a thing like that? Just don't make any sense. Anyhow, I saw the tracks in the snow next morning myself, big as you please. That's a coyote, all right."

Harry nodded knowingly. "Sounds like the same devil Hal Rolfson's been having trouble with. He's a damned smart one, all right. Say, Bill, have you tried luring him with one of those phony rabbit scents? It's real simple—all you do is get the s.o.b. downwind and you've got him. Then when he shows up you just plug him with buckshot. Nothing to it. I've done it a dozen times."

"We tried that," Bill said, shaking his head helplessly, "but it didn't work. That's what's so damn frustrating, nothing works. That coyote just *knows*. You name it, we've tried it—mixed baits, those newfangled tapes, you know, the ones that make a sound like a rabbit squealing—you can't fool the bastard. Then damned if that same animal don't sneak in right under my nose and make off with my best cotton cake feed. Now don't go telling me that's your regular coyote. The devil, Lucifer, that's what he is."

Harry regarded his friend with genuine sympathy. After all, it could be his turn next. "Sure wish Clint Hammett was here. I've never seen a guy like Clint when it came to getting rid of coyotes. That troublemaker of yours wouldn't have stood a chance against Clint."

"Hammett? Well, he can't help now, wherever he is. Don't get me wrong, no disrespect for the dead, but he hassled me plenty over that damn fence of his. Let's forget him. Listen, Harry, you, me, Hal, the rest of the guys, if we all put our heads together we can outsmart that animal. Dammit, we can't have a stupid coyote making fools out of the whole bunch of us."

"Damn right we can't. You put out poison, did you?"

"Sure, you always put a little poison in the bait, have to."

"No, no, I'm talking about a *real* poison trap, not that old-fashioned kind you've been messing with. This'll get him."

"Are you sure? Lord knows we put down plenty of the stuff already."

To tell the truth, Bill didn't enjoy using these methods. Years ago one of his own collies had been poisoned by mistake and it had taken him a long time to get over her agonized death. But now that his very livelihood was threatened, well, that's where a fellow had to draw the line.

"Oh, sure," Harry was saying, "but my way's the best. It's what you might call a refinement. Come on outside, I'll show you what I'm talking about. I've got a spare one in the shed if you want to give it a try."

Bill emptied his glass and followed his friend through the house out to the tool shed. "I sure appreciate it, Harry. Damned if I'm going to lose everything to a coyote. Just give me enough of what it takes to fix that sneak."

Bill left in far higher spirits than when he had arrived. He knew exactly where to lay the trap, next to a fence post on his property line where he had recently caught a glimpse of Lucifer rubbing his back. Early the next morning he set out with Carlos and Javier, his two farmhands. He was surprised to see how simple the trap really was, no more than a piece of reeking mutton bait covered with an old jacket. Underneath was hidden a spring device which at the appropriate moment shot a cyanide cartridge right into the mouth of the predator. Simple and effective. All he had to do now was wait.

The next morning Bill set out barely after sunrise. No sooner had he reached the fence when he spied fresh tracks in the soft snow. In his excitement he broke into a labored run. He could already make out a furry form huddled at the foot of the post. As he bounded the last few yards through the snow, elation turned to bitter frustration. Of course those weren't coyote tracks, any fool could see that. There, unmistakable with its black-ringed tail and yellow-black fur, lay the inert body of a raccoon.

The rancher was furious with himself as he retraced his steps. What on earth would Jeanie think when she heard his, well, sheepish confession? He was so certain the trap would work that he had rushed out of the house without his gun. Now, likely as not, Lucifer had seen the way the trap was rigged and would shun all such contrivances in the future. Bill had heard of legendary coyotes with storehouse memories of places and things to avoid. But try as he may, he couldn't recall a single one to come close to Lucifer.

He reached the end of the fence and started gingerly across the frozen rill at the edge of the field that lay between him and the farmhouse. In his bones he felt that he was being watched intently. There, to the right of the ice-coated rivulet, he could make out the snowy-grey form of some animal. Probably the mate of the dead raccoon, he guessed. But somehow the size and posture were all wrong. And then, just as suddenly, he realized that it was Lucifer—the devil!—following his every movement.

Bill had never seen him so close before. Relaxed, unafraid, Lucifer crouched perfectly still, making no attempt to escape. Rather he seemed to be eyeing the farmer more in puzzlement than in fright. Bill, at first spellbound at the sight of his cunning adversary, took a few tentative steps toward the creature who slowly straightened to his full height. The rancher could clearly discern the straw-colored vitreous eyes focused on him. With a peculiarly uneasy feeling, he sensed that the canine was somehow taking his measure, as if making a mental note of his human foe. Despite himself, Bill was strangely moved by the feral intelligence that illumined those lyncean eyes. And then, just as stealthily as the encounter had begun, the coyote shook himself free of snow and headed toward the open country.

In the nights that followed Bill heard Lucifer at all hours. Pinpointing the actual source, even the direction, of those eerie wails that would rise to a staccato pitch only to subside to a piteous yelp, was well-nigh impossible. Often the mournful cry sounded as if came from right under his and Jeanie's bedroom window, only to fade to a derisive echo from some distant butte. Bill had long known what ventriloquists coyotes were; he also knew that this one had selected him, William Bakewell, for piecemeal destruction. One morning Carlos reported that a sturdy ewe and her day-old lamb, the first-born of the season, had been found mauled to death. That did it. For Bill it was now a fight for survival.

It was Jeanie's idea to invite the neighboring ranchers round for a war council. All else had failed, maybe together they could find a way to outwit the beast.

"A bounty hunt's the only way to get him," Tom Calderwood declared. "That's what Clint Hammett did the last time this happened, a hundred bucks to the guy that shot him. If I remember right, that coyote didn't last the day."

"You're doggone right," Harry Lind agreed. "Tomorrow's Sunday, let's get a snow hunt together while the stuff's still on the ground. We can all have a little fun while we're at it. Hey, how about each of us chipping in ten bucks for the prize—wha'd'ya say?"

The proposal was approved unanimously. Winter had been long and dreary, and a snowmobile hunt, especially for such a worthy cause, promised welcome relief. At last Bill was confident of ridding himself of this uninvited guest who had so arrogantly feasted at his expense these past three months.

No sportsman could have asked for better hunting weather the next morning. A light sprinkling of snow had fallen overnight, leaving a fresh cover under a radiant sky. The parka-clad hunters, further warmed by a generous dram or two from their hip flasks, mounted their motorized sleighs. To a roar of open throttles and exuberant shouts the riders headed toward the open range. As the machines skimmed across the white expanse, small groups of sheep could be seen dotted around pawing the snow where the crust was thinnest. Carlos and Javier on horseback, accompanied by sheep dogs, were out scrutinizing the heavy ewes, one or two of which had already lambed and were busy suckling their ungainly offspring. Soon the snow would melt, and with the spring thaw the lambing season would begin in earnest. This would be the last chance of the year to rev up the snowmobiles and charge over the gently undulating prairie.

In the brisk morning air the motors' whine interspersed with the hunters' whoops of excitement reverberated for miles around, enough to terrify even the most courageous of beasts. Such was the crystal visibility that the furthest ridge and butte stood out with knifelike clarity. The hunters now rode abreast of one another, scanning the horizon, each anxious to be the first to spot and shoot the culprit and so claim the bounty. Other coyote tracks were imprinted in the fresh snow for miles around, but so far the quarry had eluded his pursuers.

Bill's practiced eye spotted him first. "There he is, over by that ridge! I'd recognize that bastard anywhere. First shot's mine!" he shouted, wheeling to give chase.

No more than a quarter of a mile off to their left stood a solitary coyote.

"That's him all right," Hal Rolfson confirmed, raising his binoculars. "That's the one we're after."

The entire posse made a half turn and spurred on their powered steeds. Lucifer, seemingly unafraid until now, bounded away toward the brow of a low hill. Where could he run to now? This time he'd been caught out in the open with nowhere to hide. Even the smartest ones slip up in the end.

But the view from the crest was not what the hunters had expected. In the declivity below stood a flock of some four or five hundred sheep that had strayed from their bedground. And somewhere in the middle of that ovine mass was a killer coyote. For the ranchers there was no other recourse than to dismount and survey the sea of dirty brown backs and blank faces for any sign of the interloper. Caught between a coyote and the armed men, the sheep raised their voices in a bleating cacophony. Of Lucifer there was no sign.

It was Harry who decided how to break the impasse.

"We've got to drive 'em and break 'em up. Dammit, it's even possible he went right through them and out the other side. Anyway, it's worth a try."

Now reduced to workaday wranglers, the hunters proceeded to divide the flock between them, keeping their guns at the ready.

"There he is!" came a shout.

"Where?"

"There, over there. No, not there, *there.*"

The air resounded with the sharp crack of rifle fire. The sheep, by nature the most quiescent of creatures, darted in every direction, following any of a hundred leaders. It took fully half an hour to restore some semblance of order. Four sheep lay on the ground, bleeding profusely.

"My God!" Bill swore as he turned over a carcass. "Just look what that damned coyote did."

"That wasn't your coyote," Tom corrected him. "These two look like they've been trampled to death."

Harry made the most mournful discovery. "I hate to say it, guys, but this ewe's been shot right through the head. Look at that. One of us got a bit hasty, I guess."

"For God's sake," Bill exploded. "Let's quit standing around shooting sheep and get that bastard. He must've left a trail somewhere. Not even Lucifer can fly," he added, none too hopefully.

Sure enough, a brief search beyond the outer reaches of the sheep hoofmarks divulged fresh coyote tracks. The imprints led directly to Black's Butte, an outcrop that lay close to the limits of their herding ranges. Exultantly the ranchers astride their bounding machines saw the paw traces flash by as they gained on their quarry. And there he was, the loner, his bushy tail waving unmistakably less than a quarter of a mile away, as he vainly sought to outdistance the huntsmen.

The gap narrowed to less than three hundred yards as the hunters squeezed off the first salvo. A weaving target, the bumping motion, small wonder the shots went wide of the mark. So wide in fact that the darting animal had the audacity to glance over his shoulder as if to measure the distance between himself and his pursuers. Two hundred yards, a hundred and fifty, a hundred.... there was no missing him now, however much the rascal might zig and zag. Less than.... and he'd gone, vanished from the face of the earth!

That very instant the lead snowmobilers, though they tried desperately to keep their vehicles on a straight course, found themselves sailing through space. With a sickening impact they crash-landed on the far side of the gully which they had failed to notice in their eagerness. Those behind were only marginally more fortunate. Applying their brakes at the last moment, some skidded out of control, while others toppled over the bank and into the shallow ravine.

Peacefully the snow settled and the motors died. The only sounds on the plain were the voluble curses of the drivers. Except for some bruises, no one had been seriously hurt. The machines were another story, a twisted control handle here, a snapped chain there. Guns, broken sleigh runners, and other paraphernalia were strewn about the field and along the gully.

A safe half mile away Lucifer trotted jauntily along the bed of the rivulet. To look at him, one might think that he was out on a Sunday morning stroll without a care in the world. Which couldn't be said of Bill and his friends.

"Some son of a gun," Tom exclaimed, not without a tinge of respect in his voice. "He sure led us a merry chase, didn't he?"

His companions were less charitable.

"Dammit," Harry exploded. "I just wish old Clint could have been here. He'd have fixed that devil in no time flat, none of this would have happened. Geez, just look at this mess."

The trip back to Bill's place was indeed a sorry retreat. Only two of the snowmobiles managed to return to the farm under their own power. Three more had to be left at the bottom of the gully for the time being. The remainder were somehow coaxed along by their perspiring owners.

And watching the straggling line of men and machines, a solitary coyote stood just over the brow of a hillock.

Clint Hammett was a very puzzled man. Somehow he just wasn't feeling his old self. Outwardly he looked the same as ever—the powerful musculature of the lifelong rancher, a slight stoop acquired from years of heavy toil, the parched face whose deep wrinkles seemed etched as deeply as any furrow he had ever turned. Clint ran his hand over his features just to make sure. The thick iron-grey hair, the rugged nose protruding from the weatherbeaten landscape that formed his face, the square jaw that lent a strength of granite to the whole, everything was reassuringly in place as it ever had been.

And yet Clint was uncomfortably aware that something was missing. Uncomfortably? Hardly the right word. In truth he had never felt better in all his fifty-seven years. Missing? Now that came closer to Clint's real unease. Quite unaccountably, a veritable host of bodily afflictions had suddenly vanished. Some of these over the years had become, well, if not old friends, at least dogged companions. A nagging stomach condition, the twitches of lumbago caused by constant bending and lifting, the angina attacks that often made life plain miserable, all had deserted him as if by magic. Most incredibly, the throbbing pain in his right hand—one day his rifle had backfired as he was loading it—was completely gone. Of the resultant scar that ran the length of his forefinger there wasn't the slightest trace.

In a way his presence in this strange room was even more mystifying than his perfect health. Clint tried hard to reconstruct the immediate past. Just a few minutes ago he had gone out into the crisp evening air to check on that Dorset Horn ewe. For some days now—it was less than a week after Christmas—his experienced eye had told him it would be a tricky early delivery, which is why he and Donald had decided to bring her into the barn. He had taken another look at the ewe's distended stomach and had gotten the heat lamps ready for the newborn lamb who would need drying and all the extra warmth it could get. Right now there was nothing else he could do. He closed the sliding door of the barn and headed back toward the house.

As he leaned into the biting wind a flurry of thoughts crossed his mind. Over the past thirty-five years he had assisted at hundreds of difficult births, many of them on the open range during a howling snowstorm. You had to make sure the lamb didn't become chilled after birth, that the ewe recognized and nursed her offspring. As often as not Martha had come out to help him. No sheepman was ever blessed with a better wife, he reflected. How many women nowadays would be content to raise a family and run a ranch in such an isolated spot?

He was more than halfway across the open space that separated the barn from the house. The swirling wind gave a glacial hint of the blizzard that on the radio had been reported on its way down. Clint glanced around him. The scattered outbuildings, the silo with his name painted vertically in large letters, a couple of tractors and other machinery, the dipping vat and water troughs, the sheepfolds that radiated out from the farm, all testified to years of unremitting labor. You worked hard, and this was your reward. He knew he'd have to quit some day, but thank goodness Don was there to take over. That is, if his son didn't sell out like so many other sheepfarmers had done. As it was, Beth, his daughter had left to get married eight years ago and rarely came back to visit the homestead.

It hadn't been any easy life. At times it had all seemed utterly useless. One winter some years back had been so bittercold that only a handful of ewes had pulled through. That's when the coyotes had swept down and devoured God knows how many of the flock. One night he'd gone out with Manolo, his Basque herdsman, and together they'd shot a good dozen of the marauders. Not a pretty sight, but that was the only way to keep the herd from being decimated. Once Señor Coyote got the upper hand, you might as well quit and go out of business. That was one thing Clint Hammett had no intention of ever doing.

He was practically across the yard. Bundled up though he was against the late December cold, Clint felt himself buffeted by the cutting wind that blew in straight off the plains. No doubt about it, he simply didn't have the strength he once had. Whenever he saw Don, a brawny giant who thought nothing of hoisting an eighty pound ram onto a flatbed, he knew he was getting on. He kept forgetting Don was no longer a boy and now had a wife and two kids of his own. Amazing the way those grandchildren were shooting up. Martha had urged him to take things easier and let Don and the farmhands do the heavy work. As usual, she was probably right. He had now reached the front porch of the house. He could already savor the hot meat stew that was simmering on the stove. Up a couple of steps and he'd be home.

Yet here he was. A place further removed from his own living room he could hardly imagine. To judge by the prim correctness of the newfangled furnishings, he guessed it must be some kind of waiting room or office. Clint tried hard to recollect if he had ever been here before. Certainly it wasn't Doc Ullstrom's place, always crowded with waiting patients. Here Clint was on his own. Nor had he the slightest idea how he had made the trip. One minute he was reaching out to open the front screen door, and the next instant—well, somehow he'd ended up here. Only minus the aches and pains. Pretty good doctor, he reflected.

In the absence of any company there was little to do but survey the room. A pity there wasn't an outside window, that at least would have enabled him to take his bearings. The upholstery, the carpeting and walls were all done in pastel variations of celestial blue with only a few flecks of cloudy white to offset the overall cerulean effect. Even the ceiling was designed with a matching flocculent theme, bathing the room in a supernal atmosphere. Surprisingly, there were no paintings or decorations of any kind to offset the predominant azure tones. The furnishings were minimal. In the middle of the room stood a large desk of impersonal modernistic design, and behind it, a matching swivel chair with blue padding.

As for himself, he was seated on a plush sofa covered with a velvety fabric. Blue everywhere, with just the odd touch of white. Whoever devised this color scheme must have been up in the clouds, he thought with a wry grin and shake of the head.

His reverie was interrupted by the silent entry of what he took to be a secretary or receptionist. Understandably enough, Clint had failed to notice at the far end a door barely distinguishable from the rest of the wall. No sound intruded the stillness, only an imperceptible gliding movement as a graceful young woman crossed the carpeted room. Again the all-pervasive blue, this time a light-blue blouse and dark-blue skirt which reached demurely to mid-calf. Clint sensed something dreamlike, almost incorporeal, about her whole being. Before he could frame a question the young lady was addressing him in the most dulcet voice he had ever heard.

"We've been expecting you, Mr. Hammett. Your file is now complete. You will be attended to in just a moment. Sorry to have kept you waiting." With that she placed a folder on the desk, gave Clint what could best be described as an ethereal smile, and left him alone again.

At least the place was inhabited. Other than that, he was no whit the wiser. The total silence was uncanny, no whir of an air-conditioner or heating system, not even the faintest hum of distant traffic or passing voices outside in the corridor. He was positive he had never been here before. Yet evidently his arrival had been anticipated.

Suddenly it all fell into place. Of course!—he was in some hospital. He'd had another heart seizure, this time he'd passed out, and Doc Ullstrom had ordered him brought to..... no, that didn't make much sense either. Martha would never have left him alone. And besides—

His attention was riveted by the appearance of a short stocky man of late middle age who was surveying him with polite interest. There was no telling how long the newcomer had been standing there; it could have been a matter of seconds or minutes. The man was neatly groomed and dressed city-style, an attire that invariably aroused Clint's country scorn. Some damn bureaucrat, one of those fellows who'd never done an honest day's work in his life. Before Clint knew it, the man had reached forward to grasp his hand in an effusive handshake.

"So glad you made it, Clint. Oh, by the way, my name's Peter. We're very informal here, no fancy titles or anything. Make yourself comfortable—I'll just need a minute or two to have a look at your papers, then we can begin." Releasing the rancher's hand, he walked round the desk, sat down, and began to peruse the contents of the folder.

While Peter immersed himself in the papers, Clint took the opportunity to study him more closely. The features were definitely of southern stock—he'd seen many a Mexican farmhand of the same swarthy cast and angular facial structure—but the newcomer had none of the deferential hesitancy that marked the rootless alien. Quite the contrary. Certainly he couldn't fault Peter's impeccable English, if anything a bit too citified for his taste. Despite this shortcoming, the man's demeanor and inner confidence had favorably impressed him. But as to who or what he was, Clint hadn't the faintest notion. A government official was as good a guess as any. Plenty of those around.

Peter glanced up to indicate he was through with his reading.

"Mostly sheep raising with some general farming on the side, eh, Clint? Well, I might as well come to the point right away. The fact is, yours is a very tricky case—which is why it was referred to my department."

For the first time Clint felt decidedly uneasy. "I'm afraid I don't understand," he began defensively. "And while we're at it, I'd appreciate knowing a thing or two about this outfit. First, I'd like to know how I got here, and second, where in hell *am* I?"

"Where in hell? Oh dear, I see we do have a little misunderstanding," the official noted as he began to check off some random items in the open folder before him. "A very tricky case indeed. Far more complicated than I thought. Now let's see. Started a small sheep farm when you came back from Vietnam, built it up with your brother, and then took over the whole operation when he decided to quit."

"Nothing wrong with that, is there? Anyway, what's that got to do with it? Hell, I demand to know what's going on."

"Hell again?" Peter gave him a disapproving look. "Really, you shouldn't keep evoking that place. Ah, here I see someone's added a note: 'Inclined to lapse into unfortunate phraseology, especially when agitated or intoxicated.' Uses cuss words when uptight or drunk, in other words. Moderately serious, but hardly a decisive factor. After all, we can't turn down three-fourths of our applicants, can we?"

Clint was far from mollified by this non-response. He shifted to the edge of his seat, trying to plant his booted feet firmly on the cloud-soft carpeting.

"Who the—I mean, who in—who are you? Look, I've had enough of this runaround. I want to see your boss."

The Mexican or whoever he was could barely repress a smile.

"I'm afraid you presume somewhat. Now where was I? Ah yes, I see you belong to the local church board, the Woolgrowers' Association, of course, farmers' coalition.... and a number of activities concerned with animals—besides sheep, I mean. Ducks, geese, elk, deer, raccoons, rabbits, squirrels, and so on. Quite a long list. And coyotes. Especially coyotes. Seems you've quite a fixation about coyotes, Clint."

"Fixation, is that what you call it? Now don't tell me you're another one of them bleeding hearts. I'm telling you, the coyote has got to be the sneakiest, dirtiest, meanest sonofabitch on God's green earth."

"So you would presume to criticize God's creation, would you?" Peter interjected with some asperity.

"Who, me? Heck no. All I'm saying is that your coyote's a real vicious killer. Those critters don't think nothing of slitting the throat of a sheep or a goat. I'm telling you, they're real devils, they don't hesitate one second to hamstring a deer and eat it alive."

"You're speaking from personal experience, of course?"

"Well, I heard from Hal Rolfson it happens all the time on his ranch. Then there's Bill Bakewell, I know for a fact that—"

"Rolfson? Bakewell?" Peter took scant trouble to hide his distrust. "I'll make a note of those two when the time comes. Now Clint, before we proceed, let's get one thing straight. You do know where you are, don't you?"

"Frankly, I haven't a clue."

"You haven't? Ah, I see I should have told you earlier. Clint, you won't like this, but I'm afraid you're as dead as they come. This outfit, as you so picturesquely call it, happens to be the Purgatory Investigation Center—PIC for short. As a matter of fact, the Pearly Gates are straight through that door and a little off to the right."

"Well, I'll be damned."

"There's always that risk, of course, but hopefully we can avoid it in your case. Perhaps you've now figured out which Peter I am—you know, the fellow with the keys. Still don't recognize me?"

"The beard… the robes, the rest of it—*that* Peter? Why, you just don't look, uh, biblical somehow."

The saint looked a mite crestfallen.

"We do our best to keep up with the times. Every so often I pop down to Savile Row to get fitted out. But back to your case." Peter reached into the folder, pulled out a punched card, and handed it across the desk. "It seems our central computer spotted you immediately. See for yourself."

Clint stared incredulously at the bold print. There, stamped diagonally across in black capitals was the annotation REFUSED ENTRY - LACK OF REVERENCE FOR LIFE. It took half a minute for the full impact of the words to register. It was Peter, however, who resumed the conversation.

"Believe me, it's never an easy decision for us to make. As you can see, you have passing grades all across the board except for that one. You're not a bad man at all, Clint, in fact rather a good one. It's just that you didn't show enough respect for your fellow creatures on earth."

Clint's patience with this sanctimonious bureaucrat was rapidly reaching an end.

"That's ridiculous. No guy's ever risked his neck more than I have to help his sheep when they get into trouble."

"Mountain sheep?"

"Well, no, not mountain sheep, they're not good for anything."

With a saintly sigh Peter closed the file that lay before him, pushed it aside, and looked Clint straight in the eye.

"Tell me, Clint, what makes you so certain you have a right to dominate all creatures on earth, to inflict pain and death at will? Maybe you can tell me what sets you apart from your fellow beings."

A hurt look crossed the farmer's face.

"Well, I mean, it's kinda obvious, isn't it? To start with, I'm not an animal, I'm human."

"I'm not."

"You're something else, uh, no disrespect meant. What I'm trying to say is you're a saint, why, that's even better than a human. But even you've got to admit that a human's way ahead of an animal."

"Oh, must I?"

"For Pete's sake! Uh, sorry, Your Sanctity, that just slipped out. But the fact is those poor animals don't have emotions or feel pain the way we humans do. Besides, an animal doesn't have a soul, so it can't be saved. You ought to know, you were a fisherman once."

The celestial gatekeeper tried hard to keep his composure.

"Human theology never ceases to amaze me. May I point out that the word 'animal' comes from the Latin 'anima', meaning 'soul', if I may show off my little bit of learning. In one respect you're right, though. Yes, I did fish for food before I decided to become a fisher of men. For a people that subsist largely on fava beans, lentils, and grains the occasional fish is a real treat. But tell me, Clint, what interest did you have in coyotes as food?"

"Food? You've gotta be kidding. Now sheep, that's something else. Let me tell you something, keeping those goddam—beg your pardon, keeping them coyotes away from the sheep's not that easy. No sir, it's not easy. Just last fall I had to put up a fence to protect them."

"I'm sorry to contradict you, Clint, but from up here I got the idea you didn't want your sheep wandering onto Bill Bakewell's property. Isn't that the real reason you built it?"

Clint saw he'd been caught in his own trap.

"Damn that Bakewell. He's always encouraging other people's sheep to wander onto his land. As for paying a single penny toward the fence, oh no, not him. That guy makes me sick."

"I take it then you don't love thy neighbor as thyself?" Peter observed slyly.

"Let's forget that jerk," Clint replied heatedly. Then in a conciliatory vein: "Say, Pete, getting back to my score card, how about my church attendance? Pretty good, eh? And how many guys have been as faithful to the little lady as I have?"

"That's not what it says here," Peter noted, tapping the closed folder.

"Okay then, one or two slipups. I never said I was a saint."

"I should think not."

"Now looky here, Saint Pete, I'm just what you might call a regular down to earth type of guy."

"Down to earth, you say? Why, that's exactly what I had in mind. Tell me, Clint, did you ever hear of a King Lycaon?"

"Can't say I ever have. But then me being a registered Republican…"

"No, no, this was ages ago, before my time even. Back when God was called Zeus. Do you want to hear the story?"

"Fire away. Uh, I mean, go ahead."

"Well, apparently this Lycaon fellow was one of the most insensitive kings who ever lived, so one day Zeus had enough and changed him into a wolf. *Lupus redivivus* is the technical term, I think. What do you say to that?"

"Beats me."

"More Latin, my friend. Forgive me for showing off my modest erudition, but you must remember I was the first bishop of Rome. I really meant to say coyote, but the Latin word escapes me for the moment. These Nahuatl words are the very devil to translate, if I may borrow one of your more repeatable expressions." He paused for a moment. "Now back to your case. I'm afraid I must pronounce you a practitioner of cruelty due to ignorance. The only remedy I can suggest is along the lines of *Mens humana in corpore coyote*, if I remember my rusty Latin." Peter settled back in his chair and folded his hands in his lap with an air of resigned authority.

Clint was sweating visibly. The saint's Latin pronouncement had left him more befuddled than ever.

"Come on, Your Saintness, I don't know what you have in mind exactly, but I know you're the sort to give a guy a chance."

"A chance indeed. You'll have a far better chance than any you gave a coyote, I promise you that. By the way, Clint, your name's changed to Lucifer until you have completed your penance and we meet again. Most appropriate for someone about to fall from a great height, don't you think? You know, the fallen angel bit? Adiós, ¡hasta la vista! Oops, sorry, wrong language. Seeya!"

At the same time the saintly man pressed a concealed button under the desk. All at once Clint experienced an uncanny sensation of tumbling through a boundless void, his body shrinking and changing as he spun around, falling ever downwards through a vortex which defied both time and space.

And then, just as abruptly, it was all over. Clint looked around with relief. He was back on earth again. Funny, but everything appeared in far sharper detail than he remembered it. Why did his nose capture every fragrance, his ear the faintest rustle in a way that had never happened before? And why was he so low to the ground, as if on his knees? Without thinking he glanced down at his feet. There, instead of the old familiar farm boots, two black-furred paws rested gently on the powdery snow.

※

He, Clint Hammett, reduced to a common cur! The degradation inflicted on him by that pseudo-saint was beyond belief. Yet once he had recovered from the initial shock, his practical sense quickly reasserted itself.

From the low angle of the winter sun and the long shadow cast by the snow-covered sagebrush he surmised that it must be late afternoon. Directly in front of him, no more than a quarter mile away, stood the familiar farmhouse and outbuildings. Not a soul in sight. Strange. He noted that the station wagon was gone. Where could they all be at this time of day? Of course, the funeral, *his* funeral! He wryly recalled the old joke about being late for one's own funeral. Pity he'd missed it, though. If only he could slough off this ridiculous coyote pelt, why *he'd* have a thing or two to tell the preacher about divine justice.

Facing his new reality wouldn't be easy. True, his sight and sense of smell were uncommonly sharp, as were his teeth and claws. In his favor there wasn't a square inch of land for miles around that he didn't know as well as the back of his….paws. That was fine, but what of his family? There must be some way of communicating with them. That was it! He'd wait for Martha and the others to return from church, then he'd throw himself at their mercy and explain his ghastly—ghostly would be more accurate—predicament.

But wait, how would he say it? His mind and memory were as keen as ever, but what about his voice? More to the point, did he even *have* a voice? Involuntarily, he squatted on his haunches, pointed his long nose skywards, and attempted to enunciate a soul-felt plea. Instead, he only emitted a drawn-out mournful howl that rent the still evening air. His son, Don, would have only one answer to that sort of coyote cacophony; he'd been trained by his father only too well.

On the distant road Clint could make out a vehicle followed by a swirl of kicked-up snow heading for the farmhouse, his family already on the way back from the service. Impelled by irresistible curiosity, Clint bounded across the open field toward the house where he had spent his entire adult life. He marveled at his ease of supple movement, the fluid motion of his stretched-out limbs as he sped over the firm crust. Suddenly he stopped in his tracks. Why were those sheep of his careening wildly in obvious terror? Of course. Nothing was the same now. His every move would be fraught with danger. Making a wide detour to skirt the chicken run, Clint squeezed his lithe body through a gap left by a loose board under the front porch. All he could do now was wait.

Minutes later he heard the wheel chains of the station wagon crunch the packed snow in front of the house. Squinting through a crack in the wooden steps, he saw the doors open and the family get out one by one. There was Martha as he'd always remember her, round-faced, radiating a good-natured if uncritical optimism. He could see his son Don, tight-lipped and uncharacteristically serious, get out on the driver's side, then walk around to help Ruth and the two boys, Will and Simon. Ruth had made Don a good wife, Clint reflected, but something told him she wasn't prepared to stay here forever. As to the youngsters, they were still at an age when they cheerfully accepted everything, but that too would change.

Now he could hear the approaching murmur of voices as the car doors slammed shut and the family filed up the icy path to the house. A new anxiety gripped him: would he understand a word of what they said? What was he, man or beast, Clint or Lucifer—or both?

"That really was a beautiful service," Ruth was saying, "simple but moving." Clint grasped each word without the slightest trouble.

"It certainly was," Martha agreed. "When the reverend said that Clint had found rest in a far happier place I was on the verge of tears. At least he's now at peace with no more worries."

"I wonder what Bill Bakewell was doing there," Don said with some asperity as he unlocked the front door. "I overheard him tell Tom Calderwood and some of the other guys that Dad was nothing more than a hard-drinking, cussing coyote hunter who knew next to nothing about sheep. Now why would a neighbor go around telling a bunch of lies like that, especially about someone who's dead?"

"Don't listen to what Bill says," Martha chided her son gently. "He's always been a little jealous of your dad. And that tiff over who should pay for the fence didn't help either. Now you two boys, make sure you clean your boots before you go into the house, that's it, wipe them good."

Above him Clint could hear the vigorous scraping of soles and the banging of the screen door. Some more foot stamping, the front door closing, and everyone was inside the warm house. He could just imagine the family sitting down later to a filling meal of T-bone steaks and boiled corn on the cob. The irony of it all! The injustice! He who had made this all possible now huddled alone under his own porch, an outcast from friend and foe alike.

For the first time he realized how hungry he was. He must find food, the same as any other creature. What would a coyote do in his place? So far he hadn't given the matter a moment's thought. To Clint, a coyote was a predator pure and simple, the sheepman's remorseless enemy to be eradicated at all costs. God knows he'd seen enough evidence of their depredations over the years, the mauled carcasses, the scattered entrails, horrible proof of the animal's ruthlessness. And now through some outrageous quirk he was one of them.

The sun was slipping fast over the horizon. Above him he could hear indistinct voices and the shuffle of feet on the squeaky floor boards. No one would be outdoors at this hour. Cautiously he crept out of his hiding place, keeping to the shadows as he made his way to the side of the house. What of his paw marks? Don would see them first thing in the morning and know what to do. In his mind's eye Clint already visualized the traps and poisoned bait.

The bait. He couldn't be too careful. No carrion, at all costs he must avoid carrion, anything that might be tainted. He knew only too well how deadly effective the latest poisons were. A chicken perhaps, plenty of those, but they were penned too close to the house and besides were sure to squawk to high heaven. Heaven? Good, keep that jerk of a Peter awake, Clint mused. But back to earth. It all added up to a grim fact of coyotean life—he really had no other choice but to kill a live sheep. They at least weren't poisoned. But whose?

Certainly not his own. He'd rather starve to death than touch his flock, some of whom he had helped bring into the world with his own hands. If that self-righteous Peter got him back as a famished coyote, so be it, serve him damn well right. As Clint watched the crescent moon ride higher into the night sky he became all the angrier at the saint with the perverse sense of humor. Punishment presumed guilt; Peter had not even hinted at a specific crime. What purpose could he have in mind, if any?

He had to act, and quickly. He was now ravenous, not having eaten since—when was it? Two, three days? He certainly did not relish the idea of seizing an innocent animal by the throat and killing it with his own teeth, much less of masticating the blood-filled raw meat. Well, enough of that; someone's sheep had to go, that was all there was to it. And who more deserving than Bill Bakewell?

As Clint loped off in the direction of the adjoining farm he was filled with a surprising, almost delectable sense of anticipation. So Bakewell was now going around telling everyone what a drunken deadbeat his late neighbor had been? A damn lie, of course. Come to think of it, he'd never been able to stand Bill's sly digs at him. A coyote hunter who didn't know the first thing about sheep, eh? Then there was that matter of the fence; neighbors were supposed to share costs, not simply let the other fellow pay it all. Clearly a nocturnal visit to Bill was indicated.

By now Clint was well into his backbiter's territory. Despite the chill night wind, he was surprised how warm he felt in his tawny mantle. Incredibly, he could distinguish even the smallest object against the blackness of the sky. And there, silhouetted in the snowy waste, stood the greyish shapes huddled closely together on their winter bedground. Taking care to stay downwind of the unsuspecting flock, Clint belly-crawled toward his prey. It seemed the most natural thing in the world to do. Not a sheepherder in sight; he knew full well that Carlos and Javier much preferred the protection of the sheep wagon to the stinging cold outside.

He had advanced to easy springing distance from the nearest sheep. For some moments he remained poised motionless, eyeing his prey. Just then one of the outermost ewes rose up, only to find herself facing the crouching coyote. A contagious alarm-filled bleating filled the night air as the sheep struggled one by one to their feet and sought escape. Already Clint was bounding toward a more mature ewe, some five years old, whom he judged to be one of the flock's natural leaders. In no time at all he had separated her from the others and was wheeling for the final attack. As he closed in for the kill the ewe spun round with unsuspected speed and dealt her assailant a well-aimed kick in the ribs. Stunned, it took him a good half minute to regain his breath and resume the chase. Again he was thwarted as he felt the powerful hoofs rattle his sore rib cage. It was only the ewe's gradual exhaustion and a clever feint on his part that enabled him to penetrate her defenses and sink his sharp teeth into her neck.

Clint could hardly believe what he had done. It had all happened so naturally, if a little painfully. Before he knew it he was tearing his prey apart in search of the most succulent pieces of meat. Hell, if Peter meant him to be a coyote he would act like a coyote. He was just doing what any other hungry predator would do. Without giving the matter further thought, he squatted down and feasted on his victim.

The dead ewe was far too big for him to finish. Before leaving the carcass, he took a few extra mouthfuls which he could later regurgitate if need be. The process came to him quite spontaneously. Now he must distance himself from his kill. In the morning the body would be discovered, the coyote tracks spotted, the countryside scoured for any trace of the marauder. For Clint, the best thing was to return the way he had come, this time keeping to the ridgeline where the wind had swept the soil bare of snow.

That first night back on earth he spent in the shelter of a creek bottom. Far in the distance rose the soulful cadences of other coyotes. To his surprise, the voices sounded clear and sonorous, not the grating howls he had hitherto disdained, but individual calls that transmitted a meaningful message, songs that pleaded, communicated, reassured. As he curled up under the protective lip of a cutbank, for the first time in his new existence Clint felt that he was an integral part of his surroundings.

He was awake long before the first sun's rays cast their watery light over the frosted land. The ewe had provided welcome sustenance, but already he felt the need to forage further afield. The corrals and stockmen were clearly to be avoided during broad daylight. Much as the idea of plaguing Bill Bakewell appealed to him, some inner intelligence—human or canine—warned him to keep his distance. Survival was everything.

It was still early that morning when he sighted the grey female coyote picking her way along the frozen river bed. As far as he could tell she was on her own. With some hesitancy he decided to approach her. But how would they communicate? He could understand well enough—the sounds in the night had proved that—but could he reply? At that moment his musings were cut short by a violent blow to the hip. A male coyote, the other's mate, was snapping and snarling in his face, challenging him to a fight. Clint had completely forgotten that one of a pair often followed the other at some distance for greater safety. This was no time to display his courage. Acknowledging his defeat, he hung his head low in submission and slunk off. Unsociable creatures! No wonder he'd never liked them.

The rest of the day was more successful. He soon discovered that many tussocks close to the surface tasted unexpectedly good. Several times he pounced on a field mouse exposed by a sheep's footprint in the snow, a most savory appetizer he found to his delight. There was only one minor disappointment: the jackrabbits, so easy to bag with a rifle, were the very devil to chase and impossible to catch darting up a slope with those powerful hind legs of theirs.

A couple of times he caught sight of his family away in the distance. Once in fact young Simon carrying his slingshot passed no more than a hundred yards or so from where he lay hidden. Off rabbit hunting, no doubt. Clint would gladly have revealed himself to Martha, but his wife—perhaps widow was more appropriate—stayed close to the farm buildings or else was always accompanied by Don or one of the farmhands.

Encounters with other coyotes became more frequent. Some, he noted, looked frightfully emaciated as if unable to procure their own food. One reddish-brown male in particular ran with a decided limp, while his companion appeared to have part of her lower jaw missing. A few barely had the strength to haul themselves through the deep powdery snow. And yet without exception, none of them wanted anything to do with the newcomer in their midst.

Clint was both annoyed and puzzled. Unfairly deprived of any companionship of his own kind—whatever that was—and for want of anything better to do, he decided that Bill Bakewell stood in need of a further lesson, one closer to home this time. Truth is, his neighbor's words still rankled. A lightly overcast night suited his intent perfectly. By midnight he had surveyed the Bakewell homestead from every direction. It was exactly as he last remembered it. The traps presented no problem—indeed, Bill had even once consulted him as to their best location. As to the wire fence, his neighbor had been typically tightfisted when it came to laying it deep enough. Then the side gate leading to the sheep pens, why, ridiculous, all it needed was knowing how the latch worked and then sliding the bar back.

Even so Clint waited another hour to make sure that everyone was asleep. Silently he dug his way under the wire and crept to the side gate. Rearing up on his hind legs, he worked the latch mechanism with his forepaws and teeth until the gate swung open with a faint creak. In the pen he could make out the broad form of the unsuspecting ram. It was all so easy. A stealthy crawl, a moment to poise himself for the strike, and then…. once, twice, right into the jugular, and it was all over. Not a sound, not so much as an expiring bleat. Clint listened carefully, his ears pointed toward the farmhouse whose shadow loomed directly over him. Nothing. Bill, Jeanie, fast asleep, counting sheep. With grim contentment he could just picture the scene in the morning, Bill bewailing the demise of Jack, his prize ram. Serve him right!

That nocturnal foray was but the first of many. For the sake of variety Clint once stole a couple of plump chickens from Hal Rolfson's place, and another time sank his teeth into an old gummer over at Tom Calderwood's. Nothing, however, was quite as satisfying as Bill's livestock. As to those new legtraps he was setting, so obvious really, exactly where Clint would have placed them himself. What pleasure it gave him springing them shut with a long stout twig and then hearing the harmless clang of the metal jaws!

His first face-to-face meeting with Bill in broad daylight was totally unplanned. Truth to tell, he'd become somewhat careless of late, what with pickings coming so easy. Of course, Bill not having a gun with him was a huge stroke of luck. As Clint stood motionless on the edge of the swale, looking his old neighbor in the eye, he was briefly overcome by an unexpected feeling of compassion. Maybe I have been a trifle hard on the old so-and-so, he said to himself. But then how else was a guy, a coyote, that is, to survive? Wasn't that his mission on earth?

A few weeks later matters came to a head. Clint had no one to blame but himself. The previous day he had killed a full-grown ewe of the Bakewell flock. Only afterwards did he notice the day-old lamb which in its terror had strayed from the mother. The poor thing had broken a foreleg, no doubt the result of being trampled on. Clint knew from experience that the lambkin's chances for survival were almost nil; better to end its misery then and there. With a heavy heart he delivered the fatal strike. Never in all his life, or rather lives, had he felt more despicable.

As chance would have it, the next night he found himself close to Bill's farmhouse. No doubt it was all those car lights that had attracted him. A foolish risk, of course, but he simply had to find out what was going on. The crawl space under the house provided an ideal covert. Drifting down came the delicious smell of home cooking such as he had not savored for many a day. Above the clink of cutlery on plates he recognized the sound of familiar voices.

"A bounty hunt's the only way to get him," Tom Calderwood was telling the others. "That's what Clint Hammett did the last time this happened, a hundred bucks to the guy that shot him. If I remember right, that coyote didn't last the day."

"You're doggone right", Clint heard Harry Lind concur. "Tomorrow's Sunday, how about getting a snow hunt together while the stuff's still on the ground? We can all have a little fun...."

That was all Clint needed to hear. The smart thing, of course, was to get away as far as possible, well out of range of the snowmobiles, perhaps even to an entirely new part of the state. There wasn't a moment to lose. In the morning they would spot his tracks and easily outrun him. He hadn't a chance—or had he? No sooner had he crept out from under the house and into the open than a diabolical stratagem worthy of Lucifer occurred to him. Dammit, he'd show that lamebrain bunch a thing or two. The more he thought of pitting mind against machine, the more the idea appealed to him. As he scurried across the snow, the outline of a mischievous plan began to form in his mind.

In the end, it was all too easy. Clint had often observed a jackrabbit seek refuge in a flock of sheep, so why not a coyote? As for the shooting, well, his friends had always been a bit hasty when it came to claiming bounty. And the snowmobile chase? Nothing to it really, just a little calculation and knowing the lay of the land. He could always rely on the hunters' impetuousness. Even so, it had been far more successful than he had dared hope. Watching the snowmobilers trudge home in disarray, Clint could not refrain from smiling at his vulpine, or rather coyotean, superiority over the mechanized humans. Was this what Peter had in mind, he wondered? Or was there some more subtle intent?

At that moment he became aware that he was not alone. Directly in his path stood a pair of distrustful coyotes. The bitch was obviously with pup, while her mate seemed bent on protecting her from the unwelcome attentions of others. Clint was uncertain how to react. Instinctively he sensed that this male was not seeking a scuffle but merely to assert his right to the female. Clint lay down in the snow as a gesture of conciliation. The effect was immediate; the newcomers crouched down facing him no more than a few feet away.

The next move took him completely by surprise. A few hoarse growls, that was to be expected, but certainly not a meaningful exchange. To his utter astonishment, he found himself being addressed in reproachful tones by the male.

"What makes you do it? I don't understand. You're one of us, and yet not one of us. We're all puzzled by your behavior. Why do you kill more than you'll ever need? It's about time you explained yourself to us."

Whatever Clint had expected, it certainly was not this. Just as amazingly, he found that he was able to express himself with total fluency.

"It's you who puzzle me. I've only done what any of you would do. I was hungry, so I took whatever was close at hand. Now what's wrong with that, brother coyote?"

The female could hold back no longer. "You're really a strange one in every way. We're content with a field mouse or maybe a ground squirrel, sometimes even a rat or a rabbit, rodents in other words. We take what we need for ourselves and our young, but no more. Yet we've seen you kill full-grown ewes and healthy lambs. What makes you do it?"

"Listen, I kill as nature intended us to kill," Clint replied without a trace of apology in his voice, which only further aroused the male's indignation.

"No coyote wishes to associate with a wanton killer. Haven't you wondered why all of us have avoided you since you came here?"

"But I thought all coyotes went after sheep," Clint pleaded.

"All? Who taught you that? The sheep carcasses, yes, we glean those. That's how so many of our number die from carrion poisoned by the sheepmen. If only they understood us!"

"But you do kill sheep, I know you do," Clint persisted.

The other gave a pained twitch of his brows.

"In a bitterly cold winter such as this I've known some of our starving brothers to attack the sick and the older ones of the flock. That I can't deny. But believe me, few of those would have survived until spring. You see, we select our prey, not like others. Look here, you'll see what I mean."

The two newcomers had now stood up. For the first time Clint noticed that the female had an entire forepaw missing. With every step her sleek frame lurched forward as she struggled to keep her balance.

"How did that happen?" Clint asked, uncomfortably aware that he already knew. The male pointed his muzzle in the direction of Clint's farm.

"Down there one night she caught her leg in a trap. I saw at once she had no chance of prying it loose. There was only one thing to do and I did it."

"What was that?"

"I bit the foot off myself. The pain was terrible for her, but she didn't dare howl for fear that the farmer might hear and shoot her. I'll never forget that night as long as I live. The suffering.... Well, we'd better be off now. Farewell, strange friend."

Clint caught the inexpressibly sad look of the female and glanced down to find himself staring at the stump of her leg. He no longer had any doubt why Peter had sent him back to earth. As he watched her limp away he vowed that he would do whatever lay in his power to help what he joyously perceived as his fellow creatures on earth.

The days were noticeably lengthening as the sun readied its death blow to the long winter. Where the snow only recently had shrouded everything, the sedge now pushed up in thousands of places through the sodden ground. In no time the potrero was decked in all its spring vesture, the newborn lambs gamboling among their watchful mothers. It was also the season for the coyote bitches to whelp and launch their cubs on an uncertain career that, likely as not, would end tragically for most before the year was out.

One morning Clint was startled by a noise from a totally new quarter. He guessed at once—for he had been expecting it—that a helicopter was out searching for him. Even as he glanced upwards the supreme irony of his predicament struck him, he who in the past had so often piloted the same craft in pursuit of game. Had the hunters spotted him? From their methodical circling he didn't think so; they were still scouring the flat expanse below. Luckily the topsoil grasses had dried sufficiently to hide any telltale tracks. Clint found himself surrounded by a stand of greasewood shrubs, poor protection indeed against a 12 gauge shotgun blast, but just enough to camouflage him—that is, if he froze and blended in with his background. As the helicopter swept low, he lay stretched out like a log, still, not so much as a hackle stirring. Again and again the machine swept down from the sky, determined to flush out the hell-hound on earth. Only with the undisturbed rustle of the prairie breeze did Clint dare raise his aching body once more.

The helicopter was gone, but he knew that the men had no intention of giving up. A vicious killer was in their midst, and they in turn would not rest until he was destroyed. Clint tried to place himself in their position, to predict the next step. Traps and poison had failed, the helicopter had not driven him from cover, only one method remained: a night hunt. Strictly speaking, it was illegal, but then so was it not to check the traplines regularly. He knew that neither law was observed too scrupulously—in his time he'd been no better or worse than the others. Once the ground firmed up they'd be out again after his pelt.

He thought of fleeing, anywhere to escape, but he knew that he would be invading the territory of other coyotes who might well band together to attack him. Then there was the question of innate stubbornness, pride, vanity—call it what you will—but this was *his* terrain, *his* life's work, *his* spot on earth. No, he would stand and fight here and nowhere else. If he should die, then so be it.

He hadn't long to wait. He was only surprised how many of them there were that night, surely every four-wheel-drive and pickup in the county. As the headlights came closer he could hear the frenzied baying of the dogs. Clearly they had picked up his spoor. How strange that these canine cousins were now enlisted on the side of men! They were now closing in on him from three sides. He could outrun any hound, nor was there anything to fear in single combat—but a dozen of them! And then the trucks. Despite his spurts of over forty miles an hour he knew there was no way of outdistancing those mechanical monsters.

Already he could distinguish voices shouting in the darkness. There was Harry Lind barking out orders on his walkie-talkie, Bakewell urging the others forward, as if they needed any prodding. That voice—Oh my God, wasn't that his son Don yelling at the others to keep the line straight? But what child's piping treble was that? Yes, he knew it well. Young Simon, his own grandson, had been brought on his first coyote hunt. This last was horrible, too horrible.

They were gaining on him, no doubt about it. Shaking them off this time would be well-nigh impossible. Try as he might, Clint couldn't reach a single gully or rill to throw them off his scent. Besides, he was now in full view of the marksmen as he sprinted for all his worth. Clint saw it all: the blood, the entrails, the final shot to the head. Nor would that be the end. As he gasped for breath he could already envision his limp body hogtied across the hood of a truck, a proud trophy to be displayed before a gawking public.

There was just one last chance, an outside one at best. Last autumn he had put up that fence to discourage his sheep from wandering onto Bakewell's acreage. To get there and slip underneath would take a prodigious effort. Over the years he'd heard of coyotes throwing up their food to run faster, often losing as much as ten of their thirty-five or so pounds. Summoning his last reserves of strength, Clint forced up the food and spat it out. It was as good as a second wind. Ahead he could make out the wooden posts and wire strands of the fence. A final bound and he was there, wriggling under the wire to safety, then off to the side and beyond the glare of the headlights of the halted vehicles.

Behind him all was confusion. The dogs, uncertain what was expected of them, awaited their masters' orders. Shots were fired in all directions at any shadow that moved, which only further disconcerted the hounds. Crouched a few yards to one side, Clint watched Hal Rolfson and Harry Lind pull out the stakes to provide passage for the trucks. As they rolled across, an exhausted coyote slunk back under the wire fence a mere stone's throw away. In the disorder no one had noticed. He had fooled the lot of them, man, mastiff, and machine.

Clint contemplated the scene with wry satisfaction. It had been a close call, but well worth it. What idiots those friends of his were, outwitted by a coyote, a mere animal! Still, they would soon realize their mistake and resume the hunt. Not a moment was to be wasted. He must make for the swampland at once. He turned round. The sight was sickening. For there, next to Martha, stood his grandson Simon toting his child's rifle, now aimed straight at him.

"Don't, don't!" he pleaded, yet unable to utter a word.

"Now, Simon, now!" he heard his wife cry excitedly. The barrel kicked upwards as the report rang across the prairie. "Simon, you got him, you got him! Good boy, you've got your first coyote. I'm so proud of you!"

Clint knew he was mortally wounded. Already the blood was spurting from a gash just below his eye. His strength was rapidly ebbing, the end just moments away. The men came hurrying over from their vehicles as the word spread. In his death throes Clint dimly saw himself surrounded by a semi-circle of rifle barrels glinting in the moonlight.

"Do you think he's hurting?" he barely heard Simon ask the others with childlike naïveté.

"Heck no," came Bill's immediate reply, "coyotes like that Lucifer there don't feel nothing."

His spirit was rapidly slipping away. With each second the hunters' words sounded more and more distant.

"You done good, son," Don said as he inspected the inert form on the ground. "That's the most vicious brute I've ever seen. Just look at his size. Why, that one has to be the granddaddy of them all."

Beyond All Barriers

*Diviner than the dolphin is nothing yet created;
for indeed they were aforetime men and lived in
cities along with mortals, but by the devising of
Dionysos they exchanged the land for the sea and
put on the form of fishes.*

                            Oppian, ca. 200 A.D.

*But on the dolphin, alone among others, nature
has bestowed this gift which the greatest philosophers
long for: disinterested friendship. It has no need of
any man, yet it is the friend of all men, and has often
given them great aid.*

           Plutarch: "On the Intelligence of Animals"

Beyond All Barriers

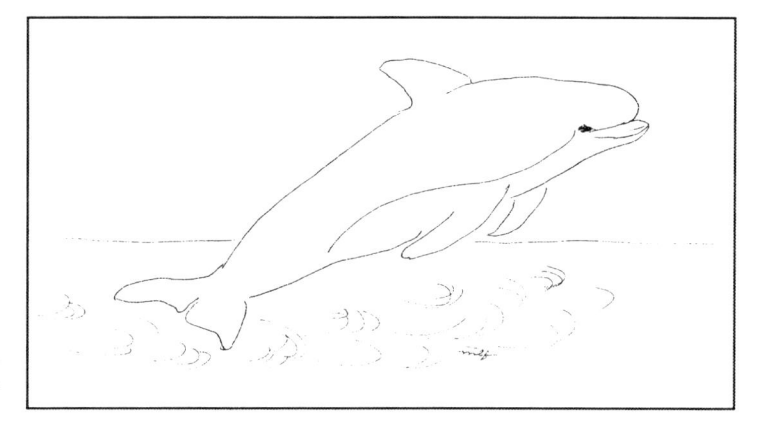

Grey, grey upon grey. The leaden sky dissolved imperceptibly into roiling ranks of whitecaps which pounded the gunwales of the seiner, now pitching unsteadily in the swell of the bucking ocean. Overhead, dirt-grey seagulls screeched and wheeled, occasionally swooping down to snatch an unwary fish from the bleak waters. The birds, at least, were enjoying modest success. The seinermen, now four weeks out of San Diego, so far had little to show for their efforts. Today was like so many others. Rain had hung in the air since early morning, and by mid-afternoon the first heavy drops flattened themselves against the superstructure of the fishing boat. For all concerned, the skipper and crew, as well as the boat's owners on land, it was a depressing experience; close to thirty days of the same grim muggy weather, scratching for just three sets—lowering and raising the fishing gear—in all that time, and not even one well full of fish to show for it. Would their *mala suerte* ever change on this trip? Or was the boat cursed with a *praga*, as all devout crewmen rightly feared?

The year had begun quite differently. The *San Rafael*, a thousand tonner and just celebrating its twentieth year at sea, had started the new season in a way that fishermen dream of, a quota trip "inside the line" in settled weather with plentiful catches every day. At times the tuna had jumped from the net into the beckoning wells so quickly that the seiner was back in harbor before the month was out. A couple of weeks for minor repairs and to resupply the boat, and with only a couple of deckhand changes—lucky crews stay together—the *San Rafael* was already passing Ballast Point and heading out into the open ocean beyond Point Loma. With a bit of luck they might even manage another trip close to shore off Central America and so beat the quota deadline in March. Born dreamers, fisherfolk.

One of these was Manuel Avila. Just turned twenty, this was already his third season on a tuna boat, his second on the *San Rafael* under skipper João da Silva. San Diego *barrio* born and bred, Manuel reflected many of the changes that had happened to the tuna fleet in the last few years. More and more *chicanos* and "down-south" *hispanos* were being signed on as crew, no longer exclusively Portuguese and Italian as in the early days. From deckhand Manuel had risen to speedboat driver on the *San Rafael*, but a bad back injury suffered while helping dolphin escape the purse seine in rough seas now reduced him to working as a brailer. Better than hanging round the docks back in San Diego, he mused. The pain was still there, but the pay was good, if erratic, and you couldn't beat the meals that Tonio, the cook, served up day after day.

The days at sea without a set gave Manuel plenty of time in which to think about the future. It was no secret that these were difficult times. The *San Rafael*, modern enough in its day, simply hadn't kept up with the latest technology. The skipper was always complaining to anyone who cared to listen about foreign boats, some calling themselves "seagoing processing ships" (here he would invariably pause to spit overboard to show his contempt), all better equipped—some even had their own helicopter to scour for fish—and American owners flying under flags of convenience just to depress wages. The bosses on shore and the stockholders, whoever they were, all they could think about were good hauls and profits. No wonder skippers "got hungry" and took risks which plain common sense and experience told them they shouldn't.

By now the watery sun was dipping lower toward the horizon. The wind had abated somewhat, the skies had begun to clear, and the waves were noticeably lower than earlier in the day. Even if they were to spot a school of fish, it was too late for a set that day. Manuel had spent dreary hours under the direction of Agostinho, the moody deckboss, working on the net pile, checking on the seine net with its buoys and rings, and doing odd maintenance jobs. Just before the bell sounded for dinner he was only too glad to go up top to the deck, anything to get away from the clatter and whine of the diesel auxiliaries. There, on the search platform halfway up the mast, he knew that his friend, Sebastian, his sole confidant on board ship, would be scanning the deep troughs and billows through his powerful binoculars for any telltale signs of tuna.

"Well, *viejo, ¿has visto algo?*" he greeted the old man perched some twelve feet above him in the multilingual mix typical of all crews.

"Not yet. But I will", the *anciano* shouted down from the platform. Then somewhat cryptically, "I know the signs."

Manuel believed his friend implicitly. Sebastian knew everything there was to know about the sea and all that lived therein. He was one of the few who still remembered catching tuna from the old baitboats, using the simple technique of pole and line, spending many arduous months without setting foot on land. In his day the nets were still made of jute and cotton, natural fibers which enabled the dolphin to locate them more easily and with a sharp bite to break free if entangled. What chance did they stand now with the nylon filament nets and all that modern machinery? Sebastian could tell stories of driftnets breaking loose and sailing through the oceans "ghost fishing" until they finally sank to the bottom of the sea, weighed down by the marine creatures trapped in the fine mesh. But even he had to admit that far fewer dolphin were being trapped and killed now than in the "good old days" that maybe hadn't really been all that good. The grizzled mariner, despite his years—none of the crew dared venture his age—had kept a mobility of body and agility of mind that were the envy of all. His knowledge of folklore and history was as boundless as the sea itself, and no man alive knew more about fish and dolphins. Especially dolphins.

By now the sun hovered but a few degrees above the horizon, and the warmth of the day was rapidly giving way to the faint chill of the early evening.

"Come on, Sebastian. You're wasting your time. Let's get some chow."

"You go, *amigo mío*. I will wait for them. I know they will come."

Manuel shrugged his shoulders for want of a better answer. No matter how diligently he scanned the blue-grey expanse on all sides, save for the half dozen seagulls and two frigate birds that followed the boat's foamy wake in hope of catching some trash fish from the bilge, there was no sign of life. Suddenly he saw Sebastian straighten up and gesticulate with his right arm.

"There they are, off to starboard. Manolo, just look at them!"

And there, coming in at a tangent toward the ship's bow, a school of graceful dolphins cut through the water effortlessly, leaping and arching as they came ever closer. From the gunwale Manuel looked down on the carefree underwater barrel roll of the dark-grey-backed, white-bellied creatures who seemed to revel as they rode the seiner's bow wave. He now found Sebastian standing at his side, with a knowing smile as he watched his aquatic friends below.

"Nature's hitchhikers," he said, chuckling. "Oh, they're fast swimmers, all right, but not that fast, at least not hour after hour." He paused for a moment to admire their performance. "You see what they're doing? Catching a free ride! And do you know something else? The smart ones stick to starboard, they know that the cranes and nets are on the other side. No, Manolo, don't ask me how, but the older fellows just seem to know from experience. Just like an old fox, or should I say, *un delfín viejo*".

The old man chuckled at his little joke, and Manuel dutifully went along with a jovial grin to make his friend happy. Five minutes later the dinner bell rang, and with a cheery wave the two men bade the silent seagliders goodnight. "*¡Qué duerman bien! Nos vemos mañana,*" Manuel tossed in cheerfully as he and Sebastian headed for the galley and Tonio's gourmet cooking.

For Manuel the evening meal was the highlight of the day, not just for the fine cuisine, but for the chance to relax and chat with Sebastian. The other crew members had little to say and kept to themselves. The two Italians, Luigi and Pietro, had never bothered to learn more than the rudiments of another language and only dreamed of making a small fortune and returning to Sicily. As for the half dozen or so *hispanos*, they came from at least four different countries and somehow had little in common other than being scared of losing their job. Manuel had tried to strike up a friendship with Jonathan, the taciturn Chief Engineer and the sole gringo on board, but it just hadn't worked out. Poor Tonio—no one had figured out exactly where he came from—was always too busy rushing around the galley to stay and chat. That only left João, the skipper, and Agostinho, the deckboss. Both were Portuguese to the core and felt superior to the others, not so much due to their rank, but out of a sense of long tradition and shared language that went back to their ancestors from the Azores, forming a bond that outsiders could not penetrate. They were friendly enough to the rest of the crew, but in a formal sort of way.

As a junior crewman Manuel had been given a lower berth and the midnight watch assignment. The movie after dinner was a typical action-packed thriller which at least got round the language problem. After the third—or was it the fourth?—gratuitous act of screen violence, Manuel decided that a quick shower and a final chat with Sebastian would be a better investment of time before going up on deck for his watch.

His evening conversations with the veteran seaman always gave him special pleasure. Manuel greatly admired the way Sebastian by sheer dint of will power had taught himself to read and learn everything there was to know about dolphins and the sea. Maybe it was the old man's awareness of the natural world, his love of lore and legend, whatever it was, he felt an unbreakable bond with these gregarious sea creatures. Sebastian could recount dolphin stories for hours, telling his listeners how playful and intelligent they were, how some even recognized the sound of diesel engines and alerted their companions to a ship's approach, how one had played tricks on human divers and gently pushed them around, another had "sprung right over a ship's mast"...... countless anecdotes.

That evening was no different from dozens of others. Fueled by two snifters of cognac Sebastian hit his stride, regaling Manuel with story after story. Some were so fanciful that the young man could not suppress a smile.

"I see you don't believe me, young friend. But it's true what I say, *cada palabra*. We can learn a lot from the dolphins. Let me give you an example. When humans come up from a deep dive, there's always the danger of the 'bends', you know, those deadly gas bubbles in the blood stream, just like Luigi's champagne over there. Not with dolphins, though. Somehow they just make their bodies collapse to withstand the pressure. And they're really smart, I can tell you. Did you know they can mimic the human voice? Well they can. Some have led their trainers a merry dance."

He paused to refresh himself before continuing.

"The trouble is, we never get to know the real dolphins, I mean, as they really are. Let me explain. With all the space in the world around us, on this boat we can't get more than fifty feet away from anyone. Now just imagine what it would be like if we never set foot on land, like some permanent Flying Dutchman. Me, I'd go crazy! But that's what we do to dolphins in captivity, putting them in pools full of chlorine with peering faces staring through portholes and boomboxes blasting away. For such highly intelligent creatures these are freak conditions! *¡Hijo, eso me pone furioso!*"

Manuel nodded in agreement. He recognized his good luck in having this sensitive soul mate on board. A quick glance at the clock. It was getting late, and he still had to get ready for his watch duty. He took leave of Sebastian with an old-fashioned handshake and invocation to the powers that protect those far from land. For the next two hours he would commune with the sea, the stars, and the dolphins.

By daybreak the sea had settled down to a gentle swell, and at last the rainclouds had broken up. Breakfast was noticeably more tense than usual as Sebastian went around telling everyone that the previous evening's herd of dolphins and the presence of large man-of-war birds diving and swooping down were good omens, and that, *Dios mediante*, today would see a good set. It proved to be a hasty pronouncement. No sooner had he gone on deck than he sensed that the wind was freshening from the northern quarter, an ominous sign that boded ill. Just then a strong gust swept under a loose hatch cover and flipped it over with a clatter. No more proof was needed that a *praga*, the old sailor's curse, was at work. "*Tal vez mañana, pero hoy no,*" he declared to his shipmates as he, like the gathering squall, shifted his position. "To go fishing today is to disturb the spirits. I feel it in my bones." Which should have been the end of the matter.

But it wasn't. Skippers are notoriously tight-lipped and rarely given to consulting with others, unless with fellow skippers over the ship radio. As for the crew, well, better to keep on the boss's good side, after all, he does the hiring and firing, he's the one who counts when it comes to divvying up the shares at the end of the trip. Besides, skippers are the guys who've heard the weather forecast on the shortwave and know everything.

João da Silva was no different from the other skippers. Tired of "skunking" for weeks without a catch he was determined not to return to home port and face his boss with empty wells. As he surveyed the surrounding ocean from high up in the crow's nest atop the mast, it was with the look of a hungry man. The waves were now a little higher than an hour ago, but down below riding the bow wave he could clearly see the dolphins disporting themselves. And there, running below them and a little way back, unmistakeably were the tuna cutting through the clear water. It took little more than half a minute for the skipper to make up his mind. He turned on the intercom and flipped the public address system switch. "*Vámanos, muchachos,*" he said matter-of-factly, "let's go. Agostinho, everyone ready to start in twenty minutes. I want the first rig in the water when I give the word."

Whatever their apprehensions—for Sebastian's warning had struck a deep chord in the minds of the more superstitious—most of the crew welcomed the excitement of a set. Truth to tell, it was just what they needed after the days of boredom and inactivity. As always at times of danger, several of the deck hands went down to the small shrine on board and lit a candle before the portrait of the young man at the helm protected by Christ. Others less strict in their formal faith besought the spirits to ward off *la mala suerte*.

No more motley a crew was ever seen as they reported to their stations dressed in swimming trunks, T-shirts, and athletic shoes. It was still too early to put on their safety helmets and nylon windbreakers. Climbing into their aluminum pongos, only the four speedboat drivers wore their padded jackets and headgear. At the radio order of the skipper, the speedboats revved up their outboard motors and were lowered one by one by the side booms into the onrushing waves, each craft hitting the surface with a fearsome shudder that jarred its occupant before setting off. ¡Qué les vayan bien! Manuel implored, mindful of his own past experience, as he watched the small boats bounce over the crest of the waves. Soon the speedboat quartet had formed a semicircle and was pushing the dolphins and tuna into an ever-tightening circle. The *San Rafael* in turn approached the school on its port side. Despite the heavy swell, everything was going to plan.

Five minutes later João da Silva gave the order to start playing out the half-mile length of seine net. Immediately the heavy skiff with its powerful diesel engine was winched into the water under the direction of the deckboss, then with the net in tow, began to circle what had by now become a thoroughly confused collection of every sea creature imaginable. As the seine closed and winches secured the oertzas, the two thick steel rings at each end of the net, on board the seiner the engine noise of the hydraulic block drowned out the clatter of the plastic corks, the clanking of chains and iron rings, and the shouts and profanities of the crew in half a dozen languages and dialects. Lost in all the deafening din was the staccato clicking of the dolphins vainly trying to escape the strangling net.

Sebastian and Manuel stood side by side working the corkline. Soon the skipper would give the order for the "back-down" and put the seiner in reverse. This tricky maneuver would elongate the net for a few precious minutes and so give the dolphins a chance to escape. In recent years this had saved the lives of thousands of the mammals, at the risk of straining the equipment and even endangering the crew who did their utmost to help.

Sebastian was becoming more agitated. The main winch took the strain of the heavy net as the purse drew in the fish below water.

"No, Manuel! Something in here tells me it's all wrong."

"It'll be O.K. Don't worry, *viejecito*."

"The spirits. They won't allow it," the old man mumbled to himself dejectedly.

His forebodings were interrupted by the skipper's shout from the crow's nest, "Back 'er down!" Immediately the chief engineer stopped the main engine which cut the forward cruising speed from twelve knots down to six, then three, until the *San Rafael* rocked at a standstill in the rising swell. Now all four of the speedboats were in line at the front of the net. The skipper barked the order to reverse the seiner's powerful engine. As the net lengthened, the drivers from one side and the crew from the other reached over to urge and help the bewildered dolphins escape over the top. Many succeeded, along with a few lucky tuna, but others were so disorientated that they swam around in ever decreasing circles within the net.

Worse still, the *San Rafael* was now beginning to roll perceptibly from side to side, buffeted by ever increasing winds. And still the catch had not been brought on board. Glancing at the mounting seas, the skipper and crew knew it was now a race against time. All were anxious to "sack up," to haul the catch on board, dangerous at the best of times, but extremely hazardous on a swaying ship in a rising sea. Below them, Manuel and Sebastian could see the confused mass ensnared in the purse-seine net, fish of all shapes and sizes including the occasional shark drawn by the odor of blood. Some of the smaller fish were hopelessly caught in the mesh, while at least two of the dolphin had drowned and were weighing down the already heavy net.

For Manuel, working the brailing nets was nearly as painful as riding the bouncing speedboats. This meant separating the sharks and dolphins from the tuna while still in the net, no job for the fainthearted. Today's set was no different from dozens of others in the past. The thing was to get in there, do your damn best, and trust in your gear and God. No one had ever taught you how, you somehow just picked it up, the same as with the hundred and one other skills that made up the day's work. No sooner had the "sack up" order been given than Manuel with three or four other crewmen found himself reaching, pulling, lifting, throwing anything that wasn't a yellowfin back into the sea. God, it was difficult work, his back was killing him, but—irony of ironies for a fisherman—he was at least saving life.

He had no idea when he first saw her. In this hectic business one dolphin looks like any another. True enough, in time you learn the different types, the Spotted in the deep tropical ocean, the Spinners and Duskies out by the islands, the Bottlenoses closer to shore, and all the rest, but when you looked at them down in the net, well, except for their length, they looked pretty much the same with that fixed smile and little beak. But not this one.

Manuel saw at once that she was in trouble. With her calf pitifully clinging to her side, the Bottlenose was floating just below the corkline of the tightening net. From the row of disk scars and tooth marks on her back, as well as the sizeable nicks on her dorsal fin, Manuel knew that she had battled many a shark while protecting her young. And now that same age-old instinct prevented her from making her escape, even as the seine rose higher in the water. No doubt she had tried again and again to lift her youngster over the net with her beak but, exhausted, had finally given up.

There was not a moment to lose. Manuel jumped into that maelstrom of despair, and lunged forward to reach the dolphin. Pushing his way through flailing fins and snapping jaws, he clawed his way across the enveloping net and reached out to the stranded mother. It was a sight he would never forget. A jagged cut just under the left eye and some crescent-shaped scar tissue to the side of the spiracle testified to some bygone vicious skirmish with a shark or a ship's propeller. But that same eye in the expressionless face bespoke a silent gratitude that transcended language. Without offering any resistance, the dolphin allowed Manuel to lift her calf, then herself, over the barrier that stretched between life and death. As she surfaced on the far side, she turned for a brief moment, raised her rostrum in salute, and with a flick of her tail, disappeared beneath the churning water.

In less than a minute Manuel was back on board. Awaiting him was a smiling Sebastian.

"*Híjole,*" he beamed, "you did it! You saved a daughter of Dionysus."

"Later, Sebastian. Save your stories for tonight. *Manos a la obra, viejo.*"

The *San Rafael* was beginning to pitch wildly, and any attempt to winch the skiff in at the stern or haul up the speedboats would have to wait for calmer seas. All attention was now focused on getting the catch on board and down the chutes into the well hatches. The skipper had been right in one thing, at least; it was going to be a "big jag" with plenty of fish. Already the powerblock at the end of the main boom was taking the strain as the bulging net slowly lifted out of the water. On both sides the crew were readying the brailers, the fish scoops that would relieve the pressure and start sorting the catch before dropping it into the hopper. Here timing and teamwork were everything; one slip, and the next thing you knew, thousands of sea creatures would be squirming all over the deck.

So far so good. Agostinho, the deckboss, whatever his moods—his fearsome outbursts were famous throughout the fleet—certainly knew his job. At great risk to himself he put on the cable clamps and got the choker thrown round the net for added support. "O.K. boss," he yelled up to the skipper, "ready to haul away!" João da Silva took in the scene from the swaying crow's nest and barked out the order to proceed. With a tremendous strain the purse cables and winches began to lift the net ever higher. With a bit of luck in another hour or so it would all be over, the speedboats and skiff back on board, and the decks swept clean. All depending, of course, on luck, the weather..... As the first drops of rain turned into a steady drizzle and then thickened into pouring rain, every mind and muscle concentrated on the immediate work.

Already the brailers and every available deckhand were busy freeing the wide net, separating the tuna with their jagged fins from the crabs, jellyfish, and assorted flotsam, while tossing the odd hammerhead down the separate shark slide. By now, the *San Rafael* was lurching dangerously from side to side, and more than one of the crew lost his footing on the slick deck and careened into a companion or railing. More ominously still, the rising net had begun to develop fits and starts, flapping like a sail in the gusty wind, making the job of stacking it that much more difficult. No one dared pronounce the word, but all feared the worst nightmare, a "roll-up" when part of the webbing gets caught round the purse cable, requiring hours to undo the resultant tangle.

Suddenly, the seiner was struck side-on by a high comber that caused it to pitch crazily to starboard. With a sickening crack the mainboom buckled, twisted grotesquely, then snapped near the middle, amid frantic cries of "*¡Ojos arriba!*" The deck became a chaotic mass of spars and netting, with debris hurtling down as men and fish slithered in all directions. Amid the confusion Manuel felt himself thrown helter-skelter against one of the brailing hoppers and then skidding across the planking into the stack of chains. He knew immediately that his back was done for.

How long he lay helplessly on the deck he never knew. At some point he must have lost consciousness, for when he recovered his senses, he found himself stretched out on his bunk and Sebastian looking anxiously down at him.

"Still alive, I see. Well, *hijito*, how do you feel?"

"Could be a lot worse, I suppose. What happened?"

Sebastian pondered his friend's question for a moment.

"The *praga*. We should never have begun the set with the curse upon us. It's all a matter of *suerte*. Ours ran out on us, that's all."

Within minutes Manuel had learned all he needed to know. The catch had been a near total loss, and the main net would need days of work to repair the rips and tears once the *San Rafael* made it back to port. One of the speedboats had had to be abandoned, though they had managed to save the skiff. As for the crew, not one of them had escaped without some sort of injury, including a couple of broken arms and a severe concussion. Sebastian was one of the luckier men—other than a sprained wrist and a glancing blow to the head, he had not fared too badly. Manuel was not so lucky with his wrenched back. Strangely enough, despite the pain, his thoughts were far away. Somewhere, somewhere in that vast expanse was a dolphin whose gaze he would never forget.

Sebastian lived with his anglo wife Sarah some half dozen blocks away from the area along San Diego Bay referred to as Tunaville by the locals. Being of Spanish (rather than of Portuguese or Italian) background, he had felt somewhat out of the mainstream of tunamen despite his near half-century before the mast. For that reason he preferred to live further up the peninsula rather than in Tunaville itself. Their three children had grown up and followed careers far from the sea, but they and their children unfailingly visited the aging couple, especially in the two months before Christmas when the tuna fleet remained in harbor for refitting.

And now, in Manuel, they had acquired another grandchild, so to speak. Fishermen look after fishermen, at least among the older generation, and Sebastian and Sarah had immediately offered their home to the homeless young man. Manuel's back was now in a brace, making him immobile and an easy victim of Sebastian's endless yarns. As for the old seaman, he grudgingly admitted that perhaps the time had come to hang up his sou'wester. The owners of the *San Rafael* had concluded that repairing the damaged equipment just wasn't worth it and had sold off the boat for what they could get. In this business it was simple: no boat, no job.

Often the subject came back to dolphins. To Sebastian, there was no real mystery about them; thousands of years ago they had been created by the god Dionysus and thereby had acquired godlike attributes themselves. Once—and here Sebastian was uncharacteristically vague—they had emerged from the sea onto land, "probably didn't like what they saw," and had returned forthwith to their aqueous home. Where the other gods fitted in wasn't altogether clear, but the old man never doubted that a dolphin had helped Poseidon woo his recalcitrant bride and as a reward had been given his own constellation in the northern sky. Equally certain was the adventure of the poet Arion who, in mortal danger from pirates, had sung a high-pitched song which attracted a passing dolphin. Whereupon Arion had unhesitatingly thrown himself into the sea and, sitting astride the selfsame dolphin, was safely brought to land. Another dolphin had saved the life of Telemachos, the son of Odysseus; small wonder that the Greek sages, such as Aristotle and Plutarch, held them in great reverence and affection, so much so that the friendly mammals were collectively given the nickname of Simo, meaning snub-nosed. Nor was that all. Sebastian knew beyond question that dolphins had helped the early Church fathers and even brought back the bodies of saints for sacred burial, and thus fully merited their reputation for swiftness, diligence, and love.

For his part Manuel needed no convincing that dolphins were very special creatures. Even his unsentimental shipmates admitted that without them the tuna would be much harder to find, and so did their best to protect them. But Manuel was still puzzled on one score.

"Tell me, Sebastian," he asked the old man one day, "why do so many fishermen call them porpoises instead of dolphin?"

The veteran self-tutored sailor was only too happy to don his best professorial air.

"Take your pick, *hijo mío*, between Latin and Greek. If you follow the Romans, our porpoise is little more than a pig fish, a 'porcus piscis', not very flattering, if you ask me. As for myself, I much prefer the Greek 'delphis', their word for womb because that's how the dolphin young are born. Of course, you know that the oracle of

Delphi was named for them," he tossed in for effect. "That's how smart they are."

Manuel looked suitably impressed by his friend's erudition. Now was the time to spring the real question.

"Sebastian, you say that the dolphins in the old days did all sorts of wonderful things. Tell me, can they still do them?"

"*¡Claro que sí!* What makes you think they can't?"

The young man hesitated for a fraction of a second.

"Sebastian, you remember that female dolphin in the net? You know, the one we saved. Well, is she still alive? I've got to know."

The *anciano* shifted his gaze up to the window and looked toward the ocean.

"It's all so difficult. No one can really say. Manolo, I don't want to break your heart, but for a wounded mother with a young calf it's not easy. A lot depends if she caught up with the other dolphins and if the sharks didn't get her first. I'm sorry!"

With that he placed his hand on the young man's shoulder. Manuel refused to believe that such a thing could happen.

"She'll make it, I know she will. And I'm going to give her a name to make sure she does. She'll perform a miracle, just like in the old days you spoke about. What was that name—Simo? That's it, I'll call her Simo."

Sebastian smiled and gave a little cough.

"I think we need a minor change. Maybe Sima for a mother is a little more appropriate."

"Sima, then. Do you think we'll ever see her again?"

The old man weighed his words carefully before replying.

"Manolo, this will need a miracle. A very big one. You'll have to pray a lot to make it happen. But yes, it can be done," he added with a reassuring twinkle in his eye.

"How do you know?" Manuel persisted.

"Well, to start with, your Sima is a very strong Pacific bottlenose from what I saw. A *Tursiops gilli* is a little bigger than her Atlantic cousins and weighs up to four hundred pounds, though

Sima must be a little less. Oh yes, they know how to defend themselves out there. A dolphin butt to the stomach is something a shark will never forget."

"You're really sure, aren't you, Sebastian? You're not just trying to...." His voice trailed off, unable to finish the sentence.

"As I said, a lot depends whether she made it back to the other dolphins. Fortunately they have a well-defined home range. I'm sure her friends tried to find her. They always do. So you see, there's real hope."

"But that means we'll never see her again, doesn't it?"

"Probably—unless she's captured or wants to be captured, which I can't imagine. No, *amigo mío*, just be glad you did what you did, and forget the matter. Not everyone has saved a dolphin, remember."

The days passed in rapid succession as the rainy season gave way to the overcast skies of early summer. Manuel's back had responded to treatment as well as could be expected, and in a week or two he'd be out looking for work. Retirement for Sebastian offered special problems. Like many tuna men, he had never even learned how to drive a car or how to follow the thousand and one rules that structured everyday life. Yes, he missed the open ocean, the boundless freedom—but was it really freedom to stay out at sea for months cooped up with fifteen other men? Strangely enough, after more than forty years of married life, this was his first real chance to get to know Sarah and discover the joys of finding his landlegs.

It was during a morning walk along the beach that the subject first came up. Manuel watched Sebastian gaze silently out to sea.

"*¿Qué te ocurre?*" he ventured.

"I'm sorry, *hijo*, but I was far away. Far away in time and distance," he added enigmatically.

"Well, are you going to tell me?"

"Let's wait until we get back," Sebastian said. "I've got something to show you."

The half hour walk back to the modest adobe house half way up the hill was uncharacteristically silent. Whatever Sebastian had in mind would have to wait.

Manuel hurried through lunch, even volunteering to wash the dishes and help Sarah put them away to speed things up. In his excitement he forgot to take the siesta rest the doctor had ordered for his back. The meal over, with a wave of his hand Sebastian beckoned him toward the deep alcove which served as a library and study. Usually the sanctuary was curtained off, but not today. There, stacked neatly on rows of shelves, stood the treasures of a lifetime. Manuel could only stare in amazement at the ancient leather-bound volumes, the faded maps that festooned the walls, the cases of mariner's instruments, a couple of old flintlocks and musty uniforms, while suspended from the ceiling hung an array of stuffed fish and nets. Jutting out from a crowded wall Manuel saw the painted figurehead of a Spanish galleon. Amid baroque curlicues stood the central figure of a stylized dolphin rising from the churning waves. The sculptor artist had given the face a knowing smile, half animal, half human. Manuel stepped closer to admire the fine carving and ran his hand over the contours.

"Why, it's magnificent. It must be worth a fortune."

"Not really. You see, it's just a copy of the original, and probably not a very good one at that. No, the original's far away, I'm afraid. No one has seen that for close on three hundred years. It's in the best guarded museum in the world, under ten fathoms of water. Oh yes, beautifully preserved, if you don't mind a barnacle or two, and nothing's ever stolen." Sebastian paused for a moment. "It's a long, long story."

To Manuel's surprise, his friend changed tack before resuming his narrative.

"Yes, *amigo mío*, I saw you smile when I said it's a long, long story. Do you know what the *gringos* call me behind my back? The

Ancient Mariner! I see their problem very clearly. They have two words, 'story' and 'history', two words, two ideas. We poor Spaniards can only afford one, so *'historia'* has to do for both. Take this figurehead here, for example, or rather the original. Now what a story lies behind it!"

The veteran sailor bade his young friend sit down as he reached into a drawer and pulled out what looked like an old map and some mildewed papers. With a dramatic flourish he untied a ribbon and unrolled a musty document.

"Do you know what this is?" he inquired rhetorically. "No? Well, I'll tell you. *Mira*, this is a Spanish *cédula real*, a royal decree, dating from the late seventeenth century. Oh, it's genuine all right. See this old-fashioned script and this that looks like little sketches? Well, it's all about a Spanish galleon that left Manila bound for Acapulco in 1685 but was lost in a hurricane somewhere in the middle of the Pacific. See here, *"se perdió de vista,"* lost without a trace, vanished, just like a century later the two ships of La Pérouse disappeared after visiting Hawai'i. And do you know what the name of the galleon was? Well, it was called the *Serenissimi Delphini*. Does that say something to you? *Delphini, Delfín*, eh?"

"You mean the ship was named for a dolphin?"

Sebastian could barely suppress a smile.

"*Joven*, you really have dolphins on the brain! But you're nearly right. You see, the galleon was christened the *Serenissimi Delphini* during the reign of Carlos, *el hechizado*, to flatter the French and maybe fob them off. You remember the poor king who was bewitched and couldn't produce an heir? Well, the French were very much interested in placing one of their own young princes on the Spanish throne. Now, in French the word *dauphin* means both the king's eldest son and also a dolphin. That's why the ship had a dolphin as a figurehead. Of course, the crew couldn't pronounce the long Latin name so they simply called the ship the *Delfín*."

"What happened to it? I mean, does anyone know?"

Sebastian unrolled the yellowed map and laid it flat on the table. Clearly the chart with its playful dolphins was of some antiquity, and owed as much to the cartographer's artistic sense as to any quest for accuracy. Manuel could make out the general contours of the large island of Hawai'i with the two volcanoes depicted in highly imaginative fashion. Various reefs and bays with soundings were indicated, along with a few settlements, but other than its picturesque interest, the map meant little to him. Seizing his moment, with an aura of mystery Sebastian superimposed the *cédula* on the map, taking care that it overlapped exactly, and with the point of a pencil pressed down on the little sketches.

"Now you see," he said triumphantly, "that's the spot where the galleon ran aground. I'm sure, though I've never had the chance to prove it. Up to now, no one ever believed me. But you do."

Manuel, his absolute faith in the old man notwithstanding, still remained dubious.

"It's not that I don't believe you, Sebastian, but how can you tell? After all, these are just two old bits of paper."

"Not any two. You need both for *la clave*, the key, otherwise it doesn't work. You see, these were brought ashore by the sole Spanish survivor. There's an old Hawaiian legend of a *haole* sailor who was saved, just like our friend Arion, by a dolphin who in this case recognized his own likeness in the figurehead of the ship. The beach even today is called Nai'a Ke'e, which means 'the place to which dolphins are drawn.' If this is true, that means that a Spaniard was the first European to set foot in Hawai'i and not Cook as the gringos would have us believe. And that also explains how the English found the Hawaiians already acquainted with iron. It all came from the *Delfín*," he added with finality.

Manuel, elated and confused, could barely grasp what he had heard.

"Do they know what happened to the Spanish sailor?"

"Well, no one knows exactly, but if I know my ancestors he lived out a long life on the Big Island and fathered several *niños*. As for the map and *cédula*, they were handed down from one generation to the next and eventually ended up in the hands of a Catholic missionary. From there they somehow came into my father's possession. The important thing is for you, Manolo, to do what I could not. One day you will be successful and go to that beach and find the wreck of the galleon. Promise me you will. This is what I ask of you."

The young man assented wholeheartedly. One way or another he swore to himself he would repay the old mariner who had given him a home and shown such kindness. He would find the place where a dolphin, as in ancient times, had worked miracles with men.

⁂

Finding work in California, that is, a job with a future, is never easy during a recession. For some reason there's little demand for an ex-speedboat driver or brailer with an aching back, even if its owner is bilingual and a hard worker. For Manuel it was going to be an uphill struggle.

Especially if, to use Sebastian's felicitous phrase, 'you have dolphins on the brain'. Whatever else he did, Manuel was determined—possessed might be a better word—to find work around dolphins. Without a high school diploma or any experience to offer, he knew the odds were stacked against him. Yet whatever else it did, the *barrio* produced some stubborn individuals. Besides, Spain had produced Don Quixote, the craziest dreamer of them all. All of this blood flowed in Manuel's veins.

Did Don Quixote ever venture forth on a more hopeless venture? Here was Manuel Avila, bent of back, his head full of Sebastian's books and stories, a latter-day knight errant venturing forth in his trusty, or rather rusty, rattletrap hoping one day to find his lost Sima. The obvious place to start looking for work was in his home city, at Sea World, but for Manuel's purposes—porpoises might be more accurate—this offered little hope. It was now right in the summer season, and the extra help had been hired long ago. As Manuel watched the dolphin shows with their fabulously trained sleek animals it was only too obvious that they would have little use for a battle-scarred veteran like Sima. More to the point, why should she be anywhere on land, least of all in California? Common sense told him that she was hundreds of miles away in the ocean with her calf, where she would stay for the rest of her days. But then Sebastian had said never give up.....

Other than job hunting, Manuel spent his days helping out his old friend and Sarah with household chores. In his spare time he pored over library books that dealt with sea life, dreaming one day of becoming a vet and working with marine animals. It all seemed so distant, so hopeless. Once in a while he saw a Flipper rerun on TV, but as often as not turned off the program after a few minutes. Either the real thing, or nothing at all. Better Sebastian's far-off stories of Korianos and Harmias, fanciful as they were, than this aquatic Lassie.

Just as he was becoming totally discouraged, Sebastian came to the rescue.

"No, not a job, I'm afraid, Manolo. Even I can't work such miracles in these times. But you'll like this, though. You remember Miguel Asturias, you know, *el flaquito*? Well, next week he's sailing to the Laguna Ojo de Liebre down in Baja, and he's invited us to come with him on a fishing trip. You'll forgive me, I'm sure, but I said yes for both of us. So Monday it's off to sea again!"

The break was just what Manuel needed. As they chugged out of San Diego harbor, he caught sight of the dark silhouettes of two submarines moored close to shore. How rigid and mechanical, he thought, how lacking in grace when compared to Sima! Could anything created by man equal the form and carefree spirit of the dolphin? The days spent in the Baja lagoon were the happiest he had ever known. There, as the sun set over a narrow spit of land, whales, seabirds, and coyotes all came together, a divine union of sea, air, and land. Once, truly a rare occasion, they even glimpsed the small harbor porpoise, known affectionately by the locals as the *vaquita* or little cow. It was now endangered, caught in the same nets as the totoaba fish. As they sailed back to San Diego, Manuel was overcome both by the wonder and sadness of it all.

Driving up and down the coast in search of work was depressing in the extreme. Often he was taken for a wetback, and even producing his birth certificate didn't help matters much. In desperation he accepted odd jobs in hotels and restaurants, just enough to earn a few dollars and continue his search. After six months he had become quite discouraged and for the first time thought about giving up. As so often, it was Sebastian who shook him out of his gloom.

"Another hotel, I'm afraid, but guess what! It has a small lagoon, with dolphins! It's just outside L.A., a friend told me about it, and if you hurry, the job's yours. Not much, but better than nothing. ¡*Buena suerte, hijo! ¡Qué te vaya bien!*" Manuel needed no further bidding. In less than four hours he presented himself at the hotel, made a favorable impression on the Personnel Manager, and landed the job, starting the next day.

The *Costa Dorada* fancied itself as a resort-cum-playground for the *nouveaux riches* which, come to think of it, might have been a far more appropriate name for the place. The name was Spanish, but little more. The high exterior wall was of white stucco with a minaret-like tower (actually an elevator) at set intervals. In the center a vaguely Moorish patio, complete with imposing *rejas* on all four sides, took pride of place. The artificial lagoon housing the dolphins was off to the right of an imposing stretch of lawn that also served as a putting green. Apparently the hotel had recently been refurbished, with a corresponding hike in prices and, it was hoped, type of clientele.

Manuel found himself working in a back room behind the main kitchen, alternately preparing food and rinsing mountains of plates and glasses prior to loading them into the voracious dishwashing machines. A mere handful of his fellow-workers spoke more than a word or two of English, and at times he fondly imagined himself back with the crew of the *San Rafael*. Why he had been hired soon became abundantly clear; on the rare occasions the immigration officers came, the feared *migra*, the kitchen help—Mexican, Vietnamese, Thais, and a scattering of North Africans—made themselves scarce while Manuel and a couple of others were presented as the entire staff. That three workers could handle the meal preparation and cleanup for a major resort struck no one as particularly strange, least of all the government bureaucrats. But then inspection was never too rigorous in any of the hotels.

Even before he began work that first day Manuel had rushed down to see the dolphins. There they were in the enclosed lagoon, two of them, circling around endlessly in the cramped space, rising and diving in monotonous sequence. Of course Sima was not there—why should she be? By now her calf would have left her to fend for itself, and the mother could be anywhere within a hundred thousand square miles. As he surveyed the dolphin basin decorated on each side with garish *azulejos* in keeping with the pseudo-Moorish motif of the resort, Manuel felt a sense of relief that Sima was spared this indignity.

Even without Sima, Manuel wanted to learn everything he could about the dolphins. In Sebastian's home and at the library he had read every book he could lay his hands on, but still it was all rather remote. This, whatever the shortcomings, was the real thing. Every night after work, and before returning to his dingy room at the back of the hotel, Manuel would come down to the lagoon and commune with the dolphins.

Within a day or two he learned some names as well as the facts of hotel life. Their overseer—trainer would be far too dignified a name—was Rick Hadley, a powerfully built young man maybe some five years older than Manuel. Clearly this was someone who would not brook any interference or criticism with the way he ran things. Hadley somehow was related to the *Costa Dorada's* new owners, and it had been his idea to bring in Corey and Cora, the two bottlenose dolphins, to "add a new dimension" to the hotel. Already thanks to him the reception area was enlivened with a couple of endangered scarlet macaws framed in shiny brass rings as décor. Some gaily colored tropical fish swam languidly around a brightly lit aquarium in the main foyer, while in the patio an uncomprehending bunting-clad burro stood before a background of a crudely painted plywood Alhambra palace—this was Spain, don't forget—patiently supporting the spoiled offspring of the wealthy on his back while the photographer snapped the Andalucian scene for posterity.

Manuel's first encounter with Hadley at the dolphin pool was brevity itself; glad you like the big fish, now get back to the kitchen. To Manuel, it was only too clear that these confined mammals were but shadows of their real selves. What did Hadley know or care about their lack of space or proper feeding? Was he even aware how disorientating the multiple echoes in the small lagoon must be to such sensitive creatures? And what of their playfulness, their sense of humor? Had he ever heard of their need for stimulation, that as highly intelligent animals they were literally dying of boredom? Worst of all, there was nothing Manuel could do about it.

As the weeks went by, he wondered why on earth he was staying on at the *Costa Dorada*. True, he had set a modest sum aside, mainly from tips he had garnered when promoted to waiter. But his search for Sima wasn't going anywhere. Just the opposite, in fact. As he served drinks at poolside he had on occasion seen inebriated guests trying to swim with Corey and Cora, and even cuddle them. One young lady, a Hollywood starlet noticeably *embarazada*, had gone so far as to express the wish that she wanted to give birth in the same water as the dolphins. Only her flustered husband, or whatever, finally dissuaded her from performing in public.

Manuel's dilemma was unexpectedly resolved one day when, out of the blue, Rick Hadley approached him. Clearly he was in a very unhappy state of mind.

"Look here, Manual," he began. (Presumably the name was derived from some instruction booklet.) "I've been thinking about those two dolphins of ours. I'm getting fed up with all that clicking and squeaking, and nothing to show for it. After all these weeks, all they can do is push an inner tube around the pool. You'd think that after all that fish we give them they'd want to jump out of the water just like dolphins in other places, wouldn't you?" he said dolefully.

Manuel was far too polite to point out that there was a world of difference between taming and training a dolphin, or that his name was short for Emanuel. Instead he let Hadley continue his lament.

"Let me come to the point, Manual. Every time I see you, you seem to be hanging around the dolphins. They sure seem to like you for some reason."

"Maybe it's because I stop and talk to them."

"Me, I don't have time to spend with them—I've got too much to do in the front office. You know, I think we should give you some time off from waiting tables—maybe you can teach them a few tricks, you know, jumping through hoops, over a bar, stuff like that. You can always hit them with the stick if they don't cooperate. That's the only way they're ever going to learn anything, believe me." Without wasting any more time he turned round and was gone.

So that was how he, Manuel Avila, was promoted to on-the-job dolphin trainer. Back at Sebastian's place he had read the tricks of the trade, how to flash the signals to elicit responses, the reward system using whistle and fish, all about the "shaping" of the routines, and the rest of it. He knew that it was a tedious process, skill by skill, sometimes requiring a step back before the cued behavior was mastered. He had no idea how tough and frustrating it would be. Corey and Cora were both Atlantic bottlenoses, well known for their adaptability and willingness to learn, but even so it took time and patience before they overcame their distrust first of the rope, then the bar held just above the water. Nor did the cramped space help matters. Manuel knew that browbeating these intelligent creatures just wouldn't work, they'd simply go on strike or even settle down on the floor of the pool to show their disgust! The secret was to work with them, to make it fun, to place yourself in *their* situation. The biggest improvement came when Manuel switched from hand signals to underwater sound cues to which the dolphins with their sonar hearing responded almost immediately. Soon Corey and Cora were jumping in unison over the hand-held bar, no record height perhaps, but respectable enough. Just as important, Manuel soon taught them the signal when to stop their act and settle down.

From time to time Rick Hadley dropped by to check on the progress. To Manuel's surprise (and relief) the overseer expressed satisfaction with what he saw.

"Keep it up, Manual," he encouraged him. "You're doing real good with those two. We'll need them the week after next when we put on the big wedding and reception, that Japanese deal. I'll take over for the day. Just show me how you do it, you know, getting them to jump." With that he turned on his heel as before and strode away.

From the bustle and frantic activity throughout the hotel it was evident that this was to be no ordinary event. The groom was the son and heir apparent of one of the major tuna fleet owners in Japan, and his wedding to the daughter of a leading competitor was designed to be the commercial and social statement of the year. The two firms exported hundreds of thousands of tons of tuna to the States and Canada, so a positive image of the company this side of the Pacific was deemed essential for business. At considerable expense some bright spirit on Madison Avenue hit on the idea of a California Shinto/Christian outdoor wedding, complete with leaping dolphins in the background to "keep the nature-lovers happy" and show how considerate the company was of all sea creatures (tuna excepted). For home consumption, the reigning sumo champion was brought along, together with an assortment of television personalities and figures in the news. All in all it was going to be very impressive indeed with satellite coverage and the usual media hoopla.

The morning of the wedding saw the entire hotel staff abustle. The previous day's rehearsal with stand-ins for the principals had gone without a hitch (the hitching was for the next day), and Manuel had every reason to be pleased with the performance of his two charges. And now it was time for the real thing. In the bright mid-morning sunlight white tuxedos and cocktail finery were the dress of the day, and even the visible hotel help were bedecked in rented suits. No expense had been spared, least of all on the exquisite foods and wines brought in from far and wide. To judge by the boisterous laughter and individual unsteady deportment, a few of the guests had evidently jumped the gun and somehow managed to acquire a drink or two before the actual service. By the time the wedding party had gathered on the immaculate lawn it was evident that many were already in high spirits.

If only they had gone on with the program as planned, none of what followed would ever have happened. Whose fault it was is difficult to tell. Whoever thought of bringing along the two scarlet macaws for added color is still not clear. Certainly insisting that one of the bridesmaids be seated on Paquito, the burro, just for the camera, didn't help either. Nor for that matter did moving the entire wedding party closer to the pool's edge for the group picture just to get the dolphins in. Finally there was Rick Hadley insisting on taking control of everything, including giving Corey and Cora their cues. Looking back, it was a catastrophe waiting to happen.

It started well enough. Hadley was busy lining everyone up, not forgetting to gently nudge the sumo champion into a prominent place near the bridal party. The minister beamed good-naturedly at everyone, even as the photographers motioned those on each side of the group to press closer towards the middle. By now a battery of international TV and film cameras were whirring furiously. Amid the banter of the assembled guests, Rick Hadley slipped to the side of the pool and gave Corey and Cora their signal to begin leaping over the bar. It all promised to be a huge success.

One can easily blame the photographers for insisting on just one more picture. But then the tuna company paying for the shindig clearly wanted its money's worth. Whatever the cause, a perceptive observer could see that the dolphins were tiring rapidly. Their once ebullient jumps were now quite labored, and Manuel saw that their heavy landings in the water more resembled a whale's breaching than the elegant reentry of a dolphin. Earlier that morning Hadley had given strict orders that he, and he alone, was in sole command of everything, including Corey and Cora. Well, *amigo*, if that's the way you want it, so be it….

By now the splashing had thoroughly drenched some of the guests standing closest to the pool. Instinctively the dolphins seemed to recognize that a wonderful new game was afoot, and with their powerful flukes were systematically soaking the densely packed group at the water's edge. Only when he caught sight of the dispirited bride in all her sodden wedding finery did Hadley realize that things were going badly wrong. Cora, in her most playful mood, chose that moment to reach out and seize the minister's trouser leg, causing that worthy to lose his balance and topple into the pool. Corey, not to be outdone, gleefully nudged Paquito who happened to be standing at pool's edge, landing both the burro and his young lady rider in the water next to the floundering minister. Unfortunately, Paquito in his fall happened to lurch against the sumo wrestler who in turn pulled down the best man and his new father-in-law with him into the pool.

All in all, no less than half a dozen forms, both human and animal, found themselves struggling in the water. Somehow only the two dolphins really felt at home in that element.

By now confusion's masterpiece was complete. Amid all the shouting and screaming, Hadley dimly remembered Manuel having told him that there was also a signal to end the dolphin act, a sort of off-switch. By now it was far too late. The two macaws entered full-throatedly into the spirit of things with ear-splitting squawks and took passing swipes at anyone within pecking distance. One of the more intoxicated guests jumped fully clothed into the lagoon, in his alcoholic haze imagining that it was his sacred duty to follow the bridegroom's example. To Hadley's horror, he saw the TV cameras filming the chaos as the operators enthusiastically swung their equipment round to capture every moment. That evening the *Costa Dorada* would be on every screen in the nation, if not the world.

Somehow Rick Hadley and the others lived to tell the tale. The end was sad enough in its own way. No amount of cajoling and tugging could pry the sumo champ out of the pool, wedged as he was between diving board and the side, though both Corey and Cora lent a willing snout in the endeavor. It was only when a local towtruck was brought round that the waterlogged wrestler could be hoisted out. Heads had to roll, and the easiest was Manuel's. That same evening he was summarily fired as the main culprit. To get rid of further evidence, Corey and Cora were slipped at the dead of night into the ocean, the only real justice in the whole sorry affair.

So Manuel found himself out on the road again, without a job. By a stroke of luck his name was omitted from the lurid tabloid accounts under screaming headlines such as "Costa's Last Stand" and "Hotel All Wet", to cite but a couple. The lawyers were expected to have a field day, though by now Corey and Cora were over the waves and far away, so they at least could not be sued. As for Manuel, the more distance he put between himself and the *Costa Dorada*, the better. As he drove his battered clunker along the old coast road, his future could hardly have looked any bleaker.

The next few days were no better. One or two hotels did have an opening, the usual *friegaplatos*, but of dolphins there was nary a sign. After all, why should a run-of-the-mill hotel mess with temperamental creatures that needed a dozen pounds of mullet a day and were prone to all sorts of illness? For a ritzy tourist hotel it didn't make much sense either, Manuel ruefully admitted. Lots of headaches, and for what? Just to entertain a crowd of tourists who didn't understand a thing that was going on.

It was now time to head back to San Diego and Sebastian. Two thoughts made him hesitate a moment. To tell Sebastian and Sarah that he had failed was a bitter pill to swallow. And then there was Sima. Something—God knows what—kept telling him that *somewhere, somehow*, they were destined to meet again. Call it stubbornness or stupidity—*testarudez* was as good a word as any—but against all evidence he was determined to push on. Would Don Quixote ever have quit?

So instead of turning south, Manuel headed north, at least for another week or two or until his funds ran out. By now it was late in the season, and the spate of tourists had subsided noticeably. The Santa Ana hot winds had come and gone, and the first dark rainclouds were rolling in from the ocean. One day towards evening, just as he was turning a bend toward the coast, it suddenly appeared. At first he could not make out the crumbling wooden palisade to the left of the road. Out in front a dozen or so cars were parked haphazardly. But it was something quite different that caught his eye. For there, over the main entrance, was a crude neon sign that proclaimed "Davy Jones' Dolphins." Dolphins! Manuel could hardly believe his eyes. Mirage or not, it took less than a second or two to slam on the brakes and turn off the road.

Of course! A roadside show. Why hadn't he thought of it? That's where Sima would be, if anywhere. Manuel quickly strode up to the entrance. "No, Miss, I'm not a customer," he told the bored-looking girl at the counter that served as the admissions booth, "I want to talk to the owner." The girl reluctantly put down her nail file, checked her fingers briefly, then led him to a tiny back office where a middle-aged man with thinning hair rose to meet them.

"Jack Guelph, alias Davy Jones," he said affably, stretching out a welcoming hand. "How can I help you? You're not an agent from—No, far too human," he added half-jokingly but with obvious relief.

"Manuel Avila, *a sus órdenes*. No, I haven't come to check up on you," he said with a smile. "Not at all. I've come for a job."

"A job, you say? Not the best of times, I'm afraid. Another month from now and we'll be closing down for the season. Fact is, business is downright slow right now," he stated matter-of-factly.

"It's not for the money," Manuel lied bravely. "If you can feed me and find me a bed I'll be happy enough."

"Now wait a minute, young man. Let's not be in too big a hurry. I still don't know the first thing about you. Have you ever worked with dolphins? What do you know about them?" he asked with a tinge of distrust.

Manuel seized his opportunity with both hands. By the time he had poured out all his knowledge and experience, with an embellishment here and an omission there, he had more than convinced Jack Guelph of his worth.

"Well, son, I guess we can arrange something. One of my new boys had to quit a week ago, and one of my trainers got another job last month. Why don't you go and see Charley Matlock? Charley's our main trainer, or, maybe I should say our only trainer at the moment. I'm sure he could do with some help. Dina here will show you the way."

With a total lack of enthusiasm the girl took Manuel round to the back of the enclosure. The sight was anything but encouraging. Some of the holding tanks showed unmistakeable signs of rust and even slow leaks, and a peek inside one revealed algae and discolored water. The pumps had obviously seen better days, and the whole enterprise had a tacky rundown look about it. Dina apparently had read Manuel's thoughts.

"No one stays here," she stated flatly. "Not if they can help it, that is."

"Where's Charley Matlock?"

A few yards ahead stood a much larger structure with raised tiers of wooden seats in a semi-circle. Behind a sort of stage was a pool only slightly larger than the one at the *Costa Dorada*. Evidently it was just after the last show of the day, for a couple of workers were sweeping up the plastic cups and other litter left by the tourists. A sunburnt young man of about Manuel's age was busy hosing down the stage area, while in the pool itself a pair of bottlenose dolphins were lazily describing endless figure eights. From an adjacent holding pen two enquiring snouts protruded in the air periodically to take in the scene. Manuel could see at a glance that none of the four dolphins was Sima…..

"Can I help you?" The words came from the tanned young man. Evidently this was Charley Matlock, trainer, keeper, and handyman all in one. Soon Manuel had finished explaining what had brought him there, and was pleased to find in Charley an enthusiastic, if somewhat naïve, listener. Far from viewing the newcomer as a competitor, Charley welcomed him as an assistant and fellow worker.

The truth is he needed all the help he could get. Davy Jones' Dolphins was run on a shoestring budget in a state of near permanent bankruptcy. Jack Guelph had served in the Navy where, to quote his own words, he "had taken to dolphins just like some folk take to horses." The story was familiar enough; a modest pension, his lifetime's savings, an unexpected inheritance, and a couple of bank loans had all been poured into what might have made good sense in the California boom days. Now the economy had turned sour, leaving nothing but payments. Manuel suspected that was just half the story. As he followed Charley around from tank to tank it was depressingly clear that there was plenty of work ahead.

The five shows next day merely reinforced the first dismal impression. To the sound of ear-splitting electronic music, the sparse crowds were urged by Charley to have "a whale of a time" and to "get in the swim", whatever that meant. At this point Stephanie, a curvaceous young lady with little left to hide, took over the mike. A pair of California sea lions were put through their predictable paces, followed by a handful of Humboldt penguins that seemed more confused by the noise than anything else. It was now time for the dolphins to take over the show. Two of them, Wanda and Wendy, leaped gracefully out of the water to the accompaniment of "oohs" and "ahs" from the onlookers, but to Manuel it was the lack of coordination that was the most telling. Instead of jumping in unison, side by side, the performance was ragged, usually the sign of poor training. Also the "porpoising," when the dolphins were supposed to reenter the water without a splash, left much to be desired as the drenched customers in the first two rows could testify. As for the somersaulting, tail slapping, and backflips, it was all barely adequate, and more than once Wanda missed going through the hoop. At this stage some in the audience were clearly getting uncomfortable with the amateurishness of it all. Babies were screaming, while some of the older children started running up and down the steps out of control. Clearly something was needed to liven up the show. Like a well-trained dolphin, Jack Guelph bounded in right on cue.

No longer the meek manager Manuel had first encountered, Jack was now accoutered as Davy Jones, the most ferocious pirate that ever laid waste to the Spanish Main, even if a trifle over the hill, perhaps, for an active buccaneer. His mustachios, eye patch and drawn sword were calculated to strike terror into the small fry that had come to watch the show, but with a broad wink he quickly reassured them that all was well. What followed was less clear with the electronic music still going full volume. Manuel tried his best to piece together the story line boomed out by Guelph over the loudspeaker. Stephanie was some exotic princess who had been abducted by the wicked Davy Jones to a far-off desert island (actually a rickety straw-topped shack in front of the penguin tank). The dolphins had heard of her plight and managed to inform the handsome English lieutenant (Charley) of her whereabouts. But how was a penniless naval officer to rescue her?

Just then Wendy and Wanda poked their beaks out of the water and offered Charley a ride Roman chariot-style on their backs to the enchanted island. Somehow the electronic cues must have got mixed up with the sound system. Whatever the reason, the two dolphins elected to part company mid-ocean, dumping a disconsolate Charley in the middle of the pool, far from his lady love. The kids loved every moment, especially when a pair of frigate birds descended amid the confusion and made off with the fish set aside as a dolphin reward. Far more disconcerting was the fact that Wendy and Wanda had failed to pick up their signal.

But Charley was not one to give up that easily. The pirate show would have to be revamped. For some time now he had played with the idea of a grand finale, an East-West water polo game with an all-star, or rather all-dolphin cast. As Wendy and Wanda were Pacific bottlenoses, and Rusty (the only male in the quartet) and Sandy hailed from the Atlantic, Charley figured that the East-West contest was a natural. Manuel thought that the idea had promise as he held dolphin inventiveness in high esteem. A goal was rigged up at either end, and with some coaching soon all four players got the hang of the game, at least dolphin style.

Thanksgiving was now approaching, the last chance to get a decent sized crowd that season. With the pirate part out, all depended on the water polo game. In an effort to whip up enthusiasm, Stephanie hopped in and out of the pool as an aquatic cheerleader while the penguins on the sidelines clapped their flippers in unison. To round off the human part, Charley was appointed referee, with Jack and Manuel as the goalkeepers. The real attraction, of course, was the spontaneity of the event. As Charley tossed the ball into the air, all four of his charges entered into the spirit of the game with gusto. Quickly Wendy gave a snout pass to Wanda who connected with a fluke wallop that sent the ball hurtling past Manuel into the net. GOAL!! Not to be outdone, Rusty, using his extra weight, bulldozed his way down the pool and rammed the ball through at the other end. GOAL!!! But with that he seemed to lose interest in the game and started to flirt quite openly with Sandy, which meant that one team was otherwise engaged. Something obviously had to be done. After a brief moment's hesitation Charley jumped into the pool to get the Atlantic team to rejoin the game. It was a fatal mistake. Before he knew what had happened, Rusty with his rostrum had given him a ferocious butt in the butt which sent him sailing through the air, despositing him in the goal next to a startled Jack Guelph. The crowd roared their approval, but Charley for once in his life was less than amused. The match was declared a tie, much to the general disappointment. Charley's sole consolation was Stephanie's kind offer to massage any sore part.

With the season over, it was time for stocktaking. As an experienced worker, Manuel's ideas were eagerly solicited. He saw the problem as twofold: facilities and training methods. Given that there was no money, it meant falling back on their own resources. Here young volunteers would be useful. Under Manuel's direction, the tanks were cleaned every day, the salinity level was carefully monitored, and the salt and rust were removed from the pumps and other machinery as far as possible. Although no expert, Manuel checked that the wires were grounded properly to avoid any electric shocks or accidents. But the most pressing problem was to enlarge the width and depth of the main pool. Manuel outlined the need from the dolphins' point of view; without the necessary space, they couldn't be expected to give of their best. Simply put, happy and healthy dolphins make much better performers. This also provided the chance to install a small underwater viewing area with a plexiglass window. Jack and the others were quickly convinced, and that winter saw prodigious amounts of soil removed by pick and shovel. Just before Christmas, perhaps moved by the spirit of the season, a local building contractor gave them a week's free use of his bulldozer, which greatly speeded things up. By early March the enlarged pool was ready.

This came at a price, however. During the construction period the dolphins were restricted to their holding tanks and suffered noticeably from the lack of exercise. Manuel had earlier pointed out to Jack that all four of them were stressed out with five shows a day and badly needed a rest. And now they had gone from one extreme to the other. Already there were the first signs of illness; Rusty (who supposedly sounded like a rusty hinge when echolocating) had developed a nasty cough, and both Sandy and Wendy had bad breath. More alarming still, all of them now began to play with their fish instead of gulping it down. But it was Wanda who gave most cause for alarm. The Pacific bottlenose had become increasingly listless and now spent long periods sulking at the bottom of her tank. The vet came but understandably was unfamiliar with dolphins' problems. Manuel suggested adding some antibiotics to her diet, but nothing helped, not even the ministrations of Wendy, who rarely left her side. Clearly Wanda was slipping away, and one morning she failed to show any signs of life. Wendy was devastated, and for a few tense days all feared that she might follow. Thanks to the new pool and the presence of Sandy and Rusty, in a few days she pulled through.

With the season about to begin in less than a month, a replacement was obviously needed. Jack, born trouper that he was, was determined to go on with the show. Finding a Pacific bottlenose—any dolphin for that matter—was not going to be easy, especially with just a few hundred dollars in the bank. As for training the newcomer....

After several ads and phone calls, false rumors and the usual haggling, finally there was a definite prospect. It was a Pacific bottlenose all right called Dolf—so much for originality—of uncertain age, sex, and background. For Manuel it was yet another disappointment, but better than nothing. Supposedly Dolf had been caught recently (the details were vague in the extreme) and was in "pretty good shape", whatever that meant. To Jack it was clearly a case of seeing is believing. So one day it was arranged to have Dolf brought out to Davy Jones' Dolphins later that morning to see if they could clinch the deal.

Sure enough, just after eleven, a van towing a tank trailer drove up. Doors opened on both sides, and two thickset men stepped out. Advancing to meet them, Jack Guelph and his entire staff trooped out to have a look at the newcomer. After the briefest of introductions it was down to business. The knots were untied, the restraining cords removed before the tarpaulin covering the tank was lifted. There, stretched out in the narrow confines, was the familiar contour of a dolphin, rocking gently from side to side, attempting to keep his skin moist in the shallow water. But that is not what struck Manuel's attention. For there, just under the left eye and to one side of the blowhole, were the jagged cut and crescent-shaped scar tissue he had seen on the dolphin caught in the seine net of the *San Rafael* more than a year ago. A fleeting look of recognition in those eyes—it was Sima!

Everyone there might be forgiven if they thought Manuel had taken leave of his senses, gone "loco" as is well known all Latins do periodically. No one at Davy Jones' Dolphins had really taken his story about Sima seriously, however much he repeated it. Manuel reached out excitedly to touch the dolphin. For her part Sima quivered in response, though her rictus, that perpetual smile on every dolphin face, did not betray the slightest emotion. But one look into those soulful eyes convinced all those present that Manuel's quixotic quest was over at long last. As the money changed hands and the two men drove off, Sima had found a new home.

First, there were some practical considerations. Just moving Sima to the new pool was a challenge. The dolphin, out of water, was not used to the force of gravity, and so had to be properly supported along her whole length, otherwise her own weight would cut off circulation. Then care had to be taken that her delicate skin not bleed or dry out lest the body overheat. Manuel knew that newly captured dolphins could easily catch pneumonia and in some cases suffer from dehydration. Nor were they used to eating dead fish, at the very time their need for fresh food was greatest. Problems, problems! All this weighed on Manuel's mind as they carried Sima on a canvas stretcher to the newly enlarged pool. As she was lowered into her new surroundings, everyone kept their fingers crossed. They need not have worried. Wendy proved especially solicitous, and soon Sima and her new companions were getting along, well, swimmingly.

Manuel was beside himself with excitement. Once he had assured himself that Sima was all right, he hurried to give Sebastian a call.

"Guess what, *viejecito*. You won't believe it, but I've found Sima."

"*¡No me digas!* Where? How?"

It took Manuel two breathless minutes to relate the gist of what had happened. The upshot was that Sebastian and Sarah agreed to drive up early next day to see for themselves. Both were happy to do so as they had begun to worry about their impulsive young friend. The reunion was most cordial with plenty of *abrazos* on both sides. As the three of them watched Sima and her new companions circle the pool there was much to talk about.

"Just three weeks to train her," Manuel sighed. "I don't know if she'll be ready that soon. Maybe we should wait a little."

"Perhaps," Sebastian answered enigmatically.

"You should have been a dolphin," Manuel smiled. "They could have used you at Delphi. How about a real answer, now. How do you think she was caught?"

"*¿Quién sabe?* Any of a dozen reasons. Exhaustion, illness, bad luck—you name it. Seems she was on her own without a calf, that's how those fools took her for a male." He paused for a moment before continuing. "Then there are reasons none of us understand. Fate, for instance. *El sino*. Some things are just meant to be, that's all there is to it," he added with a shrug.

Over dinner that evening the conversation picked up where they had left off. Sebastian was in fine mystical fettle.

"The Church teaches miracles, but no one believes them," he commented as they waited to be served. "But they do happen, I can assure you. Take Sima. Now there's a real miracle, and don't let anyone tell you differently. And I know another one waiting to happen," he added mysteriously.

"Not again!" Sarah sighed, looking heavenwards.

"*¡Cállate, mujer!* Yes, the Spanish galleon off the coast in Hawai'i. It's as real as Sima, a wonder waiting to happen. Don't forget the promise you made!"

Manuel was a little disconcerted at the direction the conversation was taking. He sought refuge in delaying tactics.

"Sebastian, any wreck after three hundred years is going to be very difficult to get at, you know, what with the barnacles and currents. It'll need divers and money, lots of money. Without outside help it's hopeless."

"*¡Hombre!* Who said outside help? You already have the best divers in the world right here under your nose. Yes, dolphins! They don't come any better. Or cheaper."

Manuel threw up his hands in despair.

"*¡Ay Dios!* Old man, you're dreaming!"

"Dreaming? With divers like Sima who can reach depths of two hundred feet, stay down for six minutes without suffering the 'bends,' and repeat all this several times a day. You call that dreaming?"

Manuel was not convinced.

"And how does one get to Hawai'i, *por favor*? Take swimming lessons at the Y, I suppose?"

"*¡Qué tonterías!* Manolo, your trouble is, you just don't have faith. That's it, faith. You just don't believe."

"What about Sima, then? I sure believed in her."

"*De acuerdo, chico*, there you didn't give up. Just hang in and you'll see."

The next morning after a leisurely breakfast Sebastian and Sarah returned to San Diego leaving behind a very perplexed

Manuel. Treasure galleons were fine and dandy, and might even keep Davy Jones' Dolphins going one day, if, if… But the immediate need was to train, or rather retrain, a rambunctious quartet of high-strung performers.

Little by little, Manuel had taken over the main training duties from Charley, who, truth to tell, had found himself out of his depth in every sense. Some things were fairly obvious: short training sessions worked better than long ones, and anyone with any sense worked with the dolphins, not against them. Manuel had heard of dolphins in effect training their trainer, amusing enough to an outsider, but a real trap to be avoided. The secret was to break the routines down into their component parts, with each skill taught step by step. Soon Manuel found that all four of his charges were highly inventive and were soon "improving" on some of the tricks, just for the fun of it, at times even forgoing the customary fish reward in their excitement. After a few days he had "the gang of four," his pet name for them, "walking on water" in unison as they propelled themselves forward with strong thrusts of their caudal fins. The next day, to his total amazement, all four suddenly started to walk in reverse before collapsing into the water amid delirious squawks and squeaks.

Other improvements quickly followed. A system of hydrophone speakers with electronic sounds was installed to sharpen the cues (where Jack Guelph got the money from was not revealed—he jokingly claimed to have held up a bank), and the public address system was improved, in part so that the audience could hear the dolphins' clicks under water. The jarring music and Charley's desperate jokes were dispensed with, to no one's regret. Instead, Manuel informed the public, especially the kids, about the way the dolphins were fed and trained, and what made them such superb swimmers. He explained how the dolphin brain was a fantastic computer that sorted out echoes from many sources and materials, enabling them to "see with sound." The idea was simple, to make the spectators part of the show, to make them really understand what was going on. Anyone leaving a Davy Jones' Dolphin performance would have a good idea what echolocation was and know the difference between a gullet and a mullet.

No one seeing Manuel work with the dolphins could fail to notice the amazing rapport between man and animal. His favorite, much as he tried to hide it, was naturally Sima. Soon a bond was formed that transcended all previous barriers. The closeness at times bordered on intuition, more of a cooperative venture than the usual relationship between trainer and animal. This in turn made improvements to the show much easier. One trick especially was a surefire winner. Every time Manuel ostentatiously lit up a cigarette, Sima or one of the others would sneak up underwater and when he wasn't looking, push him into the pool. A thoroughly soaked Manuel tried (most unconvincingly) to look annoyed. As he loudly vowed vengeance on dolphinkind in general, he climbed up a fifteen-foot ladder to enjoy a quiet puff, whereupon Sima with a mighty jump would snatch the cigarette with uncanny accuracy right from his lips. Other tricks were perhaps more conventional, such as scooping up plastic cups in the water (a subtle hint to some of the less ecologically minded spectators) and pushing Charley and Stephanie around on surfboards. The pirate story was laid to rest, but in compensation Jack Guelph was promoted to captain of a Spanish galleon in command of a crew of dolphins. In the new version—Sebastian's hand was writ large all over the script—after several misadventures involving some spectacular dolphin leaps and dives, all ended well with the treasure saved and the captain bestowing his blessing on the cabin boy (Charley in swimsuit uniform) and a local mermaid (Stephanie in a catchy bikini) who swam off into the sunset, each holding on to a dolphin dorsal fin.

Word soon got around, and thanks to some positive reviews in the papers and on TV, the crowds started picking up. At long last Davy Jones' Dolphins was breaking even, and one month even managed a modest profit. New routines were added, including spectacular upside down arching leaps and all four dolphins swinging colored rings on their beaks before flipping them to kids in the audience. By now the hand signals and underwater cues were down to a minimum, with Sima and the others in many cases taking the lead. To Manuel it was time to try something more challenging.

The idea came to him one day as he watched Sima and Rusty through the observation window. Two days earlier a passenger plane had crashed just off Long Island, but the black boxes—actually orange—still had not been located. Sebastian's Hawaiian project immediately came to mind. Instead of Spanish doubloons, Manuel wondered, could a dolphin like Sima be trained to locate and recover these vital instruments? He had read how dolphins could distinguish between objects almost identical in size and composition before retrieving the correct one off the ocean floor. The problem was that dolphins had a natural dislike of confined spaces and the maze-like obstacle course that a plane's crumpled fuselage would present. As he watched the two dolphins circle round the pool, slowly the elements of a plan began to form in his mind.

It meant starting with Sima alone. It wasn't a matter of confidence or intelligence, she had more than enough of both. No, the challenge was to break down her innate fear of passing through narrow passages. As Manuel saw it, Sima's training would require infinite patience all around, involving a high degree of trial and error. Slalom courses with various configurations were tried and just as quickly discarded when Sima became hopelessly confused. If only man and mammal spoke a common language other than mutual love and affection! Changing roles for a moment, would a human know how to follow a dolphin's detailed instructions to the letter? How could Manuel ever hope to get Sima to learn something so totally unnatural to a dolphin?

Something in the training plan clearly was not working. At times there was a desperate plea in Sima's eyes as if to say "I'm doing my best, but you've got to tell me how." That was the difficulty. At the bottom of the tank—and the reality in the ocean would be far deeper—there was no way of offering any immediate reward in recognition of a newly learned skill. Reality! Suddenly the truth hit Manuel. Of course! Why hadn't he thought of it much earlier? If they were to get anywhere, Sima had to be removed from the pool and returned to the ocean. That's what she had been trying to tell him all along!

Jack and Charley were surprisingly enthusiastic after some initial doubts. The five daily shows must be kept going with the other dolphins while Sima acquired the new skills. Getting her to a local bay was more challenging than anyone had imagined, and setting up the various underwater partitions presented unexpected difficulties at first. No one feared for a moment that she would try to escape. Quite the contrary. Sima proved to be a quick learner in her natural environment, and soon mastered a series of twists and turns before reaching the submerged training target and sounding a bell placed by the divers. Within the week she was regularly retrieving small objects, to everyone's delight. If anything, she seemed to enjoy the outings more than anyone else. It was if she were aware that she had broken through one more barrier.

Jack Guelph was no slouch when it came to getting the word around. Several journalists and TV personalities—how Manuel hated that word!—were invited to witness the performance. Their enthusiastic reports in turn attracted the visit of several well-known cetologists and other experts. Within a matter of weeks Sima was featured on several radio and TV programs, besides the Sunday supplement of half a dozen newspapers. Just as gratifying was the public response at the ticket office. With tremendous relief Jack was able to pay back the sizeable loans he had taken out (he was no more a bank robber than he was a cruel pirate!) and give the whole operation a much-needed face-lift. It had been hard work all round, but in the end well worth it.

Everyone at Davy Jones' Dolphins now had to get used to a steady stream of assorted academics, delphinologists, researchers, and the merely inquisitive. Often after a performance a total stranger would sidle up to Manuel and engage him in a technical conversation about dolphins, as if he truly were the original Delphic oracle. Overnight he had become something of a celebrity. Sima's ability to thread her way through a labyrinth of obstacles was regarded by the dolphin experts as a real scientific breakthrough, and Manuel in one interview after another was questioned as to where it would all lead. Was Sima unique or could other dolphins be similarly trained to retrieve black boxes? (Yes, in time) Did Sima have a boyfriend? (Rusty so far had made no advances) Could Sima singlehandedly (they really meant singleflipperly) attack and destroy a whole enemy fleet at anchor? (No, she had far better things to do) And what about sunken treasure? Here Manuel chose to be evasive and laugh it off as a big joke. There had to be *some* secrets, after all.

One late afternoon, just after the last show of the day, Manuel was approached by a middle-aged tall man in a smart Navy uniform. The stranger had the disciplined bearing of a career officer, one used to taking and giving orders. Clearly he had come with some precise purpose in mind.

"Captain Mike Breasely, U.S. Navy," he introduced himself with the minimum of fuss. "Mr. Avila, could I have a few words with you? I can see you're busy—I won't take more than a few moments of your time."

There was nothing in the newcomer's demeanor to indicate the reason for his visit. The last few weeks had seen several enlisted men come from as far away as San Diego, so a man in uniform was nothing out of the ordinary. But this one seemed somehow different. Manuel shook the proffered hand.

"Won't you come to Mr. Guelph's office? He's the owner, you know."

"No, Mr. Avila. You're the one I want to talk to. About Sima. That was a really impressive performance she gave, and I know who deserves the credit. Now, don't be modest. That was really something the way she threaded her way through those obstacles you had set up. I read recently that she can also tell the difference between steel and copper. Very impressive, if I may say so."

"What brings you here, Captain?" Manuel asked, somewhat defensively.

"Mr. Avila, I won't beat about the bush. I don't have to tell you about the TWA 800 crash. Sad business in every way. They had to wait several days before they located the two black boxes. Well, in today's world that's not good enough." He paused a moment to let his words sink in. "Mr. Avila, we need you. Your country needs you."

Whatever Manuel had expected, it certainly was not this. Noting his silence, Breasely continued.

"Well, maybe you've guessed, I'm with Navy research. We're very much interested in dolphin potential, in fact we have several porpoises working for us right now. I might as well tell you, several of our boys are very interested in the work you've done with Sima. Very interested."

So that was it. Despite his reservations about large institutions, Manuel had to admit being intrigued.

"What are you proposing, Captain? I assume that you have something specific in mind?"

Breasely smiled for the first time.

"Darn right I do. Mr. Avila, we'd like you and Sima to work with us. In Hawai'i."

Manuel could hardly believe his ears. Hawai'i? Sebastian! Could the old salt really be on to something? All that talk of galleons and treasure and miracles and…. Captain Breasely looked uncharacteristically puzzled.

"Mr. Avila, is something wrong? Can I…."

"Not at all! Just the opposite. You've said something wonderful. Yes, I certainly would be interested."

In retrospect Manuel was amazed at his impetuous decision. Breasely had not gone into any detail, other than a vague appeal to patriotic duty. It was now Manuel's sad task to break the news to Jack and the others. Maybe they had sensed that something of the sort was in the wind, for none of them registered any surprise.

They were all very unhappy to see him go. Charley had learned a lot from Manuel, and Stephanie had also come a long way. As for letting Sima go, the check from the U. S. Navy would provide for at least two more dolphins. Jack gave Manuel an affectionate hug, and Dina took time off from her beautification program to give him a quick peck on the cheek. Saying goodbye to Wendy, Sandy, and Rusty proved to be the most difficult. No words were exchanged, but who can deny that the language of gestures, plaintive cries, and airborne barks was any the less fervent? For Manuel and Sima it was to be a new life. Four weeks later, as the Navy transport plane took off and wheeled toward the open Pacific, he could only guess what the future held in store for both of them.

As the plane descended over O'ahu Manuel admired his new island home through the window. Below him unfolded a tropical tapestry such as he had never seen before. The cobalt blue of the limitless ocean merged a half mile offshore into the somber shadows and turquoise waters of the coral reefs. In the distance, rain clouds over green-clad mountain ranges disgorged their plenitude on the peaks, leaving the coastal plain with its pineapple fields and numerous golf courses to bask in the sun. To the right rose an incongruous mass—mess might be more accurate—of skyscrapers and high rises right in the very middle of the Pacific. This was Honolulu in all its sultry heat and excitement.

Manuel was greeted at the terminal by Captain Breasley who had preceded him to Hawai'i by a couple of weeks. For Manuel, it had been a busy time. The Navy project was apparently top secret, which meant that anyone involved in the work needed to get security clearance first. Thanks to Breasely, who seemed to carry a lot of clout in Washington, the background check was no problem, though Manuel was closely questioned about possible drug use, it being a well-known "fact" that all Latins are potential drug runners. Eventually someone in the CIA decided that the Republic was not in danger, and Manuel found himself in possession of a sheaf of impressive looking papers, all duly stamped and signed. He was now a full civilian employee of the Navy as, in her cetacean way, was Sima who had reached Hawai'i as a V.I.P.—Very Important Porpoise—on a special aircraft.

"Good to see you," Breasely said. "Here's some homegrown *aloha* to welcome you," whereupon he placed a colorful floral lei around Manuel's neck. "We tried a plastic lei with Sima, but she threw it off almost immediately. She'll have to get used to having things round her neck, though," he added without offering any further explanation. Within twenty minutes they had picked up Manuel's luggage and were heading across the *pali* to the other side of the island. An hour later Manuel was ensconced in his new quarters.

His first care, of course, was to see how Sima was housed. He had no need to worry. Sima, along with half a dozen other dolphins of various types, was cruising around an extensive saltwater lagoon, swimming alternately on her back and side before righting herself. By her spontaneous leaps and dives Manuel could see that she was thoroughly enjoying herself, so much so, that it took several minutes before she became aware of his presence. She more than made up for her tardiness with a display of acrobatics and gleeful welcoming sounds through her blowhole. Manuel was both delighted and relieved, delighted that Sima had taken to her new environment with such ease, and relieved that the month's separation had made no difference.

Hawai'i with its tropical humidity was quite different from San Diego. As he walked along the broad beach, Manuel missed the continental seabirds, the pelicans, cormorants, and gulls he had grown up with. Somehow the offshore terns and frigate birds didn't quite make up for it. But then the ever changing brilliant colors of the clouds and sea, the dramatic grandeur of the *pali* as it swooped down to the ocean, together with the most magnificent sunsets he had ever witnessed, were a feast for the eye and soul.

Working with Captain Breasely and his research team at a military base was a new challenge for Manuel. Amid the Hawaiian informality—suits and ties were strictly *kapu*—was a strong no-nonsense work ethic that he readily admired. Most were specialists in echolocation, acoustics and sonar, aquadynamics, and deep sea diving. One of them, an attractive local young lady named Lani Kaleipoki'i, was closely involved with dolphins. The specialty of two others of the team was less clear. In secret work one learns not to ask too many questions.

The daily routine did not vary greatly. Basically, the idea was that trained dolphins, with their ability to work in murky waters thanks to their uncanny echolocation skills, could be trained to find the all-important black boxes in the early hours before any salt build-up or shift of currents. The problem, as Captain Breasely—"call me Mike"—had pointed out, was the reluctance of dolphins to enter a confined space. Thanks to Manuel and Sima, that had now been resolved, at least in the case of one dolphin, though how easily others could be trained was still unclear. The rest seemed fairly straightforward. Dolphins could swim at high speeds for long periods, especially under water, thanks to their slow heartbeat and efficient use of oxygen. Nor did communications present a problem, due to the dolphins' excellent hearing and sound traveling nearly five times faster under water than on the surface. If need be, dolphins could dive up to a thousand feet, though that was the limit. Once the obstacle problem was solved, they could proceed. Then it would be just a matter of starting up the production line of trained dolphins....

It wasn't quite that simple, however. Sima became confused at times and did not seem to understand what was expected of her. The training of the other dolphins was even more disappointing. Somehow their intelligence wasn't quite the same as humans'. But why should it be? Their world, the interface of air and water, simply was not the same. Understanding remained the greatest barrier. One of the group in all seriousness suggested that maybe the dolphins could learn English—American English—seeing it was the world's language. Manuel, trying to keep a straight face, pleaded eloquently for Spanish with its more logical sound system, while Lani mischievously suggested Hawaiian. Soon in a babel of voices the whole matter was dropped. That dolphins did not have the necessary vocal equipment apparently did not occur to anyone.

As time went by, Manuel and Lani, the two civilians in the research team, were drawn closer to one another. Part of it was natural enough; in exchange for Spanish lessons, Lani taught Manuel the basics of Hawaiian. Soon language instruction blossomed into a closer relationship—all foreign tongues under the right conditions tend to become romance languages—though progress was limited at first to long walks along the beach. It was during one of these evening strolls that Lani opened Manuel's eyes.

The conversation began innocuously enough.

"How do you like Hawai'i after two months?" she asked in a well-tried opening gambit.

"Oh, I can't complain. The work, the people, everything's fine. I even like to eat poi once in a while," he smiled.

"You do? Have you tried giving any to Sima?"

"¡Caramba! She likes fish. She hasn't gone native yet."

"That's not nice of you at all."

Manuel apologized and promised to behave better in future. His slip of the tongue gave Lani her opportunity.

"How do you like Mike Breasely?" she asked. "I mean, as a boss?"

"He seems fair enough. Can't say that I'm that close to him, though."

"Manuel, there's a side to the man you don't know. I think you should, for your own sake. And Sima's."

"You mean...."

"Oh no!" she laughed, "not that! No, the man's ramrod straight, ultra correct. No hanky-panky with *that* guy! It's something else."

"Such as?"

"That guy's been through a lot in the Navy. Tail end of Vietnam, Beirut, Mogadishu, you name it. He's seen it all. What's happened is that he's become a super hawk."

"What of it? That's his affair."

"Well, not quite. Have you ever wondered what those two fellows, the ones who always keep to themselves, are doing? Let me tell you, those two have been plenty busy. Just like Mike Breasely."

"Meaning what?"

"You think Sima's being trained just to retrieve black boxes, don't you? Well, there's a lot more to it than that. Such as blowing up enemy targets and ships." She paused to let her words have their effect. Manuel clearly was shaken.

"How do you know? Are you really sure?"

"Sure I'm sure. I overheard those two men in black rubber suits talking about dolphins locking into their target as the clicks pick up in intensity. And they didn't mean black boxes. They were talking about getting through mine fields and dolphins wearing harnesses with miniaturized weapons. Manuel, you'd better face it. Mike Breasely is up to his neck in secret weapons work. *That's* his real interest in Sima."

"What can we do? How do we stop them?"

"We can't. This is a place for hush-hush projects, and we both signed on, remember. All we can do is keep our eyes open and try to make sure the dolphins don't come to any harm. I don't like it any more than you do."

The realization that Sima and her companions were in danger brought Manuel and Lani closer still. Besides the dolphins, they shared much in common. Both in a way were strangers in their own country, now minorities which long ago had been the ruling force. The signs where they lived were printed in Spanish and Hawaiian, often woefully misspelled and pronounced even worse, but the real power lay elsewhere. With Sima it was no different. A sentient creature of the pelagic wild, she now found herself in an environment that was strange to her and serving masters she could not comprehend. Did any wild being deserve to be in captivity? As Manuel and Lani watched the sunlight reflect off Sima's graceful arcing form they silently vowed that one day she would be truly free.

One evening over *mai tais* Manuel poured out his life story to Lani. She was fascinated hearing about his years out on the seiner-boats with Sebastian and his adventures, which lost nothing in the retelling. Her own life by comparison seemed overly confined—her early childhood on the Big Island, high school in Hilo, then her B.A. in Animal Sciences at the state university before landing the job working with the Navy. But to Manuel, her account seemed wonderfully exotic, the mellifluous names and fertile stories tripping off her tongue without the slightest effort. Soon they were sharing confidences with an avidity that at the beginning would have surprised both of them. One of the secrets that tumbled out was that of Sebastian and the Spanish galleon.

"The story's nothing new," Lani averred. "Stories like that have been told here in Hawai'i for generations. But an actual map, now that's something different. Let's go and find the wreck some day."

"Hold your horses, I mean dolphins," Manuel chimed in. "You don't just put on your scuba suit and hop down to the ocean floor. It's a heck of a lot more difficult."

"You're not going to give up before we even begin, are you?" she reproached him.

"Not at all. But we're not going to do the main work. Remember what Sebastian said? 'You already have the best divers in the world right here under your nose'. Sima! She's going to do it!"

"But how?"

"Lani, you're going to get to work on Breasely. He's been unhappy for some time now with the slow progress we're making. Tell him, convince him that O'ahu's too crowded for secret work, that Sima needs to work in the open ocean far away from people. Then suggest the Big Island. I think he'll go for it. Especially with you and your island charm."

"Thanks a lot, Romeo. I'll get out my grass skirt and give it a try. You just play your ukelele or guitar in the background, and we'll see what happens."

Surpringly enough, it turned out to be quite easy. For some time Mike Breasely had been thinking along similar lines, and Lani's suggestion fell on receptive ears. Cost was a problem, so it was decided that at first Sima would go on her own without the other dolphins.

Two weeks later the Navy vessel *Hawaiian Explorer* was anchored off Ke'alakeku'a Bay with a small crew and Sima aboard. As Manuel and Lani watched a school of spinner dolphins gyrate like tops in the open waters, their thoughts turned back two centuries to where Captain Cook had met his end. The hei'au and the white obelisk monument to mark the spot were all that remained, at least visibly. But what of the bones and spirits of the Hawaiian past, perhaps the great god Lono himself, that lived on in the caves high above the placid waters? And what of the dolphins whose ancestors two hundred years ago must have wondered why humans fight and kill one another?

Their reveries were interrupted by a totally unexpected piece of news. Practically without notice Captain Breasely and the two mystery men had been called urgently to Washington for a meeting. Another stroke of luck—not unconnected with Breasely's absence—was that some of the crew elected to fly to Honolulu for a boozy weekend. For Manuel and Lani it was now or never for the project. Getting the remainder of the crew members to cooperate was not the problem—to the sailors on board, one dive was pretty much the same as any other, lots of telemetric data, sonar experiments, the usual sort of thing. By Saturday afternoon, the day after Breasely's departure, the *Hawaiian Explorer* was off Nai'a Ke'e, exactly where the old map indicated the wreck of the proud galleon lay.

Preparing Sima for the great moment wasn't that easy. Already on O'ahu Manuel had shown her some facsimiles of old wooden spars and rusted ironwork to familiarize her with what she might find. The truth was, he really had little idea where to begin. If only Sebastian had kept his crazy ideas to himself! *¡Maldito viejo!* Where was the old sea dog when you needed him?

Sunday morning marked the beginning of Operation *Tesoro*, as Manuel optimistically named it. Other than Manuel and Lani, there were now only three others on board, not forgetting Sima. Soon after breakfast the sonar equipment and the underwater cameras were readied, and Sima in her holding cage lowered into the calm water. The area shown on the map was about a half mile offshore. From the fanciful chart there was no indication on what submerged object the *Serenissimi Delphini* had foundered, whether rock or coral, or if the vessel had struck the shore and by the force of the gale been forced out to sea again. As Sima disappeared beneath the waves, all Manuel and Lani could do was wait and hope.

Four minutes later she reappeared with nothing to show for her efforts. In her eyes Manuel thought he could read a note of apology as if to say, "I'll do better next time, I promise." But the next time and the next produced no better result. All they could do was to move the ship in ever-increasing circles and test the ocean floor with sonar readings and the underwater camera before giving Sima the order to dive. Once they thought they had found something, only to be disappointed yet again.

It was now past midday, the sun beating down with tropical incandescence. Lunch was consumed in dispirited silence before the operation resumed. Two more changes of location, and still nothing to show for it. By now the heat and humidity were unbearable with no escape. *Ay*, Sebastian, why did I ever listen to you?... The very sonar pings seemed to mock them, while the camera likewise failed to reveal any secrets in the endless ooze a hundred fathoms below. It was obviously time to quit the fruitless search. Sima was beginning to tire and would soon have to be lifted on board ship. It had all been for nothing. All that Manuel could do now was to give her the recall signal and…. Just then Sima's cheerful face emerged from the depths. There, unmistakeably crosswise in her mouth, like one of her favorite fish, was a jagged piece of rotted wood with markings and an iron ring at one end. She had found the galleon!

Their ecstasy was indescribable as Manuel kissed Lani on deck before the nonplussed crewmembers. The latter were even more amazed to see Manuel and Lani give Sima the biggest buss on the beak that any dolphin has ever received. Later dives brought up various artifacts including some of the crockery once used by that ghostly crew. No treasure, not for the moment at least, but a fortune if measured as a tangible tie with the past. Manuel and Lani took turns in viewing the spectral scene through the lens of the underwater camera. There, in dim outline, lay the ship's timbers and rigging, the broken masts and cannon. And what of the captain and crew? Manuel recalled the Bard's evocation of another shipwreck on another far-off island centuries ago:

> "Full fathom five thy father lies,
> Of his bones are coral made…"

Manuel prayed for a brief moment. May his Spanish ancestors on that ship all rest in peace!

As the *Hawaiian Explorer* sailed later that evening north to Kailua Kona, all aboard felt a sense of achievement. Sima, as was only right, was given a double ration of mullet as well as a mackerel or two. There was so much to tell. Mike Breasely when he came back was sure to be thrilled just as much as they were.

The reunion next day was not quite what they expected. Breasely came back from Washington a changed man. His first task was to call a meeting of the entire group.

"Listen up, everyone. We've got work to do. First thing tomorrow it's back to O'ahu. I've got new orders for all of you."

It was Lani who first broke the silence.

"Mike, while you…."

"Captain Breasely, please, Miss Kaleipoki'i. Yes, what is it?" he demanded curtly.

"You think we've been sitting on our butts, don't you? Well, we haven't. You won't believe this, but we've found the wreck of a Spanish galleon. I mean, Sima has. It's a tremendous discovery!"

"I haven't the faintest idea what you're talking about. That's the trouble with you Hawaiians, always 'talking story,' believing legends. Not enough facts, getting down to hard work. Well, all that's going to change, starting tomorrow."

"Captain, we're not just 'talking story.' This is for real. Look, see for yourself." With that Lani thrust a rusted tankard towards him. "Manuel, show him the Spanish inscription."

"I'm not interested in a bunch of dago letters. That phony junk's a dime a dozen. Get to bed early tonight, because real work begins tomorrow." With that he gave a brisk salute and was gone from the room.

"What got into him?" Manuel groaned as he sat down. "Anyone want to guess?"

Lani was the first to answer.

"I bet it's something to do with the dolphin program. The top brass in Washington isn't happy, so we're the peons who get it in the neck. It's called chain of command."

"Well, tomorrow's the moment of truth. As the good captain said, we'd better get Sima loaded on the boat and hit the hay early. *Hasta mañana.*"

The trip to O'ahu the next day was no more cheerful. The thrill at the discovery of the galleon had completely evaporated. As they drove back to base there was no joking or light talk. Everyone looked forward to the Captain's briefing with dread.

Breasely was not one to beat about the bush.

"There's been a change," he announced brusquely without offering any explanation. "No more of this black box business. We're gonna do what we came here for in the first place. Enemy targets. Find 'em and hit 'em. Training the dolphins to get through the minefields and decoys, that's your job. I want results, and I don't mean next year or the year after. I mean within a couple of months at the most. Any questions?"

Obviously he did not encourage any. To his surprise and barely concealed annoyance, Nat Singleton, one of the veteran researchers, raised his hand.

"Captain, with all due respect, you've just outlined half the problem. Thanks to Sima, I'm sure we can train dolphins to reach a target, however well guarded. The real challenge is bringing them back after they've attached the weapon. It won't be easy designing the harnesses and the timing devices so that the dolphins will have time to turn round and escape. I'm sorry, but this can't be rushed."

"Dr. Singleton, no one's talking about rushing you. I don't have to tell you, you guys are paid to get results. As I said, two months. That's plenty of time. Gentlemen, that will be all."

As they filed out of the room, a small group headed straight for the coffee machine.

"Nothing to beat a *cafecito*," Manuel assured the others. "Nat, any idea's what's biting *el jefe*?"

"I can pretty well guess. There's been a shake-up somewhere along the line, and Mike got caught in the middle. Probably his neck's on the block if we don't get results."

"It can't be done in two months," Manuel protested. "We all know a dolphin can't carry heavy bulky weights and still keep its hydrodynamic form. And that's not all. It's one thing showing Sima the profile of an enemy target and making her memorize it and the obstacles like a Cruise missile. Getting her back is something else. And she's damn well coming back."

"You bet she is," Lani chipped in. "We're seeing the real Mike—sorry, Captain Breasely—in action. Manuel, I told you about him some time ago. Now you can see for yourself. It's bye-bye Dr. Jekyll, *aloha* Mr. Hyde."

"Come on now, he's not *that* bad. He's also got a job to do. Nat, let's get on with that escape harnass of yours. Just to inspire everyone, how about you and Lani coming over to my place for a drink. Let's drink to Sima and many happy returns. From enemy targets, that is."

The next few days and weeks were the most hectic any of them had ever experienced. Everything to be carried by the dolphins—the harnasses, the limpet mines, the release devices—had to be miniaturized to reduce weight and tested for absolute reliability. Then there was the matter of training other dolphins to follow in Sima's pioneering path. Nat Singleton reckoned that, with luck, they might have everything ready in a month to six weeks, then the actual tests would last maybe another couple of weeks, after which Sima could retire with full honors.

After returning to O'ahu, Manuel had immediately phoned Sebastian.

"*Viejo*, it's one of those good news and bad news deals. The good news is that we found the galleon right where you said it would be. The bad news is they want Sima to be some sort of torpedo and blow up enemy ships. Sebastian, I think you and Sarah should come out here and see for yourselves what's going on. I'm not allowed to go into any details about the military work, but I can tell you I'm not happy."

Five days later, Manuel was chatting with his friends out on the lanai of their hotel. For good measure he brought Lani along with him.

"What happens to the galleon now?" Manuel began. "How do we get to her?"

Sebastian smiled at his young friend's impatience.

"*¡Ay, muchacho!* She's been down there home to dolphins for over three centuries, and you want to raise her immediately. No, she's going to have to wait a little longer. I can tell you one thing, though. From what I've read, the ship's worth a fortune in gold and silver. But first things first. Tell me more about Sima."

"That's just it. There isn't much to tell. No, we're not keeping any military secrets from you. The fact is, we simply don't know what's going to happen or what's on Breasely's mind."

"Whatever they're working on, it's going to happen soon," Lani volunteered. "I've never seen so many SEALS around in my life. And I don't mean the cuddly kind with fins and flippers."

The day they had all waited for dawned clear and muggy, with only a narrow band of cotton wool clouds on the horizon to break the cerulean vault of the sky. Overnight the target ship had been towed into place, and the scientists were now busy putting the finishing touches to a veritable maze of underwater partitions and hazards. On a promontory jutting out into the ocean all was feverish haste as monitoring equipment and telephoto cameras were checked and rechecked. In a holding pen abutting on to the shed that housed men and machines, Sima swam around in quiet anticipation, even as Manuel and Lani spoke words of encouragement. Finally the speedboat brought the scientists in from the target area, some last minute checks were made before Breasely announced that everything was ready to go.

This was also the signal for Manuel to join the group of men gathered at the shed. Everyone had been carefully briefed and knew what to do. The weapon that Sima carried was a dummy warhead which she was to carry through the obstacle course, plant on the ship's side before turning sharply and escaping before any real weapon would explode.

That morning Breasely had been at his most taciturn, which everyone attributed to the pressure the people back in Washington were putting on him. So no one was surprised when he called one of the Navy officers over to him.

"Lieutenant, there's been a change," he stated flatly. "We're changing the warhead. We're going for real, no messing around with a dummy. You've got five minutes to set it up and fix it to that animal there. Sharp now, snap to it."

"But Captain, I thought—"

"You're not here to argue, but obey. Lieutenant, that's an order."

It was more than Manuel could stand.

"Captain Breasely, you can't do it. You can't suddenly change everything. We're just not, well, ready for the real thing."

"Not ready? Then when the hell will you be ready?"

"Captain, you can't rush these things. We need time."

Breasely laughed scornfully.

"Time? You want time? And what the hell do you think those terrorists out there are doing? You think *they're* taking time? Listen, young man, my first assignment was out in Beirut back when those marines were killed, two hundred and forty three of them. That's something you'll never forget the rest of your life. And then after that Saudi Arabia, not to mention 9/11 and al-Qaeda. I'm fed up with this messing around, we've got a job to do and we're damn well going to do it. If the dolphin comes back, good, if it doesn't, too bad. That target's going, though." He glanced at his watch. "Lieutenant, one more minute."

Manuel refused to give up.

"Sima!" he shouted. "Captain, you're not going to kill an innocent creature—I won't let you!"

Breasely barely moved a muscle.

"You two men," he said, turning to some sailors, "hold this man until I tell you to release him." Manuel immediately found himself restrained with his arms pinioned on each side. "Are we ready now? Good! Everyone to their stations. Ready? Five, four, three, two, GO!"

Right in front of him Manuel could see the hatchdoor of the floating pen raised and Sima bound out toward the open ocean. Try as he might, he could not free himself from the firm grip of the two navy men. Out of the corner of his eye he caught sight of Lani approaching with a heavy wooden pole used for setting up equipment. The two sailors were taken completely unaware by the ferocity of Lani's attack and with shouts of pain released their prisoner. Manuel needed no further bidding. With one bound he hurtled past the startled onlookers and sprinted headlong toward the jetty and the speedboat which a few minutes earlier had returned the scientists. In seconds he was back to his first seinerboat days as a speedboat driver. With a practised hand he opened wide the throttle of the outboard engine, sending the boat bounding over the crest of the waves, ignoring the searing back pain caused him by the sudden acceleration. Ahead, as the sunlight glinted off Sima's back, he could see her swiftly narrow the distance to the looming wall of gray steel ahead.

Slowly, ever so slowly it seemed, machine gained on mammal. With her head start, Sima was already more than halfway to her object, straining every sinew to obey the whims of her masters. Like every dolphin from the days of antiquity, her sole aim was to please those humans with whom she came in contact. With a singleness of mind she was rapidly closing in on the target, already beginning to thread her way through the maze of cunningly placed obstacles.

It was now that past skills came to Manuel's aid. Flinging the speedboat to the right in a tight circle, he threw the craft into a path that would cut off Sima's knifelike advance. The gap between them was less than fifty feet. Now the danger was to avoid a collision that could maim and possibly kill the dolphin. For the first time Sima became aware of the boat and hesitated for a fraction of a second. Manuel, at risk to life and limb, stood up and yelled at the top of his lungs, "Sima! Stop! Stop! *¡Ven acá, por el amor de Dios!*" At the same time he threw himself at the dark form in the water and grasped Sima by her dorsal fin. But in doing so his weight dislodged the harnass and its lethal cargo which now, guided only by its momentum, drifted implacably toward its target.

Sima, with her intuitive intelligence, understood immediately that they were in peril. Together, man and mammal, as in the days of old, were fused for one brief moment into one being as they sped away. It was already too late. With an explosion that rent the air, machine detonated against metal, hurling a tidal wave in all directions. Manuel felt his eardrums split, his head reel, his lungs fill with water. And yet he still felt the pull of that powerful heart below him, even as consciousness was ebbing away. Disturbed thoughts flashed through his mind for the briefest of instants. No longer was Poseidon a sea god, come to help mortals in distress, but a weapon of destruction in the arsenal of Man. And now he himself was about to leave Planet Earth. But why call it Earth, he mused in his delirium, why not Planet Water? And why only "All creatures that on *earth* do dwell?" What of those in the oceans? He was now slipping away, slipping ever closer to a far distant shore…..

Early next morning, even before sunrise, a fisherman found the two bodies lying side by side on the beach. The police were called, the Navy informed, an autopsy ordered. In Manuel's case, it was straightforward enough: massive internal bleeding, water in the lungs, and perhaps also a stroke. In that of Sima it was far less clear. One expert thought she might have stranded herself, another mumbled something about an 'impaired echoranging system' or a 'biological clock confused in a geomagnetic field.' Try as they might, the vets could not find anything organically wrong and finally gave up in despair. It was left up to Sebastian, even in his grief, to make the correct diagnosis.

"I don't care what any doctor says," he protested, turning to Sarah and Lani, "Sima died of a broken heart. The ancients knew that, but we've gotten too smart for our own good. Here," at which point he began to rummage furiously in his pockets until he triumphantly held up a scrap of well-worn paper, "here's what the Greek poet Oppian had to say:

> Now, of the ways of dolphins, this wonder
> too I hear,

For which I do them honor. When there
at last draws near
The sickness that shall end them, unpitying,
well they know
Their life is done; then coastward from the great
deeps they go
And running themselves ashore on the beach's
yielding sand,
There breathe their last; preferring to meet their
doom on land…

Oppian goes on, but I won't bore you with the rest. You see, Sima instinctively knew that she and Manuel had come to the end of the road, or should I say, sea. They know these things."

Lani reached out to thank the old man for his kindness. Words did not come easily.

"Sebastian, you know Manuel thought the world of you. Well, if ever we recover anything from the *Delfín*, I want it to be yours. I know Manuel would have wanted it that way."

Sebastian placed a paternal hand on her shoulder.

"No, my dear. Sarah and I, we're a couple of ancient relics, just like those on the galleon. No, it's all yours, and yours alone."

Lani paused a moment before answering.

"It's not right, I mean disturbing everything down there. It's now the home of the dolphins. I'm sure that's what Manuel would have liked more than anything else. Sima as well. Let's just leave well enough alone."

The three of them continued their sorrowful walk along the beach. Then with a singularly beautiful expression in his voice, Sebastian turned to Lani.

"You see the surf pounding the coral reef? The breakers out there? Now look beyond the barrier. That's where they are."

Some weeks later an astronomer high up in the observatory on Mauna Kea was studying some computerized photographs of constellations close to the horizon. It was a fairly routine job offering little in the way of excitement. The occasional faint asteroid shower or fuzzy blur was the most they could hope for, and that night promised to be no different.

Suddenly, something unusual caught the young scientist's sharp eye. What was that in the constellation of Delphinus, the Dolphin, that wasn't quite right? The astronomer quickly consulted his charts to check on Gamma, a well-known telescopic double star with golden yellow components. As he checked through a high-powered telescope, there could be no doubt about it: the double had acquired a new magnitude, far eclipsing all the other stars in the constellation and in the surrounding sky.

When Sebastian and Lani read about it some days later in the papers, they fully grasped what had happened. From now to eternity Manuel and Sima would gambol their way together through the heavens, beyond all worldly cares, beyond all barriers.

ISBN 1-41205274-2